The narrow corner

William Somerset Maugham was born in 1874 and lived in Paris until he was ten. He was educated at King's School, Canterbury, and at Heidelberg University. He spent some time at St Thomas's Hospital with the idea of practising medicine, but the success of his first novel *Liza of Lambeth*, published in 1897, won him over to letters. *Of Human Bondage*, the first of his masterpieces, came out in 1915, and, with the publication in 1916 of *The Moon and Sixpence*, his reputation as a novelist was established. His position as a successful playwright was being consolidated at the same time. His first play, *A Man of Honour*, was followed by a series of successes just before and after World War I, and his career in the theatre did not end until 1933 with *Sheppey*.

His fame as a short-story writer began with *The Trembling of a Leaf*, sub-titled *Little Stories of the South Sea Islands*, in 1921, after which he published more than ten collections. His other works include travel books such as *On a Chinese Screen* and *Don Fernando*, essays, criticism, and the autobiographical *The Summing Up* and *A Writer's Notebook*.

In 1927 Somerset Maugham settled in the South of France and lived there until his death in 1965.

Also by W. Somerset Maugham
in Pan Books

W. Somerset Maugham

The narrow corner

Pan Books in association with
William Heinemann

First published 1932 by William Heinemann Ltd
This edition published 1976 by Pan Books Ltd,
Cavaye Place, London SW10 9PG, in association with
William Heinemann Ltd
9 8 7
All rights reserved
ISBN 0 330 24462 0
Made and printed in Great Britain by
Richard Clay Ltd, Bungay, Suffolk

Short, therefore, is man's life,
and narrow is the corner of the earth wherein he dwells

Preface

The characters of fiction are strange fish. They come into your mind. They grow. They acquire suitable characteristics. An environment surrounds them. You think of them now and again. Sometimes they become an obsession so that you can think of nothing else. Then you write of them and for you they cease to be. It is odd that someone who has occupied a place, often only in the background of your thoughts, but also often in the very centre of them, who then perhaps for months has lived with you all the waking hours of the day and often in your dreams, should slip your consciousness so completely that you can remember neither his name nor what he looks like. You may even forget that he ever existed. But on occasion it does not happen like that. A character whom you had thought you were done with, a character to whom you had given small heed, does not vanish into oblivion. You find yourself thinking of him again. It is often exasperating, for you have had your will of him and he is no longer of any use to you. What is the good of his forcing his presence on you? He is a gate-crasher whom you do not want at your party. He is eating the food and drinking the wine prepared for others. You have no room for him. You must concern yourself with the people who are more important to you. But does he care? Unmindful of the decent sepulchre you have prepared for him, he goes on living obstinately; indeed, he betrays an uncanny activity, and one day to your surprise he has forced his way to the forefront of your thoughts and you cannot help but give him your attention.

The reader of this novel will find Dr Saunders in a brief sketch in *On a Chinese Screen*. He was devised in order to act his part in the little story called *The Stranger*. I had space there to draw him but in a few lines and I never expected to think of him again. There was no reason why he, rather than any other of the many persons who made an appearance in that book, should go on living. He took the matter into his own hands.

And Captain Nichols was introduced to the reader in *The*

Moon and Sixpence. He was suggested by a beachcomber I met in the South Seas. But in his case I was conscious soon after I had finished that book that I was not finished with him. I went on thinking about him and when the manuscript came back from the typist and I was correcting errors, a little piece of his conversation struck me. I could not but think that here was the idea for a novel and the more I thought of it the more I liked it. When the proofs at last reached me I had made up my mind to write it and so cut out the passage in question. It ran as follows:

'About other parts of his career he was fortunately more communicative. He had smuggled guns into South America and opium into China. He had been engaged in the blackbird business in the Solomon Islands and showed a scar on his forehead as the result of a wound some scoundrelly nigger had given him who did not understand his philanthropic intentions. His chief enterprise was a long cruise he had taken in the Eastern seas, and his recollections of this formed an unfailing topic of his conversation. It appeared that some man in Sydney had been unlucky enough to commit a murder and his friends were anxious to keep him out of harm's way for a time, so Captain Nichols was approached. He was given twelve hours to buy a schooner and find a crew, and the following night, a little way down the coast, the interesting passenger was brought on board.

' "I got a thousand pounds for that job, money down, paid in gold," said Captain Nichols. "We had a wonderful trip. We went all through the Celebes and round about the islands of the Borneo Archipelago. They're wonderful those islands. Talk of beauty, vegetation, you know, and all that sort of thing. Shooting whenever you fancy it. Of course we kept out of the beaten track."

' "What sort of man was your passenger?" I asked.

' "Good fellow. One of the best. Fine card player too. We played écarté every day for a year and by the end of the year he'd got all the thousand pounds back again. I'm a pretty good card player myself and I kept my eyes skinned too."

' "Did he go back to Australia eventually?"

' "That was the idea. He'd got some friends there and they

reckoned as how they'd square his little trouble in a couple of years."

' "I see."

' "It looked as if I was going to be made the goat."

'Captain Nichols paused for a moment and his lively eyes seemed strangely veiled. A sort of opaqueness covered them.

' "Poor fellow, he fell overboard one night off the coast of Java. I guess the sharks did the rest. He was a fine card player, one of the best I ever saw." The Captain nodded reflectively. "I sold the schooner at Singapore. What with the money I got for that and the thousand pounds in gold I didn't do so badly after all." '

This then was the incident that gave me the idea for this novel, but it was not till twelve years later that I began to write it.

chapter one

All this happened a good many years ago.

chapter two

Dr Saunders yawned. It was nine o'clock in the morning. The day lay before him and he had nothing in the world to do. He had already seen a few patients. There was no doctor on the island and on his arrival such as had anything the matter with them seized the opportunity to consult him. But the place was not unhealthy and the ailments he was asked to cure were chronic, and he could do little; or they were trifling, and responded quickly to simple remedies. Dr Saunders had practised for fifteen years in Fu-chou and had acquired a great reputation among the Chinese for his skill in dealing with the ills that affect the eye, and it was to remove a cataract for a rich Chinese merchant that he had come to Takana. This was an island in the Malay Archipelago, a long way down, and the distance from Fu-chou was so great that at first he had refused to go. But the Chinese, Kim Ching by name, was himself a native of that city and two of his sons lived there. He was well acquainted with Dr Saunders, and on his periodical visits to Fu-chou had consulted him on his failing sight. He had heard how the doctor, by what looked like a miracle, had caused the blind to see, and when in due course he found himself in such a state that he could only tell day from night, he was prepared to trust no one else to perform the operation which he was assured would restore his sight. Dr Saunders had advised him to come to Fu-chou when certain symptoms appeared, but he had delayed, fearing the surgeon's knife, and when at last he could no longer distinguish one object from another the long journey made him nervous and he bade his sons persuade the doctor to come to him.

Kim Ching had started life as a coolie, but by hard work and courage, aided by good luck, cunning, and unscrupulousness, he had amassed a large fortune. At this time, a man of seventy, he owned large plantations on several islands; his own schooners fished for pearl, and he traded extensively in all the products of the Archipelago. His sons, themselves middle-aged men, went to see Dr Saunders. They were his friends and patients. Two or three times a year they invited him to a grand dinner, when they gave him bird's-nest soup, shark fins, *bêche de mer*, and many other delicacies; singing girls engaged at a high price entertained the company with their performances; and everyone got tight. The Chinese liked Dr Saunders. He spoke the dialect of Fu-chou with fluency. He lived, not like the other foreigners in the settlement, but in the heart of the Chinese city; he stayed there year in and year out and they had become accustomed to him. They knew that he smoked opium, though with moderation, and they knew what else there was to be known about him. He seemed to them a sensible man. It did not displease them that the foreigners in the community turned a cold shoulder on him. He never went to the club but to read the papers when the mail came in, and was never invited to dinner by them; they had their own English doctor and called in Dr Saunders only when he was away on leave. But when they had anything the matter with their eyes they put their disapproval in their pockets and came down for treatment to the shabby little Chinese house over the river where Dr Saunders dwelt happily amid the stenches of a native city. They looked about them with distaste as they sat in what was both the doctor's consulting-room and parlour. It was furnished in the Chinese style but for a roll-top desk and a couple of rocking-chairs much the worse for wear. On the discoloured walls Chinese scrolls, presented by grateful patients, contrasted oddly with the sheet of cardboard on which were printed in different sizes and combinations the letters of the alphabet. It always seemed to them that there hung about the house faintly the acrid scent of opium.

But this the sons of Kim Ching did not notice, and if they had it would not have incommoded them. After the usual compliments had passed and Dr Saunders had offered them cigarettes from a green tin, they set forth their business. Their father had bidden them say that now, too old and too blind to make the journey to Fu-chou, he desired Dr Saunders to come to Takana and perform the operation which he had said two years before would be necessary. What would be his fee? The doctor shook his head. He had a large practice in Fu-chou and it was out of the question for him to absent himself for any length of time. He saw no reason why Kim Ching should not come there; he could come on one of his own schooners. If that did not suit him he could get a surgeon from Macassar, who was perfectly competent to perform the operation. The sons of Kim Ching, talking very volubly, explained that their father knew that there was no one who could do the miracles that Dr Saunders could, and he was determined that no one else should touch him. He was prepared to double the sum that the doctor reckoned he could earn at Fu-chou during the period he would be away. Dr Saunders continued to shake his head. Then the two brothers looked at one another and the elder took out from an inner pocket a large and shabby wallet of black leather bulging with the notes of the Chartered Bank. He spread them out before the doctor, a thousand dollars, two thousand dollars; the doctor smiled and his sharp, bright eyes twinkled; the Chinese continued to spread out the notes; the two brothers were smiling too, ingratiatingly, but they keenly watched the doctor's face and presently they were conscious of a change in his expression. He did not move. His eyes kept their tolerant good humour, but they felt in their bones that his interest was aroused. Kim Ching's elder son paused and looked inquiringly into his face.

'I can't leave all my patients for three solid months,' said the doctor. 'Let Kim Ching get one of the Dutch doctors from Macassar or Amboyna. There's a fellow at Amboyna who's quite all right.'

The Chinese did not reply. He put more notes on the table. They were hundred-dollar bills and he arranged them in little

13

packets of ten. The wallet bulged less. He laid the packets side by side and at last there were ten of them.

'Stop,' said the doctor. 'That'll do.'

chapter three

It was a complicated journey. From Fu-chou he went on a Chinese vessel to Manila in the Philippines, and from there, after waiting a few days, by cargo boat to Macassar. Thence he took passage on the Dutch ship that ran every other month to Merauke in New Guinea, stopping at a great many places on the way, and thus at last landed at Takana. He travelled with a Chinese boy who acted as his servant, gave anaesthetics when required, and made his pipes when he smoked opium. Dr Saunders performed a successful operation on Kim Ching, and now there was nothing for him to do but sit and twiddle his thumbs till the Dutch ship called on her way back from Merauke. The island was fairly large, but it was isolated and the Dutch Régisseur visited it only at intervals. The government was represented by a half-caste Javanese, who spoke no English, and a few policemen. The town consisted of a single street of shops. Two or three were owned by Arabs from Baghdad, but the rest by Chinese. There was a small rest-house about ten minutes' walk from the town which the Régisseur inhabited on his periodical visits, and here Dr Saunders had installed himself. The path that led to it ran on through plantations for three miles, and then was lost in the virgin jungle.

When the Dutch ship came in, there was a certain animation. The captain, one or two of the officers, and the chief engineer came ashore, and the passengers if there were any, and they sat in Kim Ching's store and drank beer, but they never stayed for more than three hours and when they got back into their boats and rowed away the little town went to sleep again. It was in the doorway of this store that Dr Saunders sat now. There was a rattan awning that protected it from the sun, but in the street the sun beat down with a harsh

14

glare. A mangy dog sniffed about some offal over which a swarm of flies was buzzing and looked for something to eat. Two or three chickens scratched about in the roadway and one, squatting, ruffled her feathers in the dust. Outside the shop opposite, a naked Chinese child with a distended belly was trying to make a sand castle out of the dust in the road. Flies flew about him, settling on him, but he did not mind them, and intent on his game did not try to brush them away. Then a native passed, with nothing on but a discoloured sarong, and he carried two baskets of sugar-cane suspended to each end of a pole balanced on one shoulder. With his shuffling feet he kicked up the dust as he walked. Inside the store a clerk, hunched over a table, was busy with brush and ink writing some document in Chinese characters. A coolie sitting on the floor was rolling cigarettes and smoking them one after the other. No one came in to buy. Dr Saunders asked for a bottle of beer. The clerk left his writing and going to the back of the store took a bottle out of a pail of water and brought it along with a glass to the doctor. It was pleasantly cool.

Time hung somewhat heavily on the doctor's hands, but he was not discontented. He was able to amuse himself with little things, and the mangy dog, the thin chickens, the pot-bellied child all diverted him. He drank his bottle of beer slowly.

chapter four

He looked up. He gave a cry of surprise. For there, strolling towards him, down the middle of the dusty road, were two white men. No ship was in and he wondered where they had come from. They walked idly, looking to right and left of them, like strangers visiting the island for the first time. They were shabbily dressed in trousers and singlets. Their topis were grimy. They came up, saw him sitting in the open shop and stopped. One of them addressed him.

'Is this Kim Ching's.'

'Yes.'

15

'Is he here?'

'No, he's sick.'

'Bad luck. I suppose we can get a drink.'

'Surely.'

The speaker turned to his companion.

'Come on in.'

They entered.

'What'll you have?' asked Dr Saunders.

'A bottle of beer for me.'

'Same here,' said the other.

The doctor gave the order to the coolie. He brought bottles of beer and chairs for the strangers to sit on. One of them was middle-aged, with a sallow, lined face, white hair, and a scrub of white moustache. He was of the middle height, spare, and when he spoke he showed hideously decayed teeth. His eyes were cunning and restless. They were small and pale and set somewhat close together, which gave him a foxy look, but his manner was ingratiating.

'Where have you come from?' asked the doctor.

'We just come in on a lugger. From Thursday Island.'

'A goodish way. Have fine weather?'

'Couldn't want better. A nice breeze and no sea to speak of. Nichols' my name. Captain Nichols. Maybe you've 'eard of me.'

'I can't say I have.'

'I been sailin' these seas for thirty years. There's not an island in the Archipelago I ain't put in at one time or another. I'm pretty well known around 'ere. Kim Ching knows me. Known me for twenty years.'

'I'm a stranger myself,' said the doctor.

Captain Nichols looked at him, and though his face was open and his expression cordial, you had a feeling that there was suspicion in his glance.

'I seem to know your face,' he said. 'I could swear I seen you somewhere.'

Dr Saunders smiled but did not volunteer any information about himself. Captain Nichols screwed up his eyes in the effort to remember where he had run across the little man. He scanned his face with attention. The doctor was short, only just over five foot six, and slight, but with something of a paunch. His hands were soft and podgy, but they were small, with tapering fingers, and if he had been vain it was possible to suppose that once upon a time he had been not a little pleased with them. They had still a sort of well-bred elegance. He was very ugly, with a snub nose and a large mouth; and when he laughed, which he did often, you saw big, yellow, uneven teeth. Under his bushy grey eyebrows his green eyes gleamed bright, amusing, and clever. He was not very closely shaved and his skin was blotchy; he had a high colour which over the cheek-bones spread into a purple flush. It suggested some long-standing affection of the heart. His hair must once have been thick and black and coarse, but now it was nearly white and on the crown very thin. But his ugliness, far from being repellent, was attractive. When he laughed his skin puckered round the eyes, giving his face infinite vivacity, and his expression was charged with an extreme but not ill-natured malice. You would have taken him then for a buffoon, but for the shrewdness that gleamed from his shining eyes. His intelligence was obvious. And though merry and bright, fond of a joke and amused both at his own and at others', you had an impression that even in the abandon of laughter he never quite gave himself away. He seemed to be on his guard. For all his chattiness and however hearty his manner, you were conscious (if you were observant and did not allow yourself to be taken in by his superficial frankness) that those merry, laughing eyes were watching, weighing, judging, and forming an opinion. He was not a man to take things at their face value.

Since the doctor did not speak Captain Nichols went on:

'This is Fred Blake,' he said, with a gesture of his thumb towards his companion.

Dr Saunders nodded.

'Makin' a long stay?' continued the captain.

'I'm waiting for the Dutch packet.'

'North or south?'

'North.'

'What did you say your name was?'

'I didn't mention it. Saunders.'

'I've knocked about too long in the Indian Ocean to ask

questions,' said the captain, with his ingratiating laugh. 'Ask no questions and you won't be told no lies. Saunders? I've known a lot of chaps as answered to that name, but whether it was theirs or not by rights nobody knew but theirselves. What's the matter with old Kim Ching? Fine old sport. I was lookin' forward to 'avin' a bit of a chin-wag with 'im.'

'His eyes went back on him. He's had cataract.'

Captain Nichols sat up and held out his hand.

'Doc Saunders. I knew I'd seen your face. Fu-chou. I was up there seven years ago.'

The doctor took the proffered hand. Captain Nichols turned to his friend.

'Everyone knows Doc Saunders. Best doctor in the Far East. Eyes. That's his line. I 'ad a pal once, everyone said 'e'd go blind, nothing could stop it, 'e went to see the doc and in a month 'e could see as well as you or me. The Chinks just swear by him. Doc Saunders. Well, this is a joyful surprise. I thought you never left Fu-chou from one year's end to the other.'

'Well, I have now.'

'It's a bit of luck for me, this. You're the very man I wanted to meet.' Captain Nichols leaned forward and his cunning eyes fixed the doctor with an intensity in which there was something very like menace. 'I suffer from dyspepsia something awful.'

'Oh, Christ!' muttered Fred Blake.

It was the first time he had spoken since they sat down and Dr Saunders turned to look at him. He slouched in his chair, gnawing his fingers, in an attitude that suggested boredom and ill-humour. He was a tall young man, slight but wiry, with curly, dark brown hair and large blue eyes. He did not look more than twenty. In his dirty singlet and dungarees he looked loutish, an unlicked cub, thought the doctor, and there was a surliness in his expression that was somewhat disagreeable; but he had a straight nose and a well-formed mouth.

'Leave off bitin' your nails, Fred,' said the captain. 'Disgustin' 'abit, I call it.'

'You and your dyspepsia,' retorted the young man, with a chuckle.

18

When he smiled you saw that he had exquisite teeth. They were very white, small, and of a perfect shape; they were so unexpected a grace in that sombre face, their beauty was so dazzling, that you were taken aback. His sulky smile had great sweetness.

'You can laugh because you don't know what it is,' said Captain Nichols. 'I'm a martyr to it. Don't say I'm not careful what I eat. I've tried everything. Nothin' does me any good. This beer now. Do you think I shan't suffer for it? You know just as well as I do that I shall.'

'Go on. Tell the doctor all about it,' said Blake.

Captain Nichols asked nothing better. He proceeded to narrate the history of his malady. He described his symptoms with a scientific accuracy. There was not a revolting detail that he omitted to mention. He enumerated the doctors he had consulted and the patent remedies he had tried. Dr Saunders listened in silence, an expression of sympathetic interest on his face, and occasionally nodded his head.

'If there's anyone as can do anythin' for me it's you, doc,' said the captain earnestly. 'They don't 'ave to tell me you're clever, I can see that for meself.'

'I can't work miracles. You can't expect anyone to do much in a minute for a chronic condition like yours.'

'No, I don't ask that, but you can prescribe for me, can't you? There's nothin' I won't try. What I'd like you to do is to make a thorough examination of me, see?'

'How long are you staying here?'

'Our time's our own.'

'But we're pushing off as soon as we've got what we want,' said Blake.

A quick look passed between the two men. Dr Saunders noticed it. He did not know why he had an impression that there was something strange in it.

'What made you put in here?' he asked.

Fred Blake's face once more grew sullen, and when the doctor put his question he threw him a glance. Dr Saunders read suspicion in it, and perhaps fear. He wondered. It was the captain who replied.

'I've known Kim Ching donkey's years. We wanted some

stores, and we thought it wouldn't do us any 'arm to fill up our tank.'

'Are you trading?'

'In a manner of speakin'. If anythin' comes along we ain't goin' to miss a chance. Who would?'

'What cargo are you carrying?'

'A bit of everything.'

Captain Nichols smiled genially, showing his decayed, discoloured teeth, and he looked strangely shifty and dishonest. It occurred to Dr Saunders that perhaps they were smuggling opium.

'You're not going to Macassar by any chance?'

'We might be.'

'What's that paper?' said Fred Blake suddenly, pointing to one that lay on the counter.

'Oh, that's three weeks old. We brought it down in the ship I came on.'

'Have they got any Australian papers here?'

'No.'

Dr Saunders chuckled at the notion.

'Is there any Australian news in that paper?'

'It's Dutch. I don't know Dutch. In any case, you'd have had later news than that on Thursday Island.'

Blake frowned a little. The captain grinned craftily.

'This ain't exactly the hub of the universe, Fred,' he sniggered.

'Don't you ever have any English papers here at all?' asked Blake.

'Now and then a stray copy of the Hong Kong paper finds it way here or a *Straits Times*, but they're a month old.'

'Don't they ever get any news?'

'Only what the Dutch ship brings.'

'Haven't they got a cable or a wireless?'

'No.'

'If a man wanted to keep out of the way of the police I should think he'd be pretty safe here,' said Captain Nichols.

'For some time, anyway,' agreed the doctor.

'Have another bottle of beer, doc?' asked Blake.

'No, I don't think I will. I'm going back to the rest-house. If you two fellows would like to come and dine there tonight, I can get you some sort of a meal.'

He addressed himself to Blake because he had a feeling that his impulse would be to refuse, but it was Captain Nichols who answered.

'That'd be fine. A change from the lugger.'

'You don't want to be bothered with us,' said Blake.

'No bother. I'll meet you here about six. We'll have a few drinks and then go up.'

The doctor rose, nodded and left.

chapter five

But he did not go immediately to the rest-house. The invitation he had so cordially given to these strangers was due to no sudden urge of hospitality, but to a notion that had come into his head while he was talking to them. Now that he had left Fu-chou and his practice, he was in no hurry to get back, and he had made up his mind to make a trip to Java, his first holiday for many years, before he returned to work. It occurred to him that if they would give him a passage on the lugger, if not to Macassar, at least to one of the more frequented islands, he could then find a steamer to take him in the direction he wished to go. He had been resigned to spending another three weeks or so on Takana when it seemed impossible to get away; but Kim Ching needed his services no longer, and now that a chance offered he was seized with an immense eagerness to profit by it. The thought of staying where he was for so long with nothing to do suddenly became intolerable to him. He walked down the broad street, it was less than half a mile long, till he came to the sea. There was no quay. Coconuts grew to the water's edge, and among them were the huts of the natives of the island. Children were playing about and gaunt pigs rooted among the piles. There was a straight line of silver beach with a few prahus and dug-outs drawn up on it. The coral sand glistened under the fiery sun, and even with shoes on it was hot under the soles of your feet. Hideous crabs scuttled out of your way as you walked. One of the prahus lay bottom up and three dark-skinned Malays in sarongs were working on it. A reef a few hundred yards out formed a lagoon, and in this the water was clear and deep. A small crowd of boys were romping in the shallow. One of Kim Ching's schooners lay at anchor and not far from it was the stranger's lugger. She was very shabby beside Kim Ching's trim craft and badly needed a coat of paint. She seemed very small to rove the trackless ocean, and Dr Saunders had a moment's hesitation. He looked up at the sky. It was cloudless. No wind stirred the leaves of the coconut trees. Drawn up on the beach was a squat little dinghy, and he supposed it was in this that the two men had rowed ashore. He could see no crew on the lugger.

Having had a good look, he turned back and strolled along to the rest-house. He changed into the Chinese trousers and silk tunic in which from long habit he felt most at ease, and taking a book went out to sit on the veranda. Fruit trees grew round about the rest-house, and opposite, on the other side of the path, was a handsome grove of coconuts. They rose, very tall and straight, in their regular lines, and the bright sun, piercing the leaves, splashed the ground with a fantastic pattern of yellow light. Behind him, in the cookhouse, the boy was preparing tiffin.

Dr Saunders was not a great reader. He seldom opened a novel. Interested in character, he liked books that displayed the oddities of human nature, and he had read over and over again Pepys and Boswell's *Johnson*, Florio's *Montaigne*, and Hazlitt's essays. He liked old travel books, and he could peruse with pleasure the accounts in Hakluyt of countries he had never been to. He had at home a considerable library of the books written about China by the early missionaries. He read neither for information nor to improve his mind, but sought in books occasion for reverie. He read with a sense of humour peculiar to himself, and was able to get out of the narratives of missionary enterprise an amount of demure fun which would have much surprised the authors. He was a quiet man, of an agreeable discourse, but not one to force his conversation on you, and he could enjoy his little joke without feeling a desire to impart it to another.

He held in his hand now a volume of Père Huc's travels, but he read with divided attention. His thoughts were occupied with the two strangers who had so unexpectedly appeared on the island. Dr Saunders had known so many thousands of people in his Eastern life that he had no difficulty in placing Captain Nichols. He was a bad hat. By his accent he was English, and if he had knocked about the China seas for so many years it was likely that he had got into some trouble in England. Dishonesty was stamped on his mean and crafty features. He could not have prospered greatly if he was no more now than skipper of this shabby little lugger, and Dr Saunders let a sigh, an ironical sigh, fall on the still air as he reflected how seldom it was that the crook received an adequate return for his labours. But of course the probability was that Captain Nichols preferred dirty work to clean. He was the sort of man who was willing to put his hand to anything. You would not trust him out of your sight. You could rely on him for nothing but to do you down. He had said he knew Kim Ching. It was probable that he was more often out of a job than in one, and he would have been glad enough to take employment under a Chinese owner. He was the kind of fellow you would engage if you had something shady to do, and it might very well be that at one time he had been skipper of one of Kim Ching's schooners. The conclusion Dr Saunders arrived at was that he rather liked Captain Nichols. He was taken by the skipper's genial friendliness; it gave a pleasant savour to his roguery, and the dyspepsia he suffered from added a comic note that pleased. The doctor was glad that he would see him again that evening.

Dr Saunders took an interest in his fellows that was not quite scientific and not quite human. He wanted to receive entertainment from them. He regarded them dispassionately and it gave him just the same amusement to unravel the intricacies of the individual as a mathematician might find in the solution of a problem. He made no use of the knowledge he obtained. The satisfaction he got from it was aesthetic, and if to know and judge men gave him a subtle sense of superiority he was unconscious of it. He had fewer prejudices than most men. The sense of disapproval was left out of him. Many people are indulgent to the vices they practise, and have small patience with those they have no mind to; some, broader minded, can accept them all in a comprehensive toleration, a toleration, however, that is more often theoretical than practical; but few can suffer manners different from their own without distaste. It is seldom that a man is shocked by the thought that someone has seduced another's wife, and it may be that he preserves his equanimity when he knows that another has cheated at cards or forged a cheque (though this is not easy when you are yourself the victim), but it is hard for him to make a bosom friend of one who drops his aitches, and almost impossible if he scoops up gravy with his knife. Dr Saunders lacked this sensitiveness. Unpleasant table manners affected him as little as a purulent ulcer. Right and wrong were no more to him than good weather and bad weather. He took them as they came. He judged but he did not condemn. He laughed.

He was very easy to get on with. He was much liked. But he had no friends. He was an agreeable companion, but neither sought intimacy nor gave it. There was no one in the world to whom he was not at heart indifferent. He was self-sufficient. His happiness depended not on persons but on himself. He was selfish, but since he was at the same time shrewd and disinterested, few knew it and none was inconvenienced by it. Because he wanted nothing, he was never in anybody's way. Money meant little to him, and he never much minded whether patients paid him or not. They thought him philanthropic. Since time was as unimportant to him as cash, he was just as willing to doctor them as not. It amused him to see their ailments yield to treatment, and he continued to find entertainment in human nature. He confounded persons and patients. Each was like another page in an interminable book, and that there were so many repetitions oddly added to the interest. It was curious to see how all these people, white, yellow, and brown, responded to the critical situations of humanity, but the sight neither touched his heart nor troubled his nerves. Death was, after all, the greatest event in every man's life, and he never ceased to find interest in the way he faced it. It was with a little thrill that he sought to pierce into a man's consciousness, looking through the eyes frightened, defiant, sullen, or resigned, into the soul confronted for the first time with the knowledge that its race was run, but the thrill was merely one of curiosity. His sensibility was unaffected. He felt neither sorrow nor pity. He only faintly wondered how it was that what was so important to one could matter so little to another. And yet his manner was full of sympathy. He knew exactly what to say to alleviate the terror or pain of the moment, and he left no one but fortified, consoled and encouraged. It was a game that he played, and it gave him satisfaction to play it well. He had great natural kindliness, but it was a kindliness of instinct, which betokened no interest in the recipient: he would come to the rescue if you were in a fix, but if there was no getting you out of it would not bother about you further. He did not like to kill living things, and he would neither shoot nor fish. He went so far, for no reason other than that he felt that every creature had a right to life, that he preferred to brush away a mosquito or a fly than to swat it. Perhaps he was an intensely logical man. It could not be denied that he led a good life (if at least you did not confine goodness to conformity with your own sensual inclinations), for he was charitable and kindly, and he devoted his energies to the alleviation of pain, but if motive counts for righteousness, then he deserved no praise; for he was influenced in his actions neither by love, pity, nor charity.

chapter six

Dr Saunders sat down to tiffin and having finished went into the bedroom and threw himself on his bed. But it was very hot and he could not sleep. He wondered what the connexion was between Captain Nichols and Fred Blake. Notwithstanding his grimy dungarees, the young man did not give the impression of being a sailor; the doctor did not quite know why, and for want of a better reason surmised that it was because he had not got the sea in his eyes. He was hard to place. He spoke with something of an Australian accent, but he was evidently not a rough-neck, and he might have had some education: his manners seemed quite good. Perhaps his people had a business of sorts in Sydney, and he was used to a comfortable home and decent surroundings. But why he was sailing these lonely seas on a pearling lugger with a scoundrel like Captain Nichols was mysterious. Of course the pair of them might be in partnership, but what traffic they were engaged in remained to be seen. Dr Saunders was inclined to believe that it was not a very honest one, and whatever it was, that Fred Blake would get the thin end of the stick.

Though Dr Saunders was stark naked, the sweat poured off him. Between his legs was a Dutch wife. This is the bolster which they use in those parts for coolness' sake, and many grow so accustomed to it that even in temperate climes they cannot sleep without it; but it was strange to the doctor and it irked him. He threw it aside and rolled over on his back. In the garden round the rest-house, in the coconut grove opposite, a myriad insects were making noise, and the insistent din, which generally fell unheard on ears benumbed, now throbbed on his nerves with a racket to awake the dead. He gave up the attempt to sleep, and wrapping a sarong round him went out again on to the veranda. It was as hot there as within and as airless. He was weary. His mind was restless, but it worked perversely, and thoughts jerked through his brain like the misfirings of a defective carburettor. He tried to cool himself with a bath, but it brought no refreshment to his spirit. It remained hot, listless, and uneasy. The veranda was intolerable, and he threw himself once more on his bed. The air under the mosquito curtains seemed to stand still. He could not read, he could not think, he could not rest. The hours were leaden-footed.

He was aroused at last by a voice on the steps, and going out he found there a messenger from Kim Ching, who asked him to go and see him. The doctor had paid his patient a professional visit that morning, and there was nothing much more he could do for him, but he put on his clothes and sallied forth.

Kim Ching had heard of the lugger's arrival, and was curious to know what the strangers wanted. He had been told that the doctor had spent an hour with them that morning. He did not much care for unknown persons to come to the island, so much of which belonged to him. Captain Nichols had sent a message asking to see him, but the Chinese had replied that he was too sick to receive anyone. The captain claimed acquaintance with him, but Kim Ching had no recollection of him. An accurate description of the man had already reached him, and the doctor's account added nothing to help him. It appeared that they were staying two or three days.

'They told me they were sailing at dawn,' said Dr Saunders. He reflected for a moment. 'Perhaps they changed their plans when I told them there was no cable or wireless on the island.'

'They've got nothing in the lugger but ballast,' said Kim Ching. 'Stones.'

'No cargo at all?'

'Nothing.'

'Opium?'

Kim Ching shook his head. The doctor smiled.

'Perhaps it's just a pleasure trip. The skipper's got stomach trouble. He wants me to do something for him.'

Kim Ching gave an exclamation. That gave him the clue. He remembered. He had had Captain Nichols on one of his schooners, eight or ten years before, and had fired him. There had been some dispute, but Kim Ching did not go into any detail.

'He's a bad man,' said Kim Ching. 'I could have had him put in prison.'

Dr Saunders guessed that the transaction, whatever it was, had been far from straight, and it might well be that Captain Nichols, knowing Kim Ching would not venture to prosecute, had taken more than his fair share of the profits. There was an ugly look in the Chinaman's face. He knew all about Captain Nichols now. He had lost his certificate, there had been some trouble with an insurance company, and since then he had been glad to take employment with owners who were not particular about such things. He had been a heavy drinker till his stomach went back on him. He picked up a living as best he could. He was often on the beach. But he was a first-rate sea-man, and he got jobs. He did not keep them long, because it was impossible for him to go straight.

'You tell him he more better get out of here pletty damn quick,' said Kim Ching, to finish, breaking into English.

chapter seven

Night had fallen when Dr Saunders sauntered down once more to Kim Ching's store. Nichols and Blake were sitting there drinking beer. He took them up to the rest-house. The sailor was full of small talk, of a facetious nature, but Fred remained sullen and silent. Dr Saunders was conscious that he came against his will. When he entered the living-room of the bungalow he gave a quick, suspicious look round as though he awaited he did not quite know what, and when the house ghekko gave its sudden harsh cry he started suddenly.

'It's only a lizard,' said Dr Saunders.

'It made me jump.'

Dr Saunders called Ah Kay, his boy, and told him to bring the whisky and some glasses.

'I daren't drink it,' said the skipper. 'It's poison to me. How would you like never to be able to eat a thing or drink a thing, without knowin' you was goin' to suffer for it?'

'Let me see what I can do for you,' said Dr Saunders.

He went to his medicine chest and mixed something in a glass. He gave it to the captain and told him to swallow it.

'Maybe that'll help you to eat your dinner in comfort.'

He poured out whisky for himself and Fred Blake and turned on the gramophone. The young man listened to the record and his expression grew more alert; when it was fin-ished he put on another himself and, slightly swaying to the rhythm, stood looking at the instrument. He stole one or two glances at the doctor, but the doctor pretended not to notice him. Captain Nichols, his shifty eyes never still, carried on the conversation. It consisted chiefly of inquiries about this man and that in Fu-chou, Shanghai, and Hong Kong, and descriptions of the drunken parties he had been on in those parts. Ah Kay brought in the dinner and they sat down.

'I enjoy my food,' said the captain. 'Not fallals, mind you. I like it good and I like it simple. Not a big eater. I never been that. A cut off the joint and a couple of veges, with a bit of cheese to finish up with, and I'm satisfied. You couldn't eat anything simpler than that, could you? And then twenty minutes after – as regular as clockwork – agony. I tell you life ain't worth livin' when you suffer like what I do. D'you ever know old George Vaughan? One of the best. He was on one of the Jardine boats, used to go up to Amoy, he 'ad dyspepsia so bad he 'anged himself. I shouldn't be surprised if I didn't, too, one of these days.'

Ah Kay was not a bad cook, and Fred Blake did full justice to the dinner.

'This is a treat after what we've had to eat on the lugger.'

'Most of it comes out of a tin, but the boy flavours it up. The Chinese are natural-born cooks.'

'It's the best dinner I've had for five weeks.'

Dr Saunders remembered that they had said they had come from Thursday Island. With the fine weather they admitted that could not have taken them more than a week.

'What sort of a place is Thursday Island?' he asked.

It was the captain who answered.

'Hell of a place. Nothin' but goats. The wind blows six months one way and then it blows six months the other. Gets on your nerves.'

Captain Nichols spoke with a twinkle in his eyes as though he saw what was at the back of the doctor's simple question and was amused at the easy way he tackled it.

'Do you live there?' Dr Saunders asked the young man, a guileless smile on his lips.

'No, Brisbane,' he answered abruptly.

'Fred's got a bit of capital,' said Captain Nichols, 'and 'e thought he'd like to 'ave a look-see on the chance 'e might find somethin' in these parts 'e'd like to invest it in. My idea, that was. You see, I know all these islands inside out, and what I say is, there's a rare lot of chances for a young fellow with a

29

bit of capital. That's what I'd do if I 'ad a bit of capital, buy a plantation in one of these islands.'

'Do a bit of pearl fishing, too,' said Blake.

'You can get all the labour you want. Native labour's the only thing. Then you sit back and let other people work for you. Fine life, too. Grand thing for a young fellow.'

The skipper's shifty eyes, for a moment still, were fixed on Dr Saunders' bland face, and it was not hard to see that he was watching the effect of what he was saying. The doctor felt that they had concocted the story between them that afternoon. And when the skipper saw that Dr Saunders did not swallow it, he grinned cheerfully. It was as if he took so much delight in lying that it would have spoilt it for him if you had accepted it as the truth.

'That's why we put in 'ere,' he went on. 'There's not much about these islands that old Kim Ching don't know, and it struck me we might do business with 'im. I told the boy in the store to tell the old fellow I was 'ere.'

'I know. He told me.'

'You seen 'im, then? Did 'e say anythin' about me?'

'Yes, he said you'd better get out of here pretty damn quick.'

'Why, what's 'e got against me?'

'He didn't say.'

'We 'ad a bit of a disagreement, I know that, but that was donkey's years ago. There's no sense in 'oldin' a thing up against a fellow all that while. Forgive and forget, I say.'

Captain Nichols had the unusual trait that he could play a mean trick on a man without bearing him any ill feeling afterwards, and he could not understand that the injured party might continue to harbour malice. Dr Saunders noticed the idiosyncrasy with amused detachment.

'My impression is that Kim Ching has a good memory,' he said.

They talked of one thing and another.

'Do you know,' said the captain suddenly, 'I don't believe I'm goin' to 'ave dyspepsia tonight. Say, what was that stuff you gave me?'

'A little preparation that I've found useful in chronic cases like yours.'

'I wish you'd give me some more of it.'

'It mightn't do you any good next time. What you want is treatment.'

'Do you think you could cure me?'

The doctor saw his opportunity coming.

'I don't know about that. If I could watch you for a few days and try one or two things, I might be able to do something for you.'

'I've got a good mind to stay on 'ere for a bit and let you see. We're in no 'urry.'

'What about Kim Ching?'

'What can 'e do?'

'Come off it,' said Fred Blake. 'We don't want to get into any trouble here. We're sailing tomorrow.'

'It's all right for you to talk. You don't suffer like what I do. Look 'ere, I'll tell you what I'll do. I'll go and see the old devil tomorrow and find out what 'e's got against me.'

'We're sailing tomorrow,' repeated the other.

'We're sailin' when I say we sail.'

The two men looked at one another for an instant. The skipper smiled with his usual foxy geniality, but Fred Blake frowned with sullen anger. Dr Saunders interrupted the quarrel that was in the air.

'I don't suppose you know Chinamen as well as I do, captain, but you must know something about them. If they've got their knife into you they're not going to let you off for the asking.'

The skipper thumped his fist on the table.

'Well, it was only a matter of a couple of 'undred quid. Old Kim's as rich as be damned. What difference can that make to 'im? He's an old crook, anyway.'

'Have you never noticed that nothing hurts the feelings of a crook so much as to have another crook do the dirty on him?'

Captain Nichols wore a moody scowl. His little greenish eyes, set too close together, seemed to converge as he shot a bitter glance into space. He looked a very ugly customer. But at the doctor's remark he threw back his head and laughed.

'That's a good one. I like you, doc, you don't mind what you say, do you? Well, it takes all sorts to make a world. Keep your eyes skinned and let the devil take the 'indmost, that's what I say. And when you see a chance of makin' a bit you're a fool if you don't take it. Of course everyone makes a mistake now and again. But you can't always tell beforehand 'ow things are goin' to turn out.'

'If the doctor gives you some more of that stuff and tells you what to do, you'll be all right,' said Blake.

He had recovered his temper.

'No, I won't do that,' said Dr Saunders. 'But I'll tell you what: I'm fed up with this God-forsaken island and I want to get out; if you'll give me a passage on the lugger to Timor or Macassar or Surabaya, you shall have all the treatment you want.'

'That's an idea,' said Captain Nichols.

'A damned rotten one,' cried the other.

'Why?'

'We can't carry passengers.'

'We can sign 'im on.'

'There's no accommodation.'

'I guess the doctor ain't particular.'

'Not a bit. I'll bring my own food and drink. I'll get a lot of canned stuff at Kim Ching's, and he's got plenty of beer.'

'Nothing doing,' said Blake.

'Look 'ere, young feller-me-lad, who gaves orders on this boat, you or me?'

'Well, if it comes down to brass tacks, I do.'

'Put that out of your 'ead at once, my lad. I'm skipper and what I say goes.'

'Whose boat is it?'

'You know very well whose boat it is.'

Dr Saunders watched them curiously. His bright quick eyes missed nothing. The captain had lost all his geniality and his face was mottled with red. The youth bore a look of thunder. His fists were clenched and his head thrust forward.

'I won't have him on the boat, and that's that,' he cried.

'Oh, come on,' said the doctor, 'it's not going to hurt you. It'll only be for five or six days. Be a sport. If you won't take me I shall have to stay here God knows how long.'

'That's your look out.'

'What have you got against me?'

'That's my business.'

Dr Saunders gave him a questioning glance. Blake was not only angry, he was nervous. His handsome, sullen face was pale. It was curious that he should be so disinclined to let him come on the lugger. In these seas people made no bones about that sort of thing. Kim Ching had said they carried no cargo, but it might be the sort of cargo that did not take up much space and was easily hidden. Neither morphine or cocaine took up a great deal of room, and there was a lot of money to be made if you could take them to the right places.

'You'd be doing me a great favour,' he said gently.

'I'm sorry; I don't want to seem a rotten sport, but me and Nichols are here on business, and we can't go out of our way to land a passenger in some place we don't want to go to.'

'I've known the doctor for twenty years,' said Nichols. 'He's all right.'

'You never set eyes on him till this morning.'

'I know all about 'im.' The captain grinned, showing his broken, discoloured little teeth, and Dr Saunders reflected that he should have them out. 'And if what I 'ear is true 'e ain't got much on any of us.'

He gave the doctor a shrewd look. It was interesting to see the hardness behind his genial smile. The doctor bore the glance without flinching. You could not have told if the shaft had gone home or if he had no notion of what the skipper was talking about.

'I don't bother myself much with other people's concerns,' he smiled.

'Live and let live, I say,' said the captain, with the amiable toleration of the scamp.

'When I say no, I mean no,' answered the young man obstinately.

'Oh, you make me tired,' said Nichols. 'There ain't nothin' to be scared about.'

'Who says I'm scared?'

'I do.'

'I've got nothing to be scared about.'

They flung the short sentences at one another quickly. Their exasperation was increasing. Dr Saunders wondered what the secret was that lay between them. It had evidently more to do with Fred Blake than with Nichols. For once the rascal had nothing on his conscience. He reflected that Captain Nichols was not the sort of man who would make it easy for anyone whose secret he knew. He could not exactly tell why, but he had an impression that, whatever it was, Captain Nichols did not know but only suspected it. The doctor, however, was very anxious to get on the lugger, and he did not mean to give up the project before he need. It amused him to exercise a certain astuteness to gain his end.

'Look here, I don't want to cause a quarrel between you two. If Blake doesn't want me, let's say no more about it.'

'But I want you,' retorted the skipper. 'It's a chance in a million for me. If there's a man alive as can put my digestion right, it is you, and d'you think I'm goin' to miss an opportunity like that? Not 'alf.'

'You think too much about your digestion,' said Blake. 'That's my belief. If you just ate what you wanted to and didn't bother, you'd be all right.'

'Oh, should I? I suppose you know more about me digestive apparatus than what I do. I suppose you know when a bit of dry toast sits on me stomach like a ton of lead. I suppose you'll say it's all fancy next.'

'Well, if you ask me, I think fancy's got a damned sight more to do with it than you think.'

'You son of a bitch.'

'Who are you calling a son of a bitch?'

'I'm calling you a son of a bitch.'

'Oh, shut up,' said the doctor.

Captain Nichols gave a loud belch.

'Now the bastard's brought it on again. It's three months if it's a day that I was able to sit down after supper and feel comfortable, and now he's brought it on again. An upset like this is the death of me. Flies to me stomach at once. I'm a bundle of nerves. Always 'ave been. I thought I was goin' to 'ave a pleasant evenin' for once, and now he's gone and ruined it. I've got dyspepsia somethin' cruel.'

'I'm sorry to hear that,' said the doctor.

'They all say the same thing; they all say: Captain, you're a bundle of nerves. Delicate? You're more delicate than a child.'

Dr Saunders was gravely sympathetic.

'It's as I suspected, you want watching; your stomach wants educating. If I'd been coming with you on the lugger I should have made it my business to teach your digestive juices to function in a proper manner. I don't say I could have effected a cure in six or seven days, but I could have put you on the way.'

'But who says you're not comin' on the lugger?'

'Blake does, and from what I gather he's the boss.'

'Oh, do you? Well, you're mistaken. I'm skipper, and what I says goes. Get your kit packed and come on board tomorrow mornin'. I'll sign you on as a member of the crew.'

'You'll do nothing of the sort,' said Blake, jumping to his feet. 'I've got as much say as you have, and I say he's not coming. I won't have anyone on the lugger, and that's that.'

'Oh, won't you? And what'll you say if I run her straight up to B.N.B.? British territory, young feller-me-lad.'

'You take care an accident doesn't happen to you.'

'D'you think I'm scared of you? D'you think I've knocked about all over the world since before you was born without knowin' 'ow to take care of meself? Stick a knife in me back, would you? And who's goin' to sail the boat? You and them four black niggers? You make me laugh. Why, you don't know one end of the boat from the other.'

Blake clenched his hands again. The two men glared at one another, but in the captain's eyes was a mocking sneer. He knew that when it came to a show-down he held the cards. A little sigh escaped the other.

'Where d'you want to go?' he asked the doctor.

'Any Dutch island where I can get a ship that'll take me on my way.'

'All right, come on, then. Anyway, it'll be better than being cooped up alone with that all the time.'

He gave the skipper a glance of impotent hatred. Captain Nichols laughed good-naturedly.

'That's true, it'll be company for you, me boy. We're getting off about ten tomorrow. That suit you?'

'Suit me A1,' said the doctor.

chapter eight

His guests left early and Dr Saunders, taking his book, lay down in a long, rattan chair. He glanced at his watch. It was a little after nine. It was his habit to smoke half a dozen pipes of an evening. He liked to begin at ten. He waited for this moment, not with malaise, but with a little tremor of anticipation which was pleasant, and he would not cut this short by advancing the hour of his indulgence.

He called Ah Kay and told him that they were sailing in the morning on the strangers' lugger. The boy nodded. He, too, was glad to get away. Dr Saunders had engaged him when he was thirteen, and now he was nineteen. He was a slim, comely youth with large black eyes and a skin as smooth as a girl's. His hair, coal-black and cut very short, fitted his head like a close cap. His oval face was of the colour of old ivory. He was quick to smile, and then he showed two rows of the most exquisite teeth possible, small and white and regular. In his short Chinese trousers of white cotton and the tight jacket without a collar he had a languorous elegance that was strangely touching. He moved silently and his gestures had the deliberate grace of a cat. Dr Saunders sometimes flattered himself with the thought that Ah Kay regarded him with affection.

At ten, closing his book, he called:

'Ah Kay!'

The boy came in and Dr Saunders watched him placidly as he took from a table the little tray on which were the oil lamp, the needle, the pipe, and the round tin of opium. The boy put it down on the floor by the doctor, and himself squatting on his haunches, lit the lamp. He held the needle in the flame, and with the warm end extracted a sufficiency from the tin of opium; with deft fingers he made it into a ball and delicately cooked it over the little yellow flame. Dr Saunders watched it sizzle and swell. The boy withdrew it from the flame, kneaded the pellet again and cooked it once more; he inserted it into the pipe and handed it to his master. The doctor took it and with the strong quick pull of the practised smoker inhaled the sweet-tasting smoke. He held it for a minute in his lungs and then slowly exhaled it. He handed the pipe back. The boy scraped it out and put it on the tray. He warmed the needle again and began to cook another pellet. The doctor smoked a second pipe and a third. The boy rose from the floor and went into the cookhouse. He came back with a little pot of jasmine tea and poured it into a Chinese bowl. The fragrance for an instant overpowered the acrid odour of the drug. The doctor lay back in his long chair, his head against a cushion and looked at the ceiling. They did not speak. It was very silent in the compound, and the only sound that broke the stillness was the sharp cry of a ghekko. The doctor watched it as it stood still on the ceiling, a little yellow beast that looked like a pre-historic monster in miniature, and occasionally made a rapid dart as a fly or a moth caught its attention. Ah Kay lit himself a cigarette, and taking an odd, stringed instrument, something like a banjo, amused himself by playing softly. The thin notes straggled along the air, disconnected sounds they seemed, and if now and then you heard the beginning of a melody, it was not completed and your ear was deceived; it was a slow and plain-tive music, as incoherent as the varied scents of flowers, and it seemed to offer you but indications, a hint here and there, the suggestion of a rhythm, with which to create in your own soul a more subtle music than ears could hear. Now and then a sharp discord, like the scratching of a pencil on a slate, as-saulted the nerves with a sudden shock. It gave the soul the same delicious tremor as startles the body when in the heat you plunge into an ice-cold pool. The boy sat on the floor in an attitude of unaffected beauty and meditatively plucked the strings of his lute. Dr Saunders wondered what vague emo-tions touched him. His melancholy face was impassive. He seemed to be looking into his memory for melodies heard in some long past existence.

Presently the boy looked up, a rapid, charming smile sud-denly lighting up his features, and asked his master if he was ready. The doctor nodded. Ah Kay put down his lute and relit the little lamp. He prepared another pipe. The doctor smoked it and two more besides. This was his limit. He smoked regu-larly, but with moderation. Then he lay back and surrendered himself to his thoughts. Ah Kay now made himself a couple of pipes, and having smoked them put out the lamp. He lay down on a mat with a wooden rest under his neck and presently fell asleep.

But the doctor, exquisitely at peace, considered the riddle of existence. His body rested in the long chair so comfortably that he was not conscious of it except in so far as an obscure sense of well-being in it added to his spiritual relief. In this condition of freedom his soul could look down upon his flesh with the affectionate tolerance with which you might regard a friend who bored you but whose love was grateful to you. His mind was extraordinarily alert, but in its activity there was no restlessness and no anxiety; it moved with an assurance of power, as you might imagine a great physicist would move among his symbols, and his lucidity had the absolute delight of pure beauty. It was an end in itself. He was lord of space and time. There was no problem that he could not solve if he chose; everything was clear, everything was exquisitely simple; but it seemed foolish to resolve the difficulties of being when there was so delicate a pleasure in knowing that you could completely do so whensoever you chose.

chapter nine

Dr Saunders was an early riser. The dawn had but just broken when he went out on his veranda and called Ah Kay. The boy brought his breakfast, the little delicate bananas known as lady's fingers, the inevitable fried eggs, toast, and tea. The doctor ate with good appetite. There was little packing to do. Ah Kay's scanty wardrobe went into a brown-paper parcel, and the doctor's into a Chinese portmanteau of pale pigskin. The medical stores and the surgical appliances were kept in a tin box of moderate size. Three or four natives were waiting at the foot of the steps that led up to the veranda, patients who wanted to consult the doctor, and he had them up one by one while he ate his breakfast. He told them he was leaving that morning. Then he walked over to Kim Ching's house. It stood in a plantation of coconut trees. It was an imposing bungalow, the largest on the island, with bits and pieces of architecture to give it style, but its pretentiousness contrasted oddly with a sordid environment. It had no garden, and the ground round about it, littered with empty tins of preserved foodstuff and fragments of packing-cases, was untended. Chickens, ducks, dogs, and pigs wandered about trying to find something to eat among the refuse. It was furnished in the European style, with sideboards of fumed oak, American rockers of the kind you used to see in Middle-Western hotels, and occasional tables upholstered in plush. On the walls were enlarged photographs in massive gold frames of Kim Ching and the many members of his family.

Kim Ching was tall and stout, of a dignified presence, and he wore white ducks and a watch-chain of massive gold. He was much pleased with the result of his operation; he could see as he had never expected to, but all the same he would have liked to keep Dr Saunders on the island a little longer.

'You damn fool to go on that lugger,' he said when the doctor told him he was sailing with Captain Nichols. 'You velly comfortable here. Why you no wait? Take it easy an' enjoy yourself. Much more better you wait for Dutch boat. Nichols velly bad man.'

'You're not a velly good man yourself, Kim Ching.'

The trader, showing a row of expensive gold teeth, greeted this sally with a slow, fat smile in which there was no hint of disagreement. He liked the doctor and was grateful to him. When he saw that there was no persuading him to stay, he ceased to urge it. Dr Saunders gave him his final instructions and took leave of him. Kim Ching accompanied him to the door and they parted. The doctor went down to the village and bought provisions for the journey, a bag of rice, a bunch of bananas, canned goods, whisky, and beer; he told the coolie to take them down to the beach and wait for him, and returned to the rest-house. Ah Kay was ready and one of that morning's patients, willing to earn a trifle, was waiting to carry the luggage. When they came to the beach one of Kim Ching's sons was there to see him off, and he had brought at his father's instructions a roll of Chinese silk as a parting present, and a

39

little square packet wrapped in white paper with Chinese characters on it, the contents of which Dr Saunders guessed.

'Chandu?'

'My father say velly good stuff. P'laps you not have plenty for journey.'

There was no sign of life on the lugger, and the dinghy was not to be seen on the beach. Dr Saunders shouted, but his voice was thin and throaty and did not carry. Ah Kay and Kim Ching's son tried to make someone hear, but in vain, so they put the luggage and the stores into a dug-out and a native paddled the doctor and Ah Kay out. When they came up Dr Saunders shouted again:

'Captain Nichols.'

Fred Blake appeared.

'Oh, it's you. Nichols has gone ashore to get water.'

'I didn't see him.'

Blake said nothing more. The doctor climbed on board, followed by Ah Kay, and the native handed them up their kit and the provisions.

'Where shall I put my stuff?'

'There's the cabin,' said Blake, pointing.

The doctor went down the companion. The cabin was aft. It was so low that you could not stand upright in it, far from spacious, and the main mast went through it. The ceiling was blackened where a smoking lamp hung. There were small portholes with wooden shutters. The mattresses of Nichols and Fred Blake were lengthways, and the only place for himself that the doctor could see was at the foot of the companion. He went on deck again and told Ah Kay to take down his sleeping mat and his portmanteau.

'The stores had better go in the hold,' he said to Fred.

'Fat chance there is for them there. We keep ours in the cabin. Tell your boy he'll find a place under the boards. They're loose.'

The doctor looked about him. He knew nothing of the sea. Except on occasion on the Min River, he had never been on anything but a steamer. The lugger looked very small for so long a voyage. It was a little more than fifty feet long. He would have liked to ask Blake several things, but he had gone forward. It was plain that though he had consented to the doctor's coming it was against his will. He was sulking. There were a couple of old canvas chairs on deck, and in one of them the doctor sat down.

In a little while a blackfellow, wearing nothing but a dingy pareo, came along. He was of solid build, and his crisp curly hair was very grey.

'Captain coming,' he said.

Dr Saunders looked in the direction in which he pointed, and saw the dinghy advancing towards them. Captain Nichols was steering and two blackfellows were rowing. They came alongside and the skipper called out:

'Utan, Tom, give a hand with the casks.'

Another blackfellow came up from the hold. The crew consisted of these four. Torres Straits islanders, tall, strong men with fine figures. Captain Nichols climbed on board and shook hands with the doctor.

'Settled in all right, doc? Not much of the ocean grey'ound about the *Fenton*, but as good a sea-boat as anyone can want. She'll stand anything.'

He gave the dirty, unkempt little craft a sweeping glance in which there was the satisfaction of the workman with the tools he knew how to handle.

'Well, we'll be gettin' off.'

He gave his orders sharply. Mainsail and foresail were hoisted, the anchor weighed, and they slipped out of the lagoon. There was not a cloud in the sky, and the sun beat down on the shining sea. The monsoon was blowing, but with no great force, and there was a slight swell. Two or three gulls flew round them in wide circles. Now and then a flying-fish pierced the surface of the water, made a long dart over it and dived down with a tiny splash. Dr Saunders read, smoked cigarettes, and when he was tired of reading looked at the sea and the green islands they passed. After a while the skipper handed over the wheel to one of the crew and came and sat down by him.

'We'll anchor at Badu tonight,' he said. 'That's about forty-five miles. It looks all right in the Sailing Directions. There's an anchorage there.'

'What is it?'

'Oh, just an uninhabited island. We generally anchor for the night.'

'Blake doesn't seem any more pleased to have me on board,' said the doctor.

'We 'ad a bit of an argument last night.'

'What's the trouble?'

'He's only a kid.'

Dr Saunders knew that he must earn his passage, and he knew also that when a man has told you all his symptoms he will have gained confidence and will tell you a great deal more besides. He began to ask the skipper questions about his health. There was nothing on which he was prepared to talk at greater length. The doctor took him down into the cabin, made him lie down, and carefully examined him. When they went on deck again the grey-haired blackfellow, Tom Obu by name, who was cook and steward, was bringing aft their dinner.

'Come on, Fred,' called the skipper.

They sat down.

'This smells good,' said Nichols, as Tom Obu took the lid off the saucepan. 'Somethin' new, Tom?'

'I shouldn't be surprised if my boy hadn't lent a hand,' said the doctor.

'I think I can eat this,' said the skipper as he took a mouthful of a mess of rice and meat that he ladled on to his plate. 'What do you think of this, Fred? Seems to me we're goin' to do ourselves O.K. with the doc on board.'

'It's better than Tom's cooking, I'll say that for it.'

They ate with hearty appetite. The captain lit his pipe.

'If I don't 'ave a pain after this I'll say you're a wonder, doc.'

'You won't have a pain.'

'What beats me is 'ow a fellow like you come to settle in a place like Fu-chou. You could make a fortune in Sydney.'

'I'm all right in Fu-chou. I like China.'

'Yep? Studied in England, didn't you?'

'Yes.'

'I've 'eard tell you was a specialist, 'ad a big practice in London, and I don't know what all.'

42

'You mustn't believe all you hear.'

'Seems funny you chuckin' everything and settlin' in a lousy Chinese city. You must 'ave been makin' a packet in London.'

The skipper looked at him with his little shifty blue eyes and his grinning face was quick with malice. But the doctor bore his scrutiny blandly. He smiled, showing those large discoloured teeth of his, his eyes shrewd and alert, but gave no sign of embarrassment.

'Ever go back to England?'

'No. Why should I? My home's in Fu-chou.'

'I don't blame you. England's finished, if you ask me. Too many rules and regulations for my taste. Why can't they leave a fellow alone? that's what I'd like to know. Not on the register, are you?'

He shot the question out suddenly as though he wished to take the doctor by surprise. But he had met someone who was a match for him.

'Don't say you haven't confidence in me, Captain. You must believe in your doctor. He can't do much for you if you don't.'

'Believe in you? Why, if I didn't believe in you you wouldn't be 'ere.' Captain Nichols grew deadly serious; this was something that concerned himself. 'I know there's no one as is a patch on you anywheres between Bombay and Sydney, and if the truth was only told I shouldn't be surprised if you'd 'ave to go a long way in London before you could find anyone as could 'old a candle to you. I know you've taken every degree a fellow can take. I've 'eard tell as 'ow if you'd stay in London you'd be a baronet by now.'

'I don't mind telling you that I've got more degrees than are any use to me,' the doctor laughed.

'Funny you shouldn't be in the book. What's it called? The *Medical Directory*.'

'What makes you think I'm not?' murmured the doctor, smiling but wary.

'Fellow I knew in Sydney looked you up. Talkin' about you, 'e was, to another doctor, pal of 'is, and sayin' you was such a marvel and all that, and out of curiosity they'd 'ad a look-see.'

'Perhaps your friend looked in the wrong edition.'

Captain Nichols chuckled slyly.

'Perhaps he did. I never thought of that.'

'Anyhow, I've never seen the inside of a gaol, Captain.'

The skipper gave a little start. He repressed it at once, but he changed colour. Dr Saunders had made a shot in the dark and his eyes twinkled. The skipper laughed.

'That's a good one. No more 'ave I, doc, but don't you forget there's many a man gone to gaol for no fault of 'is own and there's many a man as might 'ave gone there if he 'adn't thought a change of air would suit him.'

They looked at one another and chuckled.

'What's there to laugh about?' said Fred Blake.

chapter ten

Towards evening they sighted the island where Captain Nichols designed to pass the night, a cone covered to its summit with trees so that it looked like a hill in a picture by Piero della Francesca, and sailing round it they came to the anchorage they had read of in the Sailing Directions. It was a well-sheltered cove and the water was so clear that as you looked over the side you saw on the ocean floor the fantastic efflorescence of the coral. You saw the fish swimming, like natives of the forest threading their familiar way through the jungle. Not a little to their surprise they found a schooner anchored there.

'What's that?' asked Fred Blake.

His eyes were anxious, and indeed it was strange to enter upon that silent cove, protected by the green hill, in the still cool of the evening and see there a sailing vessel. She lay, sails furled, and because the spot was so solitary her presence was vaguely sinister. Captain Nichols looked at her through his glasses.

'She's a pearler. Port Darwin. I don't know what she's doin' 'ere. There's a lot of 'em round by the Aru Islands.'

They saw the crew, a white man among them, watching them, and presently a boat was lowered.

'They're comin' over,' said the skipper.

By the time they were anchored, the dinghy had rowed up and Captain Nichols exchanged shouts of greeting with the captain of the schooner. He came on board, an Australian, and told them that his Japanese diver was sick and he was on his way to one of the Dutch islands where he could get a doctor.

'We got a doctor on board,' said Captain Nichols. 'We're givin' 'im a passage.'

The Australian asked Dr Saunders if he would come along and see his sick man, and after they had given him a cup of tea, for he refused a drink, the doctor got into the dinghy.

'Have you got any Australian papers?' asked Fred.

'I've got a *Bulletin*. It's a month old.'

'Never mind. It'll be new to us.'

'You're welcome to it. I'll send it back by the doctor.'

It did not take Dr Saunders long to discover that the diver was suffering from a severe attack of dysentery. He was very ill. He gave him a hypodermic injection, and told the captain there was nothing to do but keep him quiet.

'Damn these Japs, they've got no constitution. I shan't get any more out of him for some time then?'

'If ever,' said the doctor.

They shook hands and he got into the dinghy again. The blackfellow pushed off.

'Here, wait a bit. I forgot to give you that paper.'

The Australian dived into the cabin and in a minute came out again with a *Sydney Bulletin*. He threw it into the dinghy.

Captain Nichols and Fred were playing cribbage when the doctor climbed back on to the *Fenton*. The sun was setting and the smooth sea was lucid with pale and various colour, blue, green, salmon-pink, and milky purple, and it was like the subtle and tender colour of silence.

'Fixed 'im up all right?' inquired the skipper indifferently.

'He's pretty bad.'

'Is that the paper?' Fred asked.

He took it out of the doctor's hand, and strolled forwards.

'Play cribbage?' said Nichols.

'No, I don't.'

'Me and Fred play it every night. Luck of the devil 'e as. I shouldn't like to tell you 'ow much money 'e's won off me. It can't go on. It must turn soon.' He called out: 'Come on, Fred.'

'Half a mo.'

The skipper shrugged his shoulders.

'No manners. Anxious to see a paper, wasn't 'e?'

'And a month old one at that,' answered the doctor. 'How long is it since you left Thursday Island?'

'We never went near Thursday Island.'

'Oh!'

'What about a spot? D'you think it'd do me any 'arm?'

'I don't think so.'

The skipper shouted for Tom Obu, and the blackfellow brought them a couple of glasses and some water. Nichols fetched the whisky. The sun set and the night crept softly over the still water. The only sound that broke the silence was the leap now and then of a fish. Tom Obu brought a hurricane lamp and placed it on the deck-house, and going below lit the smoking oil lamp in the cabin.

'I wonder what our young friend is readin' all this time.'

'In the dark?'

'Maybe 'e's thinkin' of what 'e 'as read.'

But when at last Fred joined them and sat down to finish the interrupted game, it seemed to Dr Saunders, in the uncertain light, that he was very pale. He had not brought the paper with him and the doctor went forward to get it. He could not see it. He called Ah Kay and told him to look for it. Standing in the darkness he watched the players.

'Fifteen two. Fifteen four. Fifteen six. Fifteen eight; and six are fourteen. And one for his nob seventeen.' 'God, what luck you 'ave.'

The skipper was a bad loser. His face was set and hard. His shifty eyes glanced at each card he turned up with a sneering look. But the other played with a smile on his lips. The light of the hurricane lamp cut his profile out of the darkness, and it was astonishingly fine. His long lashes cast a little shadow on his cheeks. Just then he was more than a handsome young man; he had a tragic beauty that was very moving. Ah Kay came and said he could not find the paper.

46

'Where did you leave that *Bulletin*, Fred?' asked the doctor. 'My boy can't find it.'

'Isn't it there?'

'No, we've both looked.'

'How the hell should I know where it is? Two for his heels.'

'Throw it overboard when you done with it?' asked the captain.

'Me? Why should I throw it overboard?'

'Well, if you didn't it must be somewhere about,' said the doctor.

'That's another game to you,' the skipper growled. 'I never see anyone 'old such cards.'

chapter eleven

It was between one and two in the morning. Dr Saunders sat in a deck-chair. The skipper was asleep in the cabin and Fred had taken his mattress forrard. It was very still. The stars were so bright that the shape of the island was very distinctly outlined against the night. Distance is less an affair of space than of time and though they had gone but five-and-forty miles it seemed to the doctor that Takana was very far away. London was at the other end of the world. He had a fleeting vision of Piccadilly Circus, with its bright lights, the crowd of buses, cars, and taxis, and the crowd that surged when the theatres disgorged their audiences. There was a part that in his day they called the Front, the street on the north side that led from Shaftesbury Avenue to the Charing Cross Road, where from eleven to twelve people walked up and down in a serried throng. That was before the war. There was a sense of adventure in the air. Eyes met and then ... The doctor smiled. He did not regret the past; he regretted nothing. Then his wandering thoughts hovered over the bridge at Fu-chou, the bridge over the Min River, from which you saw the fishermen in the barges below fishing with cormorants; rickshaws crossed the bridge, and coolies bearing heavy loads, and the innumerable Chinese walked to and fro. On the right bank as you looked downstream was the Chinese City with its crowded houses and its temples. The schooner showed no light and the doctor only saw it in the darkness because he knew that it was there. All was silent on board. But in the hold where the pearl shell was piled, on one of the wooden bunks along the side, lay the dying diver. The doctor attached small value to human life. Who, that had lived so long amid those teeming Chinese where it was held so cheap, could have much feeling about it? He was a Japanese, the diver, and probably a Buddhist. Transmigration? Look at the sea: wave follows wave, it is not the same wave, yet one causes another and transmits its form and movement. So the beings travelling through the world are not the same today and tomorrow, nor in one life the same as in another; and yet it is the urge and the form of the previous lives that determine the character of those that follow. A reasonable belief but an incredible one. But was it any more incredible than that so much striving, such a variety of accidents, so many miraculous hazards should have combined, through the long aeons of time, to produce from the primeval slime at long last this man who, by means of Flexner's bacillus, was aimlessly snuffed out? Dr Saunders thought it odd, but natural, senseless certainly, but he had long made himself at home in the futility of things. Of course the spirit was a difficulty. Did that cease to exist when the matter which was its instrument dissolved? In that lovely night, his thoughts flowing without purpose, like birds, sea-gulls, wheeling over the sea, rising and falling as the wind took them, he could not but keep an open mind.

There was the sound of shuffling steps on the companion and the skipper appeared. The stripe of his pyjamas was bold enough to tell against the darkness.

'Captain?'

'It's me. I thought I'd come up for a breath of air.' He sank into the chair by the doctor's side. 'Had your smoke?'

'Yes.'

'I've never took to it meself. I've known a good many as did, though. Never seemed to do 'em much 'arm. Settles the stomach, they say. One fellow I knew went all to pieces. Skipper of one of Butterfield's boats on the Yang-tze at one time. Good position and everything. They thought a rare lot of 'im. Sent him 'ome once to get cured, but 'e took to it again the moment 'e come back. Ended up as a tout for a fantan 'ouse. Used to 'ang about the docks at Shanghai and cadge 'alf-dollars.'

They were silent for a while. Captain Nichols sucked a briar pipe.

'Seen anythin' of Fred?'

'He's sleeping on deck.'

'Funny thing about that paper. He didn't want you and me to read somethin'.'

'What d'you suppose he did with it?'

'Dropped it overboard.'

'What's it all about?'

The skipper gave a low chuckle.

'Believe me, or believe me not, I don't know any more than you do.'

'I've lived in the East long enough to know that it's better to mind my own business.'

But the skipper was inclined to be confidential. His digestion was not troubling him and after three or four hours of good sleep he felt very wide awake.

'There's somethin' fishy about it, I know that, but I'm like you, doc, I'm all for mindin' me own business. Ask no questions an' you'll be told no lies. That's what I say, an' if you get a chance of makin' a bit of money, take it quick.' The skipper gave his pipe a pull. 'You won't let this go any further, will you?'

'Not on your life.'

'Well, it's like this. I was in Sydney. I 'adn't 'ad a job for the best part of two years. And not for the want of tryin', mind you. Just bad luck. First-rate seaman I am and got a lot of experience. Steam or sail, I don't mind what it is. You'd think they'd jump at me. But no. I'm a married man too. Things got so bad my old woman 'ad to go into service, I didn't 'alf like it, I can tell you, but there, I just 'ad to lump it. I 'ad a roof over me 'ead and three meals a day, she give me that all right, but when it come to lettin' me 'ave 'alf a dollar to go to the pictures and get one or two drinks, no, sir. An' nag. Never been married, 'ave you?'

'No.'

'Well, I don't blame you. They're near, you know. Women can't bear partin' with their money. I been married twenty years, and it's been nag, nag, nag all the time. Very superior woman, my missus, that's what begun the trouble, she thought she demeaned 'erself by marryin' me. Her father was a big draper up in Liverpool, and she never let me forget it. She blamed me because I couldn't get a job. Said I liked bein' on the beach. Lazy, idle loafer she called me and said she was fair sick of workin' 'erself to the bone to give me board and lodgin' and if I didn't get a billet soon I could just get out and shift for meself. I give you my word, sometimes I just 'ad to 'old on to meself like grim death not to give her a sock on the jaw, lady though she was, and no one knows that better than what I do. D'you know Sydney?'

'No, I've never been there.'

'Well, one night I was just standin' around in a bar down by the 'arbour I used to go to sometimes. I 'adn't 'ad a drink all day, and I was just parched; my dyspepsia was somethin' awful, and I was feeling pretty low. I 'adn't got a penny in me pocket, me what's commanded more ships than you can count on the fingers of your two 'ands, and I couldn't go 'ome. I knew the missus'd start on me, and she'd give me a bit of cold mutton for me supper, though she knows it's the death of me, and she'd go on and on, always the lady, if you know what I mean, but just nasty, cuttin' and superior-like, never raisin' her voice, but not a minute's peace. An' if I was to lose me temper and tell 'er to go to hell, she'd just draw 'erself up and say: none of your foul language 'ere, Captain, *if* you please. I may 'ave married a common sailor, but I will be treated like a lady.'

Captain Nichols lowered his voice and leant over in a very confidential manner.

'Now this is quite *infra dig.*, if you know what I mean, just between you and me: you don't know where you are with women. They don't behave like 'uman beings. Would you believe it, I've run away from 'er four times. You would think a woman'd see what you meant after that, wouldn't you?'

50

'You would.'

'But no. Every time she's followed me. Of course, once she knew where I'd gone, and it was easy, but the others she didn't know any more than the man in the moon. I'd 'ave bet every penny I 'ad in the world that she wouldn't find me. Like lookin' for a needle in a bundle of 'ay, it was. An' then one day she'd walk up, quite cool, as if she seen me the day before, and not a 'ow d'you do or a fancy seein' you or anythin' like that, but: "You want a shave if you ask me, Captain," or: "Them trousers of yours is a disgrace, Captain." ... I don't care who it is, it's the kind of thing to break anyone's nerve.'

Captain Nichols was silent and his eyes swept the empty sea. In that lucid night you saw quite clearly the thin sharp line of the horizon.

'This time I been an' gone an' done the trick, and I 'ave got away from 'er. She don't know where I am and she can't find out, but I give you my word I wouldn't be surprised if she was to come rowin' over that sea in a dinghy, all neat and tidy, she's always the lady to look at, I will say that for 'er, and come on board and just say to me: "What's that nasty, filthy tobacco you're smokin', Captain? You know, I can't abide anythin' but Player's Navy Cut." It's me nerves. That's what's at the bottom of my dyspepsia, if the truth was only known. I remember, once I went to see a doctor in Singapore as 'ad been very strongly recommended to me and 'e wrote a lot of stuff in a book, you know 'ow doctors do, and he put a cross down. Well, I didn't 'alf like the look of that, so I said to 'im, "I say, doctor," I says, "what's that cross mean?" "Oh," he says, "I always put a cross when I 'ave reason to suspect domestic unpleasantness." "Oh, I see," I says; "well, you've 'it the nail on the 'ead, doctor; I bear a cross all right." Clever fellow 'e was, but 'e never done my dyspepsia much good.'

'Socrates suffered from the same sort of affliction, Captain, but I never heard that it affected his digestion.'

'Who was 'e?'

'An honest man.'

'Much good it did 'im, I lay.'

'In point of fact, it didn't.'

'You've got to take things as you find 'em, I say, and if

you're too particular you won't get anywhere.'

Dr Saunders laughed in his heart. It appealed to his sense of humour to think of this mean and unscrupulous blackguard in abject terror of his wife. It was the triumph of spirit over matter. He wondered what she looked like.

'I was tellin' you about Fred Blake,' the skipper continued, after a pause to relight his pipe. 'Well, as I was sayin', I was in that bar. I said good evenin' to one or two chaps, cordial like, you know, and they said good evenin' to me and looked the other way. You could see them just sayin' to theirselves: there's that bum again, cadgin' around for drinks; 'e ain't goin' to get one out of me. You can't wonder I was feelin' pretty low. Humiliating, that's what it was, for a man as 'ad been in a good position like what I 'ave. It's terrible 'ow near a fellow can be with 'is money when he knows you ain't got none. The boss give me a dirty look and I 'alf thought he was going to ask me what I'd 'ave, and then when I said I'd wait a bit, 'e'd say, well, I'd better wait outside. I began talkin' to one or two chaps I didn't know, but they wasn't what you'd call cordial. I cracked a joke or two, but I couldn't get 'em laughin', and they made it pretty plain that I was buttin' in. And then I saw a fellow come in I knew. Big bully of a chap. What they call a larrikin' in Australia. Name of Ryan. You 'ad to keep in with 'im. He 'ad something to do with politics. Always 'ad plenty of money. He lent me five bob once. Well, I didn't think 'e'd want to see me, so I pretended I didn't recognize 'im and just went on talkin'. But I was watchin' 'im out of the corner of me eye. He looked round and then 'e come right up to me.

' "Good evenin', Captain," he says, very friendly like. "How's the world been treatin' you these days?"

' "Rotten," I says.

' "Still lookin' for a job?"

' "Yes," I says.

' "What'll you 'ave?" he says.

'I 'ad a beer and 'e 'ad a beer. It pretty near saved my life. But you know, I'm not much of a one for believin' in miracles. I wanted that beer pretty bad, but I knew just as well as I know I'm talkin' to you, that Ryan wasn't givin' it me for nothin'. He's one of them 'earties, you know; slaps you on the back

and laughs at your jokes as though he'd fair burst, and it's
" 'Ullo, where 'ave you been 'idin' yourself?" and, "My missus
is a grand little woman and you should see my kiddies," and
all that; and then all the time 'e's watchin' you and 'is eyes
look right through you. It takes in the mugs. "Good old Ryan,"
they say; "one of the best." There are no flies on me, doc. You
don't catch me so easy as that. And while I was drinkin' my
beer I said to myself: "Now, then, old boy, you keep your eyes
skinned. He wants something." But of course I didn't let on. I
told 'im a yarn or two and 'e just laughed 'is 'ead off.

' "You're a caution, Captain," 'e said; "great old sport,
that's what you are. Finish your beer and we'll 'ave another. I
could listen to you talkin' all night."

'Well, I finished my beer and I saw 'e was goin' to order another.

' "Look 'ere, Bill," he says: well, my name's Tom, but I
didn't say nothing. I saw 'e was tryin' to be friendly. "Look
'ere, Bill," he says, "there's too many people round 'ere, one
simply can't 'ear oneself talk, and you never know who's listenin' to what you say. I'll tell you what we'll do." He called
the boss. "Look 'ere George, come 'ere a minute." And up he
comes with a run. "Look 'ere, George, me and my friend we
want to 'ave a little quiet yarn about old times. What about
that room of yours?"

' "My office? All right. You can go in there if you want to,
and welcome."

' "That's the ticket. And you bring us a couple of beers."

'Well, we walks round and we goes into the office, and
George brings us a couple of beers 'imself. In person; gives me
a nod, 'e does. And George goes out. Ryan shut the door after
'im and 'e looked at the window to see it was shut all right.
Said 'e couldn't stand a draught at any price. I didn't know
what 'e was after, and I thought I'd better get straight with 'im
at once.

' "Look 'ere, Ryan," I says; "I'm sorry about that five bob
you lent me. It's been on me mind ever since, but the truth is
I've 'ad all I can do just to keep body and soul together."

' "Forget it," he says. "What's five bob? I know you're all
right. You're a fine feller, Bill. What's the good of 'avin'

53

money if you can't lend it to a pal when 'e's down on his luck?"

' "Well, I'd do the same by you, Ryan," says I, takin' my cue from 'im. To listen to us you'd 'ave thought us a pair of brothers.'

Captain Nichols chuckled as he recalled the scene they had played. He took an artist's delight in his own rascality.

' "Chin, chin," say I.

'We both 'ad a drink of beer. "Now look 'ere, Bill," says 'e, wipin' 'is mouth with the back of 'is 'and, "I been makin' inquiries about you. Good seaman and all that, ain't you?" "None better," says I. "If you ain't 'ad a job for some time I reckon it's more by bad luck than bad management." "That's right," says I. "Now I'm going to give you a surprise, Bill," says 'e. "I'm going to offer you a job meself." "I'll take it," says I. "No matter what it is." "That's the spirit," says 'e. "I knew I could count on you."

' "Well, what is it?" I ask 'im.

'He give me a look, and though 'e was smilin' at me as if I was his long lost brother and 'e loved me like anything, 'e was lookin' at me pretty 'ard. It was no jokin' matter, I could see that.

' "Can you keep your mouth shut?" 'e asks me.

' "Like a clam," says I.

' "That's good," says 'e. "Now what d'you say to takin' a tidy little pearling lugger, you know, one of them ketches they 'ave at Thursday Island and Port Darwin, and cruisin' about the islands for a few months?"

' "Sounds all right to me," I says.

' "Well, that's the job."

' "Tradin'?" I says.

' "No, just pleasure." '

Captain Nichols sniggered.

'I nearly laughed outright when 'e said that, but one 'as to be careful, lot of people 'ave no sense of humour, so I just looked as grave as a judge. He give me another look and I could see 'e could be an ugly customer if you put 'is back up.

' "I'll tell you 'ow it is," 'e says. "Young fellow I know been workin' too 'ard. His dad's an old pal of mine, and I'm doin'

54

this to please 'im, see? He's a man in a very good position. Got a lot of influence in one way and another."

'He 'ad another drink of beer. I kep' me eyes on 'im but I never said a word. Not a syllable.

' "The old man's in a rare state. Only kid, you know. Well, I know what it is with me own kids. If one of 'em gets a pain in 'is big toe, I'm upset for the day."

' "You don't 'ave to tell me," I says. "I got a daughter me-self."

' "Only child?" he says.

'I nodded.

' "Grand thing, children," he says. "Nothin' like 'em to bring 'appiness in a man's life."

' "You're right there," I says.

' "Always delicate, this boy's been," 'e says, shakin' 'is 'ead. "Got a touch of the lungs. The doctors say the best thing 'e can do is to 'ave a cruise on a sailin' ship. Well, 'is dad didn't 'alf like the idea of 'is takin' a passage on any old ship and 'e 'eard of this 'ere ketch and 'e bought her. You see, like that, you're not tied down and you can go anywhere. Nice easy life, that's what 'e wants the boy to 'ave; I mean, you don't 'ave to 'urry. You choose your own weather an' when you get to some island what looks like you could stay there for a bit, why, you just stay. There's dozens of them islands up between Australia and China, they tell me."

' "Thousands," says I.

' "An' the boy's got to be kep' quiet. Essential, that is. His dad wants you to keep away from where there's a lot of people."

' "That's all right," says I, lookin' as innocent as a new-born babe. "And 'ow long for?"

' "I don't exactly know," says he. "Depends on the boy's 'ealth. Two or three months, maybe, or maybe a year."

' "I see," says I; "and what do I get out of it?"

' "Two 'undred quid when your passenger comes on board, and two 'undred quid when you comes back."

' "Make it five 'undred down and I'm game," says I. He never says a thing, but 'e give me a dirty look. And 'e just shoved his jaw out at me. My word, 'e looked a beauty. If there's one thing I got it's tact. He could make things pretty unpleasant for me if 'e wanted to. I knew that, and I 'ad a feeling that if I didn't take care 'e would want to. So I just shrugged me shoulders, careless like, and laughed. "Oh, well, I don't care about the money," I says. "Money means nothin' to me, never 'as. If it 'ad I'd be one of the richest men in Australia today. I'll take what you say. Anythin' to oblige a friend."

' "Good old Bill," says 'e.

' "Where's the ketch now?" says I. "I'd like to go and 'ave a look at her."

' "Oh, she's all right. Friend of mine just brought her down from Thursday Island to sell 'er. She's in grand shape. She ain't in Sydney. She's up the coast a few miles."

' "What about a crew?"

' "Niggers from Torres Straits. They brought 'er down. All you've got to do is to get on board and sail away."

' "When would you want me to sail?"

' "Now."

' "Now?" says I, surprised. "Not tonight?"

' "Yes, tonight. I got a car waitin' down the street. I'll drive you over to where she's lying."

' "What's the 'urry?" I says, smiling, but giving 'im a look as much to say I thought it damned fishy.

' "The boy's dad's a big business man. Always does things like that."

' "Politician?" says I.

'I was beginning to put two and two together, so to speak.

' "My aunt," says Ryan.

' "But I'm a married man," says I. "If I just go off like this without sayin' so much as a word to nobody, my old woman'll be makin' inquiries all over the place. She'll want to know where I am and when she can't find nobody to tell her she'll go to the police."

'He looked at me pretty sharp when I said this. I knew he didn't 'alf like the idea of 'er goin' to the police.

' "It'll look funny, a master mariner disappearin' like this. I mean, it ain't like as if I was a blackfellow or a Kanaka. Of course I don't know if there's anyone 'as reason to be inquisitive. There's a lot of nosey-parkers about, especially just now with the election comin' on."

'I couldn't 'elp thinkin' I got a good one in there, about the election, but 'e didn't let on a thing. His great ugly face might 'a' been a blank wall.

' "I'll go and see 'er meself," 'e said.

'I 'ad me own game to play, too, and I wasn't goin' to let a chance like this pass me by.

' "Tell 'er the first mate of a steamer broke his neck just as she was going out and they took me on and I didn't 'ave time to go 'ome and she'll 'ear from me next from Cape Town."

' "That's the ticket," says 'e.

' "An' if she kicks up a racket give 'er a passage to Cape Town and a five-pound note. That's not askin' much."

'He laughed then, honest, and 'e said 'e'd do it.

'He finished 'is beer and I finished mine.

' "Now then," says 'e, "if you're ready we'll be startin'." He looked at 'is watch. "You meet me at the corner of Market Street in 'alf an hour. I'll drive by in my car and you just jump in. You go out first. No need for you to go out by the bar. There's a door at the end of the passage. You take that and you'll find yourself in the street."

' "O.K." says I, and I takes me 'at.

' "There's just one thing I'd like to say to you," 'e says, as I was going. "An' this refers to now and later. If you don't want a knife in your back or a bullet in your guts you better not try no monkey tricks. See?"

'He said it quite pleasant, but I'm no fool, and I knew 'e meant it.

' "Don't you 'ave no fear," says I. "When a chap treats me like a gentleman, I behave like one." Then very casual like, "Young feller on board, I suppose?"

' "No, 'e ain't. Comin' on board later."

'I walked out and I got into the street. I walked along to where he said. It was only a matter of two 'undred yards. I thought to meself if 'e wanted me to wait there for 'alf an' hour it was because he 'ad to go and see someone and say what 'ad 'appened. I couldn't 'elp wonderin' what the police'd say if I told 'em somethin' funny was up and it'd be worth

57

their while to follow the car and 'ave a look at this ketch. But I thought p'raps it wouldn't be worth *my* while. It's all very well to do a public duty, and I don't mind bein' in well with the cops any more than anyone else does, but it wouldn't do me much good if I got a knife in me belly for me pains. And there was no four 'undred quid to be got out of them. P'raps it's just as well I didn't try any 'anky-panky on with Ryan, because I see a chap on the other side of the street, standin' in the shadow as if 'e didn't want no one to see him, and it looked to me as if he was watchin' me. I walked over to 'ave a look at 'im and 'e walked away when he saw me comin', then I walked back again and he come and stood just where 'e was before. Funny. It was all damned funny. The thing what grizzled me was that Ryan 'adn't shown more confidence in me. If you're goin' to trust a man, trust 'im, that's what I say. I want you to understand I didn't mind its bein' funny. I seen a lot of funny things in my day and I take 'em as they come.'

Dr Saunders smiled. He began to understand Captain Nichols. He was a man who found the daily round of honest life a trifle humdrum. He needed a spice of crookedness to counteract the depression his dyspepsia caused him. His blood ran faster, he felt better in health, his vitality was heightened when his fingers dabbled in crime. The alertness he must then exercise to protect himself from harm took his mind off the processes of his lamentable digestion. If Dr Saunders was somewhat lacking in sympathy, he made up for it by being uncommonly tolerant. He thought it no business of his to praise or condemn. He was able to recognize that one was a saint and another a villain, but his consideration of both was fraught with the same cool detachment.

'I couldn't 'elp laughin' as I thought of meself standin' there,' continued the skipper, 'and startin' off on a cruise without so much as a change of clothes, me shavin' tackle or a toothbrush. You wouldn't find many men as'd be prepared to do that and not give a tinker's cuss.'

'You wouldn't,' said the doctor.

'And then I thought of the face my old woman'd make when Ryan told 'er I'd sailed. I can just see 'er toddlin' off to Cape Town by the next ship. She'll never find me no more.

This time I *'ave* got away from her. And who'd 'ave thought it'd come like that just when I was thinkin' I couldn't stand another day of it. If it wasn't Providence, I don't know what it was.'

'It's ways are always said to be inscrutable.'

'Don't I know it? Brought up a Baptist, I was. "Not a sparrow shall fall –" you know 'ow it goes. I seen it come true over and over again. And then after I'd been waitin' there a bit, a good 'alf hour, a car come along and stops just by me. "Jump in," says Ryan, and off we go. The roads are terrible bad round Sydney and we was bumpin' up and down like a cork in the water. Pretty fast he drove.

' "What about stores and all that?" I says to Ryan.

' "It's all on board," 'e says. "You got enough to last you three months."

'I didn't know where 'e was goin'. Dark night and I couldn't see a thing; it must 'ave been gettin' on for midnight.

' "Here we are," 'e says, and stops. "Get out."

'I got out and 'e got out after me. He turns off 'is lights. I knew we was pretty near the sea, but I couldn't see a yard in front of me. He 'ad an electric torch.

' "You follow me," 'e says, "an' look where you're goin'."

'We walked a bit. A sort of pathway there was. I'm pretty nimble on me feet, but I nearly come arse over tip two or three times. "Nice thing if I break my bloody leg goin' down 'ere," I says to meself. I wasn't 'alf glad when we come to the bottom and I felt the beach under me feet. You could see the water, but you couldn't see nothin' else. Ryan give a whistle. Someone on the water shouted, but low, if you know what I mean, and Ryan flashed his torch to show where we was. Then I 'eard oars splashin' and in a minute or two a couple of blackfellows rowed up in the dinghy. Ryan and me, we got in, and they pushed off. If I'd 'ad twenty quid on me I wouldn't 'ave given much for my chances of ever seein' Australia no more. Australia felix, by gum. We rowed for about ten minutes, I should say, and then we come alongside the ketch.

' "What d'you think of 'er?" asks Ryan, when we got on board.

' "Can't see much," says I. "Tell you more in the morning."

' "In the morning you got to be well out to sea," says Ryan.

' "When's this poor invalid boy comin'?" says I.

' "Pretty soon now," says Ryan. "You go down into the cabin and light the lamp and 'ave a look round. We'll 'ave a bottle of beer. Here's a box of matches."

' "Suits me," I says, and down I goes.

'I couldn't see much, but I knew the way about by instinct. And I didn't go down so quick I couldn't 'ave a look behind me. I twigged he was up to somethin'. I see 'im give three or four flashes with the torch. " 'Ullo," I says to meself, "some-one's watchin'," but if it was ashore or on sea, I couldn't say. Then Ryan comes down and I 'ad a look round. He fished out a bottle of beer for 'isself and a bottle of beer for me.

' "The moon'll be gettin' up soon," he says. "There's a nice little breeze."

' "Startin' right away, are we?" I says.

' "Sooner the better, after the boy's come on board, and just keep goin', see?"

' "Look 'ere, Ryan," I says, "I ain't got so much as a safety razor with me."

' "Grow a beard then, Bill," he answers. "The orders is, no landin' anywhere till you get to New Guinea. If you want to go ashore at Merauke, you can."

' "Dutch, ain't it?" He nods. "Look here, Ryan," I says. "You know I wasn't born yesterday. I can't 'elp thinkin', can I? What's the good, why don't you come out with it straight and tell me what it's all about?"

' "Bill, old boy," 'e says very friendly like, "you drink your beer and don't you ask no questions. I know I can't 'elp you thinkin', but you just believe what you're told or I swear to God I'll gouge your bloody eyes out meself."

' "Well, that's straight enough," says I, laughing.

' "Here's luck," says 'e.

'He took a swig of beer and so did I.

' "Plenty of it?" I asked.

' "Enough to last you. I know you're not a soaker. I wouldn't 'ave given you the job if I 'adn't known that."

' "No," I says, "I like me little drop of beer, but I know when I've 'ad enough. What about the money?"

' "I got it 'ere," 'e says. "I'll give it you before I get off."

'Well, we sat talkin' of one thing and another. I ask 'im what crew there was and a lot like that, and he ask me if I'd 'ave a job gettin' out at night and I says, no, I could sail the boat with me eyes shut and then suddenly I 'eard something. I got sharp ears, I 'ave, and there ain't much goin' on that I miss that way.

' "There's a boat comin'," I says.

' "And about time, too," 'e says. "I got to get back to my missus and the kids tonight."

' "Better go on deck, 'adn't we?" I says.

' "No necessity at all," 'e says.

' "All right," I says.

'We just sat there listenin'. Sounded like a dinghy. She come up and give a bump on the side. Then someone come on board. He come down the companion. All dressed up he was, blue serge suit, collar and tie, brown shoes. Not like what 'e is now.

' "This is Fred," says Ryan, givin' me a look.

' "Fred Blake," says the young fellow.

' "This is Captain Nichols. First-rate seaman. He's all right."

'The kid give me a look and I give 'im one. He didn't look exactly what you'd call delicate, I must say, picture of 'ealth, I'd 'ave said. Bit jumpy. If you'd asked me I'd 'ave said he was scared.

' "Bad luck your crockin' up like this," I says, very affable like. "The sea air'll pull you together, believe me. Nothin' like a cruise to build up a young fellow's constitution."

'I never see anyone go so red as 'e done when I said that. Ryan looked at 'im an' 'e looked at me and laughed. Then 'e says 'e'd tip over the dibs and be gettin' off. He 'ad it in his belt and 'e took it off and paid it over to me, two 'undred golden sovereigns. I 'adn't seen gold in donkeys' years. Only the banks 'ad it. Seemed to me that whoever it was wanted to get this 'ere boy out of the way, 'e must be pretty high up.

' "Throw in the belt, Ryan," I says. "I can't leave a lot of money like that lyin' about."

' "All right," says 'e, "take the belt. Well, good luck." And before I could say a word he was out of the cabin and 'e'd

61

popped over the side and the boat was movin' away. They wasn't takin' no chances of my seein' who was in it.'

'And what happened then?'

'Well, I put the money back in the belt and strapped it round me.'

'Devil of a weight, isn't it?'

'When we come to Merauke we bought a couple of boxes and I've hid mine away so as nobody knows where it is. But if things go on like they are, I'll be able to carry all what's left without so much as feelin' it.'

'What d'you mean by that?'

'Well, we sailed all the way up the coast, inside the Bank, of course, fine weather and all that, nice breeze, and I said to the kid: "What about a game of cribbage?" Had to pass the time somehow, you know, and I knew 'e'd got a good bit of money. I didn't see why I shouldn't 'ave some of it. I've played cribbage all me life, and I thought I got a soft thing on. I believe the devil's in them cards. D'you know, I 'aven't 'ad a winnin' day since we left Sydney. I've lost a matter of seventy pounds, I 'ave. And it's not as if 'e could play. It's the devil's own luck he's got.'

'Perhaps he plays better than you think.'

'Don't you believe it. What I don't know about cribbage ain't worth knowin'. D'you think I'd 'ave took him on if I 'adn't known that? No, it's luck, and luck can't go on for ever. It's bound to change and then I'll get back all I've lost and all he's got besides. It's aggravatin', of course, but I ain't worryin'.'

'Has he told you anything about himself?'

'Not a thing. But I've put two and two together and I got a pretty shrewd idea what's at the bottom of it.'

'Oh!'

'There's politics at the bottom of it or I'll eat my 'at. If there 'adn't been Ryan wouldn't 'ave been mixed up in it. The Government's pretty rocky in New South Wales. They're 'angin' on by their teeth. If there was a scandal they'd go out to-morrow. There'll 'ave to be an election soon, anyway. They think they'll get in again, but my belief is it's a toss-up and I guess they know they can't take a risk. I shouldn't be surprised if Fred wasn't the son of somebody pretty important.'

'Premier, or somebody like that, you mean? Is there one of the Ministers called Blake?'

'Blake's no more 'is name than it is mine. It's one of the ministers all right, and Fred's 'is son or 'is nephew; and whatever it is, if it come out, he'd lose 'is seat, and my opinion is they all thought it better Fred should be out of the way for a few months.'

'And what d'you think it is he did?'

'Murder, if you ask me.'

'He's only a kid.'

'Old enough to 'ang.'

chapter twelve

'Hulloa, what's that?' said the skipper. 'There's a boat comin'.'

His hearing was indeed acute, for Dr Saunders heard nothing. The captain peered into the darkness. He put his hand on the doctor's arm and, getting up noiselessly, slipped down into the cabin. In a moment he came up again and the doctor saw that he carried a revolver.

'No 'arm bein' on the safe side,' he said.

Now the doctor discerned the faint grating of oars turning in rusty rowlocks.

'It's the schooner's dinghy,' he said.

'I know it is. But I don't know what they want. Pretty late to pay a social call.'

The two men waited in silence and listened to the approaching sound. Presently, they not only heard the splash of the water, but saw the vague outline of the boat, a little black mass against the black sea.

'Hullo, there,' cried Nichols suddenly. 'Boat ahoy.'

'That you, Captain?' a voice travelled over the water.

'Yes, it's me. What d'you want?'

He stood at the gunwale, the revolver in his hand, hanging from the end of his loose arm. The Australian rowed on.

'Wait till I come on board,' he said.

'Pretty late, ain't it?' cried Nichols.

The Australian told the man who was rowing to stop.

'Wake up the doctor, will you? I don't half like the look of my Jap. Seems to me he's sinking.'

'The doctor's 'ere. Come to the side.'

The dinghy came on and Captain Nichols, leaning over, saw that the Australian was alone with a blackfellow.

'D'you want me to come over?' asked Dr Saunders.

'Sorry to trouble you, doc, but I think he's pretty bad.'

'I'll come. Wait till I get my things.'

He stumbled down the companion and picked up a satchel in which he had what was necessary for emergencies. He climbed over the side and let himself down into the dinghy. The blackfellow rowed off quickly.

'You know what it is,' said the Australian, 'you can't get a diver for the asking, not a Jap, and they're the only ones worth having. There isn't one in the Arus out of a job now, and if I lose this chap it's going to queer my pitch good and proper. I mean, I shall have to go all the way to Yokohama, and then the chances are I shall have to hang around for a month before I get what I want.'

The diver was lying on one of the lower bunks in the crew's quarters. The air was fetid and the heat fearful. Two blackfellows were asleep and one of them, lying on his back, breathed stertorously. A third, sitting on his haunches on the floor by the sick man's side, was staring at him with eyes that had no meaning. A hurricane lamp hanging from a beam gave a dim light. The diver was in a state of collapse. He was conscious, but when the doctor went up to him there was no change in the expression of the coal-black Oriental eyes. One might have thought that they gazed already at Eternity and could not be distracted by a transitory object. Dr Saunders felt his pulse and put his hand on the clammy forehead. He gave him a hypodermic injection. He stood by the side of the bunk and looked reflectively at the recumbent form.

'Let's go up and get a little air,' he said presently. 'Tell this man to come and tell us if there's any change.'

'Is he for it?' asked the Australian, when they got on deck.

'Looks like it.'

'God, I do have bad luck.'

The doctor chuckled. The Australian asked him to sit down. The night was as still as death. In the calm water the stars from their vast distances looked at themselves. The two men were silent. Some say that if you believe a thing with sufficient force it becomes true. For that Jap, lying there, dying there, painlessly, it was not the end, but the turning over of a page; he knew, as certainly as he knew that the sun in a few hours would rise, that he was but slipping from one life to another. Karma, the deeds of this as of all the other lives he had passed, would be somehow continued; and perhaps, in his exhaustion, the only emotion that remained to him was curiosity, anxious it might be or amused, to know in what condition he would be reborn. Dr Saunders dozed off. He was awakened by a blackman's hand on his shoulder.

'Come quick.'

The dawn was breaking. It was not yet day, but the light of the stars had dwindled and the sky was ghostly. He went below. The diver was sinking fast. His eyes were open still, but his pulse was imperceptible and his body had the coldness of death. Suddenly there was a little rattle, not loud, but deprecating and conciliatory, like the manners of the Japanese, and he was dead. The two sleepers had wakened and one sat on the edge of his bunk, his black naked legs dangling, while the other, as though he wanted to shut away from him what was happening so close, sat crouched on the floor with his back to the dying man, and held his head in his hands.

When the doctor went back on deck, and told the captain, he shrugged his shoulders.

'No physique, these Japs,' he said.

Dawn now was stealing over the water, and the first rays of the sun touched its stillness with cool and delicate colours.

'Well, I'll be getting back to the *Fenton*,' said the doctor. 'I know the captain wants to sail soon after it's light.'

'You'd better have some breakfast before you go. You must be pretty peckish.'

'Well, I could do with a cup of tea.'

'I'll tell you what. I've got some eggs, I was keeping them

for the Jap, but he won't want 'em now, let's have some bacon and eggs.'

He shouted for the cook.

'I just fancy a plate of bacon and eggs,' he said, rubbing his hands. 'They ought to be pretty fresh still.'

Presently the cook brought them, piping hot, with tea and biscuits.

'God, they smell good,' said the Australian. 'Funny thing, you know. I never get tired of bacon and eggs. When I'm at home I have them every day. Sometimes my wife gives me something else for a change, but there's nothing I like 'alf so much.'

But when the blackfellow was rowing Dr Saunders back to the *Fenton*, it struck him that death was a funnier thing even than that the schooner's captain should like bacon and eggs for breakfast. The flat sea was shining like polished steel. Its colours were pale and delicate like the colours in the boudoir of an eighteenth-century *marquise*. It seemed very odd to the doctor that men should die. There was something absurd in the notion that this pearl diver, the heir of innumerable generations, the result of a complicated process of evolution that had lasted since the planet was formed, here and now, because of a succession of accidents that confounded the imagination, should be brought to death on this lost and uninhabited spot.

Captain Nichols was shaving when the doctor reached the side and he gave him a hand to help him on board.

'Well, what's the news?'

'Oh, he's dead.'

'I thought as much. What's bein' done about buryin' him?'

'I don't know. I didn't ask. I suppose they'll just throw him overboard.'

'Like a dog?'

'Why not?'

The skipper gave signs of an agitation that not a little surprised Dr Saunders.

'That won't do at all. Not on a British vessel. He must be buried in the proper way. I mean, he must 'ave a proper service and all that.'

'He was a Buddhist or Shintoist or something like that, you know.'

'I can't 'elp that. I been at sea, man and boy, for more than thirty years, and when a chap dies on a British ship he must 'ave a British funeral. Death levels all men, doc, you ought to know that, and at a time like this we can't 'old it up against a fellow that he's a Jap, or a nigger, or a dago, or anything. Hi, you men, lower a boat and look sharp about it. I'll go over to the schooner meself. When I see you didn't come back all this time I said to meself that this was going to 'appen. That's why I was shavin' when you come alongside.'

'What are you going to do?'

'I'm goin' to talk to the skipper of that there schooner. We must do what's right. Give that Jap a send-off in style. I've always made a point of that on every vessel I've commanded. Makes a rare good impression on the crew. Then they know what to expect if anything 'appens to them.'

The dinghy was lowered and the skipper rowed away. Fred Blake came aft. With his tousled hair, his clear skin and blue eyes, his springtime radiance, he looked like a young Bacchus in a Venetian picture. The doctor, tired after a night of little sleep, felt a moment's envy of his insolent youth.

'How's the patient, doctor?'

'Dead.'

'Some fellows have all the luck, don't they?'

Dr Saunders gave him a sharp look, but did not speak.

In a little while, they saw the dinghy coming back from the schooner, but without Captain Nichols. The man called Utan spoke English well. He brought them a message that they were all to go over.

'What the hell for?' asked Blake.

'Come on,' said the doctor.

The two white men climbed over the side and the remaining two members of the crew.

'Captain say everybody. China boy, too.'

'Jump in. Ah Kay,' said the doctor to his servant, who was sitting on deck, unconcerned, sewing a button on a pair of trousers.

Ah Kay put down his work and with his friendly little smile stepped down on light feet into the dinghy. They rowed over to the schooner. When they climbed up the ladder, they found

Captain Nichols and the Australian waiting for them.

'Captain Atkinson agrees with me that we ought to do the right thing by this poor Jap,' said Nichols, 'and as he 'asn't the experience what I 'ave, 'e's asked me to conduct the ceremony in proper style.'

'That's right,' said the Australian.

'It isn't my place, I know that. When you 'ave a death at sea it's the captain's place to read the service, but 'e don't 'appen to 'ave a prayer-book on board and 'e don't know what to do any more than a canary with a rumpsteak. Am I right, Captain?'

The Australian nodded gravely.

'But I thought you were a Baptist,' said the doctor.

'Ordinarily, I am,' said Nichols. 'But when it comes to funerals and that-like I always 'ave used the prayer-book and I always shall use the prayer-book. Now, Captain, as soon as your party's ready we'll assemble the men and get on with the job.'

The Australian walked forrard and in a minute or two rejoined them.

'Looks to me as if they was just putting in the last stitches,' he said.

'A stitch in time saves nine,' said Captain Nichols, somewhat to the doctor's perplexity.

'What d'you say to a little drink while we're waiting?'

'Not yet, Captain. We'll 'ave that afterwards. Business before pleasure.'

Then a man came along.

'All finished, boss,' he said.

'That's fine,' said Nichols. 'Come on, chaps.'

He was alert. He held himself erect. His little foxy eyes were twinkling with pleasant anticipation. The doctor observed with demure amusement his air of subdued gaiety. It was plain that he enjoyed the situation. They marched aft. The crews of the two boats, blackfellows all of them, were standing about, some with pipes in their mouths, one or two with the fag-end of a cigarette sticking to their thick lips. On the deck lay a bundle in what looked to the doctor like a copra sack. It was very small. You could hardly believe that it contained what had once been a man.

'Are you all 'ere?' asked Captain Nichols, looking round. 'No smokin', please. Respect for the dead.'

They put away their pipes, and spat out the ends of their cigarettes.

'Stand round now. You near me, Captain. I'm only doin' this to oblige, you understand, and I don't want you to think I don't know it's your place and not mine. Now then, are you all ready?'

Captain Nichols's recollection of the burial service was somewhat sketchy. He began with a prayer that owed much to his invention, but which he delivered with unction. Its language was florid. He ended with a resounding amen.

'Now we'll sing a 'ymn.' He looked at the blackfellows. 'You've all been to missionary schools and I want you to put your guts in it. Let 'em 'ear you right away to Macassar. Come on, all of you. Onward Christian Soldiers, onwards as to war.'

He burst out singing in a throaty, tuneless strain, but with fervour, and he had hardly started before the crews of the two boats joined in. They sang lustily with rich deep voices and the sound travelled over the peaceful sea. It was a hymn they had all learnt in their native islands, and they knew every word of it; but in their unfamiliar speech, with its queer intonations, it gathered a strange mystery so that it seemed not like a Christian hymn, but like the barbaric, rhythmical shouting of a savage multitude. It rang with fantastic sounds, the beating of drums and the clang of curious instruments, and it suggested the night and dark ceremonies by the water's edge and the dripping of blood in human sacrifice. Ah Kay, very clean in his neat white dress, stood a little apart from the black men in an attitude of negligent grace, and in his lovely liquid eyes was a look of a slightly scornful astonishment. They ended the first verse and without prompting from Captain Nichols sang the second. But when they started on the third he clapped his hands sharply.

'Now then, that's enough,' he cried. 'This ain't a bloody concert. We don't want to stay 'ere all night.'

They stopped suddenly and he looked round with severity. The doctor's eyes fell on that small bundle in the copra sack that lay on deck in the middle of the circle. He did not know why, but he thought of the little boy the dead diver once had been, with his yellow face and sloe-black eyes, who played in the streets of a Japanese town and was taken by his mother in her pretty Japanese dress, with pins in her elaborately done hair and clogs on her feet, to see the cherry blossom when it was in flower and, on holidays, to the temple, where he was given a cake; and perhaps once, dressed all in white, with an ashen wand in his hand, he had gone with all his family on pilgrimage and watched the sun rise from the summit of Fuji Yama, the sacred mountain.

'Now I'm going to say another prayer and when I come to the words, "we therefore commend 'is body to the deep," and mind you watch out for them, I don't want a hitch or anythin' like that, you just catch 'old of 'im and pop 'im over, see? Better detail two men to do that, Captain.'

'You, Bob. And Jo.'

The two men stepped forward and made to seize the body.

'Not yet, you damned fools,' cried Captain Nichols. 'Let me get the words out of me mouth, blast you.' And then, without stopping to take breath, he burst into prayer. He went on till he could evidently think of nothing more to say, and then, raising his voice a little: 'Forasmuch as it 'as pleased Almighty God of 'is great mercy to take unto 'isself the soul of our dear brother 'ere departed: We therefore commend his body to the deep...' He gave the two men a severe look, but they were staring at him with open mouths. 'Now then, don't be all night about it. Pop the bleeder over, blast you.'

With a start they leapt at the little bundle that lay on deck and flung it overboard. It plunged into the water with hardly a splash. Captain Nichols went on with a little satisfied smile on his face:

'To be turned into corruption, lookin' for the resurrection of the body when the sea shall give up its dead. Now, dearly beloved brethren, we'll all say the Lord's prayer, and no mumblin', please. God wants to 'ear and I want to 'ear. Our Father which art in 'eaven...'

He repeated it to the crew in a loud voice and all but Ah Kay said it with him.

'Now, men, that's about all,' he continued, but in the same

unctuous voice; 'I'm glad to 'ave 'ad the opportunity to conduct this sad ceremony in the proper way. In the midst of life we are in death, and accidents will 'appen in the best regulated families. I want you to know that if you're taken to the bourne from which no one ever comes back, so long as you're on a British ship and under the British flag, you can be sure of 'avin' a decent funeral and bein' buried like a faithful son of our Lord Jesus Christ. Under ordinary circumstances I should now call upon you to give three cheers for your captain, Captain Atkinson, but this is a sad occasion upon which we are gathered together and our thoughts are too deep for tears, so I will ask you to give 'im three cheers in your 'earts. And now to God the Father, God the Son and God the 'oly Ghost. A-a-men.'

Captain Nichols turned aside with the manner of a man descending from the pulpit and held out his hand to the captain of the schooner. The Australian wrung it warmly.

'By God, you done that first-rate,' he said.

'Practice,' said Captain Nichols modestly.

'Now, boys, what about a tiddly?'

'That's the idea,' said Captain Nichols. He turned to his crew. 'You fellers get back to the *Fenton* and, Tom, you come back and fetch us.'

The four men shambled along the deck. Captain Atkinson brought up from the cabin a bottle of whisky and some glasses.

'A parson couldn't have done it better,' he said, raising his glass to Captain Nichols.

'It's just a matter of feelin'. You 'ave to 'ave the feelin'. I mean, when I was conductin' that service I didn't think it was only a dirty little Jap, it was just the same to me as if it'd been you or Fred or the doctor. That's Christianity, that is.'

chapter thirteen

The monsoon was blowing hard and when they left the shelter of the land they found a heavy sea. The doctor was ignorant of sailing vessels and to his unaccustomed eyes it seemed formidable. Captain Nichols had the water-cask aft lashed down. The waves, crested with white, looked very large and in that small craft one was very near the water. Now and then a heavy sea struck them and a cloud of spoon-drift swept along the deck. They were passing islands and as they passed each one the doctor asked himself if he could swim so far if they were capsized. He was nervous. It exasperated him. He knew there was no need. Two of the blackfellows were sitting on the hatch tying rope together to make a fishing line, and, intent on their job, never so much as gave the sea a glance. The water was muddy and there were reefs all around them. The skipper ordered one of the men to stand on the jib-boom and keep a look-out. The blackfellow guided the skipper with a gesture of one arm or the other. The sun shone and the sky was bright blue, but high above them white clouds raced with a swift and even motion. The doctor tried to read, but he had to duck constantly to avoid the spray when a sea broke over them. Presently there was a dull scraping and he clutched the gunwale. They had struck a reef. They bumped over and were again in deep water. Nichols shouted a curse at the look-out man for not being more careful. They struck another reef and again bumped off.

'We'd better get out of this,' said the skipper.

He altered his course and made for the open sea. The ketch rolled heavily and righted herself each time with a peevish jerk. Dr Saunders was wet through.

'Why don't you go down into the cabin?' the skipper shouted.

'I prefer being on deck.'

'No danger, you know.'

'Is it going to get any worse?'

'I shouldn't wonder. Looks to me as if it was blowin' up a bit.'

The doctor, looking over the stern, watched a heavy sea charge down upon them, and he expected the next wave to crash before the ketch had time to recover, but with an agility that was almost human she avoided it just in time and triumphantly rode on. He was not comfortable. He was not happy. Fred Blake came up to him.

'Grand, isn't it? Exhilarating having a bit of a blow like this.'

His curling hair was all blown about in the wind and his eyes were shining. He was enjoying himself. The doctor shrugged his shoulders, but did not answer. He looked at a great billow, with overhanging, breaking crest, that came rolling towards them, as though it were not the unconscious result of natural forces, but had a malignant purpose. Nearer and nearer it came and it seemed as though it must inevitably overwhelm them. The frail craft could never withstand that monstrous mountain of water.

'Look out,' shouted the skipper.

He kept the lugger dead before it. Dr Saunders instinctively clung to the mast. It struck them and it seemed that a wall of water poured over them. The deck was swimming.

'That was a whopper,' shouted Fred.

'I needed a bath,' said the skipper.

They both laughed. But the doctor was sick with fear. He wished with all his heart that he had stayed safely on the island of Takana till the steamer called. How stupid it was to risk his life rather than endure two or three weeks of boredom! He swore to himself that if he escaped this time nothing would induce him again to do anything so absurd. He did not attempt to read any more. He could not see through his spectacles splashed with water, and his book was drenched. He watched the waves that swept on. The islands now were dim in the distance.

'Enjoyin' it, doc?' shouted the skipper.

The lugger was tossing about like a cork. Dr Saunders tried to force a smile to his lips.

'Fine thing to blow the cobwebs away,' the skipper added.

The doctor had never seen him in better spirits. He was alert. He seemed to enjoy his own competence. It was no figure of speech to say that he was in his element. Fear? He knew nothing of it, that vulgar, cheating, shifty man; there was nothing decent in him, he knew nothing of whatever gave dignity to man, or beauty, and you had only to know him for twenty-four hours to be certain that if there were two ways of doing a thing, a straight one and a crooked, he would choose the crooked one. In that low and squalid mind there was but one motive, the desire to get the better of his fellow men by foul means; it was not even a passion of evil, in which after all there might be a sinister grandeur, it was a puckish malice that found satisfaction in besting another. And yet here, in this tiny vessel in that vast desert of angry waves, without possibility of succour if catastrophe befell them, he was at ease, strong in his knowledge of the sea, proud, self-assured and happy. He seemed to take pleasure in his mastery of the little boat he managed with such confident skill; it was in his hands like a horse in a horseman's when he knows every trick and habit it has, every whim and every capacity; he watched the waves with a smile in his foxy little eyes, and he nodded with self-satisfaction as they thundered by. It almost seemed to the doctor that to him they too were living things that he found a cynical amusement in getting the better of.

Dr Saunders flinched as he watched the huge waves race after them, and clinging to the mast he swayed away from the sea as the lugger heeled over; and then, as though his weight could make all the difference, swayed back as she rolled. He knew he was pale, and he felt his face stiff. He wondered if there would be any chance of getting into one of the two dinghies if the boat foundered. There wouldn't be much chance for them if they did. They were a hundred miles away from any inhabited spot and out of the line of traffic. If anything happened the only thing was to let oneself drown quickly. It was not death he minded, but dying, and he wondered if it would be very unpleasant while he swallowed the water and choked, and, notwithstanding his will, desperately struggled.

Then the cook lurched along the deck bearing their dinner. A heavy sea had swamped out the hold, and he had not been able to light a fire, so it consisted of a tin of corned beef and cold potatoes.

'Send Utan along to take the helm,' the skipper shouted.

The blackfellow took the skipper's place, and the three men gathered round their wretched meal.

'Pretty peckish, I am,' said Nichols jovially, as he helped himself. 'How's the appetite, Fred?'

'All right.'

74

The lad was soaked to the skin, but his cheeks were bright and his eyes glistened. Dr Saunders wondered if his air of unconcern was assumed. Frightened, and angry with himself because he was, he gave the skipper a sour look.

'If you can digest this you can digest an ox.'

'Bless you, I never 'ave dyspepsia when there's a bit of a gale. Like a tonic to me, it is.'

'How long is this blasted wind going to blow?'

'Not likin' it much, doc?' The skipper chuckled slyly. 'It may drop towards sunset or it may blow up a bit.'

'Can't we get in the shelter of some island?'

'Better off at sea. These boats, they can stand anythin'. I don't fancy goin' to pieces on a reef.'

When they had finished eating Captain Nichols lit his pipe.

'What about a game of cribbage, Fred?' he said.

'I'm on.'

'You're not going to play that damned game now?' cried the doctor.

Captain Nichols gave the sea a sneering glance.

'A little bit of water; that's nothin'. Them niggers, they can steer a boat with anyone.'

They went down into the cabin. Dr Saunders stayed on deck and sullenly watched the sea. The afternoon stretched interminably before him. He wondered what Ah Kay was up to and presently he scrambled forward. Only one of the crew was on deck. The hatch was battened down.

'Where's my boy?' he asked.

The man pointed to the hold.

'Sleeping. Want to go down?'

He raised the hatch, and the doctor clambered down the companion. A lamp was alight. It was dark and noisome. One blackfellow was sitting on the floor, with nothing on but a loin cloth, mending his trousers; the other and Ah Kay were in their bunks. They were sleeping quietly. But when the doctor lurched up to Ah Kay he woke and gave his master his sweet and friendly smile.

'Feeling all right?'

'Yes.'

'Frightened?'

75

Ah Kay, smiling again, shook his head.

'Go back to sleep,' said the doctor.

He climbed up the companion and with difficulty pushed up the hatch. The man on deck helped him, and as he came out on deck a sheet of water hit him in the face. His heart sank. He swore and shook his fists at the angry sea.

'Better get below,' said the blackfellow. 'Wet up here.'

The doctor shook his head. He stood there clinging to a rope. He wanted human companionship. He knew perfectly well that he was the only man on board who was afraid. Even Ah Kay, who knew no more of the sea than he, was unconcerned. There was no danger. They were as safe on the lugger as on dry land, and yet he could not prevent the pang of terror that seized him each time that a following wave caught them up and sent a cloud of spoon-drift hurtling along the deck. The water flowed out of the scuppers in a great rush. He was terrified. It seemed to him that it was only by an effort of will that he did not curl up in a corner and whimper. He had an instinct to appeal for succour to a God he did not believe in, and he had to clench his teeth to prevent his trembling lips from uttering a prayer. The circumstance seemed to him ironical that he, an intelligent man, who looked upon himself as something of a philosopher, should be affected with this craven fear, and he smiled grimly at the absurdity. It was a bit thick, if you came to think of it, that he, with his quick brain, his wide knowledge, and reasoned view of life, he who had nothing to lose by death, should tremble while these men, ignorant like the blackfellow by his side, base like the captain or dull like Fred Blake, should remain unperturbed. It just showed what a poor thing the mind was. He felt sick with fright, and he asked himself what it was he was frightened of. Death? He had faced death before. Once indeed he had decided to make an end of himself, but painlessly, and it had needed an odd mixture of courage, cynicism, and cold reason to make him go on with a life that seemed to offer nothing desirable. He was glad now that he had had the sense. But he knew that he had no great attachment to life. Sometimes when ill he had felt his hold on it so slight that he looked forward to dissolution not only with resignation but with cheerfulness. Pain? He bore pain pretty well. After all, if you could bear dengue or a bad toothache with serenity, you could bear anything. No, it was not that, it was just some instinct over which he had no control; and he looked curiously, as though it were something outside himself, at the terror that made his throat dry and his knees shake.

'Very odd,' he muttered as he made his way aft.

He glanced at his wrist-watch. By God, it was only three. There was something horrible in that clean, wind-swept sky. Its brilliance was heartless. It seemed to have nothing to do with the tempestuous sea; and the sea, so hard and bright a blue, recked nothing of man. Strange, senseless powers that sported with him and destroyed him not from malice, but in wanton amusement.

'Give me the sea from the beach,' the doctor muttered to himself grimly.

He went down into the cabin.

'Two for his 'eels at all events,' he heard from the skipper.

They were still playing their dreary game.

'How's the weather, doc?'

'Rotten.'

'It'll 'ave to be worse before it's better, like a woman 'avin' a baby. Grand boats these are. Weather a hurricane. I'd rather go to sea in one of these Australian pearlin' luggers than in a transatlantic liner.'

'It's your crib,' said Fred.

They were playing on the captain's mattress, and the doctor, changing his dripping clothes, flung himself on the other. He could not read in the fitful light of the swaying lamp. He lay and listened to the monotonous terms of the game. They struck the ear with an insistent jar. The cabin creaked and groaned and over his head the wind roared furiously. He was shaken from side to side.

'That was a roll,' said Fred.

'Takin' it grand, ain't she? Fifteen two. Fifteen four.'

Fred was winning again and the skipper played to a running accompaniment of complaint. Dr Saunders stiffened his limbs to bear the misery of his fear. The hours passed with frightful slowness. Towards sunset Captain Nichols went on deck.

'Blowin' up a bit,' he said, when he came down again. 'I'm goin' to have a nap. It don't look to me as if I'd get much sleep tonight.'

'Why don't you lay her to?' asked Fred.

'Bring 'er up to the wind with a sea like this runnin'? No, sir. She's all right as long as everythin' 'olds.'

He coiled himself up on his mattress and in five minutes was snoring peacefully. Fred went on deck to get a breath of air. The doctor was angry with himself for having been such a fool as to take a passage on this small craft, and he was angry with the captain and with Fred because they were free of the terror that obsessed him. But when the ketch had seemed about to founder a hundred times, and each time righted herself, there stole upon him gradually an unwilling admiration for the gallant little boat. At seven the cook brought them their supper and woke Captain Nichols to eat it. He had been able to make a fire, and they had hot stew and hot tea. Then the three of them went on deck and the skipper took the helm. It was a clear night, with the stars in their myriads twinkling brightly; the sea was rough, and in the darkness the waves looked enormous.

'By God, there's a big 'un,' cried Fred.

A huge wall of green water, with a breaking crest, was rushing down on them. It looked as though it must inevitably fall on them, and if it did, the *Fenton*, powerless to rise to it, must be rolled over and over. The skipper glanced round and jammed himself against the wheel. He steered so that the wave should strike them dead aft. Suddenly the stern slewed off the course and there was a crash and a mass of water swept over the quarter. They were blinded. Then the bulwarks rose above the sea. The *Fenton* shook herself like a dog stepping on to dry land and the water poured out of the scuppers.

'Gettin' beyond a joke,' bellowed the skipper.

'Any islands near?'

'Yep. If we can keep goin' for a couple of hours we can get under their lee.'

'What about reefs?'

'There ain't any marked. Moon'll be out soon. You two chaps better go below.'

'I'll stay on deck,' said Fred. 'Stuffy in the cabin.'

'Please yourself. What about you, doc?'

The doctor hesitated. He hated the look of the angry sea and he was bored with being frightened. He had died so many deaths that he had exhausted his emotion.

'Can I be of any use?'

'No more than a snowball in 'ell.'

'Remember you carry Caesar and his fortunes,' he shouted in the skipper's ear.

But Captain Nichols, not having had a classical education, did not see the point of the jest. If I perish, I perish, the doctor reflected, and he made up his mind to get all the enjoyment he could out of what might be his last hours on earth. He went forward to fetch Ah Kay. The boy followed him back and came down with him into the cabin.

'Let's try Kim Ching's chandu,' said Dr Saunders. 'No need to stint ourselves tonight.'

The boy got the lamp and the opium from the valise, and with his accustomed nonchalance started to prepare the pipe. Never had the first long inhalation seemed more delicious. They smoked alternately. Gradually peace descended upon the doctor's soul. His nerves ceased to tingle with the roll of the lugger. Fear left him. After the usual six pipes that the doctor smoked every night Ah Kay lay back as if he had finished.

'Not yet,' said Dr Saunders softly. 'For once I'm going the whole hog.'

The motion of the boat was not unpleasant. Little by little it seemed to him that he grasped its rhythm. It was only his carcase that was tossed from side to side, his spirit soared in regions far above the storm. He walked in the infinite, but he knew, before Einstein, that it was bounded by his own thought. He knew once more that he had but to stretch his intelligence ever so little to solve a great mystery; and again he did not do it because it gave him more pleasure to know that it was there waiting to be solved. It had agreeably tantalized him so long, it was indelicate, when any moment might be his last, to ravish its secret. He was like a well-bred man who will not expose his mistress to the humiliation of knowing that he does not believe her lies. Ah Kay fell asleep, curled up at the foot of the mattress. Dr Saunders moved a little so as not to disturb him. He thought of God and of eternity, and he laughed softly, in his heart, at the absurdity of life. Scraps of poetry floated in his memory. It seemed to him that he was dead already and Captain Nichols, Charon in a tarpaulin, was bearing him to a strange, sweet place. At last he fell asleep also.

chapter fourteen

He was awakened by the chill of dawn. He opened his eyes and saw that the companion hatch was open, and then he was aware of the skipper and Fred Blake sleeping on their mattresses. They had come down and left the hatch open on account of the pungent smell of the opium. Suddenly it occurred to him that the lugger rolled no longer. He raised himself. He felt a trifle heavy, for he was unaccustomed to smoke so much, and he thought he would get into the air.

Ah Kay was resting peacefully where he had fallen asleep. He touched him on the shoulder. The boy opened his eyes and his lips broke immediately into the slow smile that gave such beauty to his young face. He stretched himself and yawned.

'Get me some tea,' said the doctor.

Ah Kay was on his feet in a minute. The doctor followed him up the companion. The sun had not yet risen and one pale star still loitered in the sky, but the night had thinned to a ghostly grey, and the ketch seemed to float on the surface of a cloud. The man at the helm in an old coat, with a muffler round his neck and a battered hat crammed down at his head, gave the doctor a surly nod. The sea was quite calm. They were passing between two islands so close together that they might have been sailing down a canal. There was a very light breeze. The blackfellow at the helm seemed half asleep. The dawn slid between the low, wooded islands, gravely, with a deliberate calmness that seemed to conceal an inward apprehension; and you felt it natural and even inevitable that men should have personified it in a maiden. It had indeed the shyness and the grace of a young girl, the charming seriousness, the indifference, and the ruthlessness. The sky had the washed-out colour of an archaic statue. The virgin forests on each side of them still held the night, but then insensibly the grey of the sea was shot with the soft hues of a pigeon's breast. There was a pause, and with a smile the day broke. Sailing between those uninhabited islands, on that still sea, in a silence that caused you almost to hold your breath, you had a strange and exciting impression of the beginning of the world. There man might never have passed and you had a feeling that what your eyes saw had never been seen before. You had a sensation of primeval freshness, and all the complication of the generations disappeared. A stark simplicity, as bare and severe as a straight line, filled the soul with rapture. Dr Saunders knew at that moment the ecstasy of the mystic.

Ah Kay brought him a cup of tea, jasmine-scented, and scrambling down from the spiritual altitudes on which for an instant he had floated he made himself comfortable, as in an arm-chair, in the bliss of a material enjoyment. The air was cool but balmy. He asked for nothing but to go on for ever in that boat sailing on an even keel between green islands.

When he had been sitting there an hour, delighting in his ease, he heard steps on the companion, and Fred Blake came on deck. In his pyjamas, with his tousled hair, he looked very young, and as was natural to his age he had awakened fresh, with all the lines smoothed out of his face, and not puckered and wrinkled and time-worn as sleep had left the doctor.

'Up early, doctor?' He noticed the empty cup. 'I wonder if I can get a cup of tea.'

'Ask Ah Kay.'

'All right. I'll just get Utan to throw a couple of buckets of water over me.'

He went forward and spoke to one of the men. The doctor saw the blackfellow lower a bucket by a rope into the sea, and then Fred Blake stripped his pyjamas and stood on deck naked while the other threw the contents over him. The bucket was lowered again and Fred turned round. He was tall, with square shoulders, a small waist and slender hips; his arms and neck were tanned, but the rest of his body was very white. He dried himself, and putting on his pyjamas again came aft. His eyes were shining and on his lips was the outline of a smile.

'You're a very good-looking young fellow,' said the doctor.

Fred gave an indifferent shrug of the shoulders and sank into the next chair.

'We lost a boat in the night. D'you know that?'

'No, I didn't.'

'Blew like the devil. We've lost the jib. Just torn to tatters. Nichols wasn't half glad to get into the shelter of the islands, I can tell you. I thought we'd never make it.'

'Did you stay up on deck all the time?'

'Yes, I thought if we foundered I'd rather be in the open.'

'There wouldn't have been much chance for you.'

'No, I know that.'

'Weren't you afraid?'

'No. You know, I think if it's coming to you, it'll come. And there's nothing to do about it.'

'I was frightened.'

'Nichols said you were in the afternoon. He thought it a hell of a joke.'

'It's a question of age, you know. The old are much more easily frightened than the young. I couldn't help thinking it rather funny at the time that I, who had so much less to lose than you who've got all your life before you, should dread losing it so much more than you did.'

'How could you think if you were as scared as all that?'

'I was scared with my body. That didn't prevent me from thinking with my mind.'

'Bit of a character, aren't you, doctor.'

'I don't know about that.'

'I'm sorry I was so short with you when you asked if you could have a passage on this boat.' He hesitated an instant. 'I've been ill, you know, and my nerves are a bit funny. I'm not crazy about people I don't know.'

'Oh, that's all right.'

'I don't want you to think I'm just a rough-neck.' He looked round at the peaceful scene. They had sailed out of the narrow arm between the two islands, and now found themselves in what looked like an inland sea. They were surrounded by low-lying islets, thickly covered with vegetation, and the water was as calm and blue as a Swiss lake. 'Bit of a change from last night. Got worse when the moon rose. How you could have slept through it beats me. There was a hell of a racket.'

'I smoked.'

'Nichols said you were going to when you and the Chink went into the cabin. I wouldn't believe it. But when we came down – huh, it was enough to take the roof of your head off.'

'Why wouldn't you believe it?'

'I couldn't imagine that a man like you could degrade himself by doing such a thing.'

The doctor chuckled.

'One should be tolerant of other people's vices,' he said calmly.

'I've got no cause to blame anybody.'

'What else has Nichols said about me?'

'Oh, well.' He paused as he saw Ah Kay, as neat as a new pin in his white dress, slim and graceful, come along to fetch the empty cups. 'It's no business of mine, anyway. He says you were struck off the rolls for something.'

'Removed from the Register is the correct expression,' placidly interrupted the doctor.

'And he says he believes you went to gaol. Naturally one can't help wondering when one sees a man with your intelligence, and the reputation you have in the East, settled in a beastly Chinese city.'

'What makes you think I'm intelligent?'

'I can see that you're educated. I don't want you to think that I'm just a larrikin. I was studying to be an accountant when my health broke down. This isn't the sort of life I'm used to.'

The doctor smiled. No one could have looked more radiantly well than Fred Blake. His broad chest, his athletic build, gave the lie to his tale of tuberculosis.

'Shall I tell you something?'

'Not if you don't want to.'

'Oh, not about myself. I don't talk much about myself. I think there's no harm in a doctor being a trifle mysterious. It adds to his patients' belief in him. I was going to give you a reflection based on experience. When some incident has shattered the career you've mapped out for yourself, a folly, a crime, or a misfortune, you mustn't think you're down and out. It may be a stroke of luck, and when you look back years later you may say to yourself that you wouldn't for anything in the world exchange the new life disaster has forced upon you for the dull, humdrum existence you would have led if circumstances hadn't intervened.'

Fred looked down.

'Why do you say that to me?'

'I thought it might be a useful piece of information.'

The young man sighed a little.

'You never know about people, do you? I used to think you were either white or yellow. It seems to me you can't tell what anyone'll do when it comes to the pinch. Of all the rotten skunks I've met I've never met one to beat Nichols. He'd rather go crooked than straight. You can't trust him an inch. We've been together a good while now, and I thought there wasn't much I didn't know about him. He'd do his own brother down if he got the chance. Not a decent thing about him. You should have seen him last night. I don't mind telling you it was a pretty near thing. You'd have been surprised. Calm as a cucumber. My opinion is that he just revelled in it. Once he said to me: "Said your prayers, Fred? If we don't make the islands before it gets much worse, we shall be feeding the fishes in the morning." And he grinned all over his ugly face. He kept his head all right. I've done a bit of sailing in Sydney harbour and I give you my word I've never seen a boat handled like he handled this one. I take my hat off to him. If we're here now it's him we owe it to. He's got nerve all right. And if he thought there was twenty pounds to be made without risk by doing us in, you and me, d'you think he'd hesitate? How d'you explain that?'

'Oh, I don't know.'

'But don't you think it's funny that a chap who's nothing but a born crook should have all that pluck? I mean, I've always heard that when a man was a wrong 'un he might bluster and bully, but when it comes to a crisis he'd just crumple up. I hate that chap, and all the same, last night I couldn't help admiring him.'

The doctor smiled quietly, but did not answer. He was amused by the lad's ingenuous surprise at the complexity of human nature.

'And he's conceited. We play cribbage all the time, fancies himself at the game. I always beat him, and he will go on.'

'He tells me you've been very lucky.'

'Lucky in love, unlucky at cards, they say. I've played cards all my life. I've got a knack for it. That's one of the reasons why I went in for being an accountant. I've got that sort of head. It's not luck. You have luck in streaks. I know about cards, and in the long run it's always the fellow who plays best who wins. Nichols thinks he's smart. He hasn't got a dog's chance playing with me.'

The conversation dropped and they sat side by side in easy comfort. After a while Captain Nichols woke and came on deck. In his dirty pyjamas, unwashed, unshaved, with his decayed teeth and general air of having run to seed, he presented an appearance that was almost repulsive. His face, grey in the light of early morning, bore a peevish expression.

'It's come on again, doc.'

'What?'

'My dyspepsia. I 'ad a snack last night before I went to bed. I knew I oughtn't to eat anything just before turnin' in, but I was that 'ungry I just 'ad to, and it's on me chest now somethin' cruel.'

'We'll see what we can do about it,' smiled the doctor, getting up from his chair.

'You won't be able to do a thing,' answered the skipper gloomily. 'I know my digestion. After I been through a patch of dirty weather I always 'ave dyspepsia as sure as my name's Nichols. Cruel 'ard, I call it. I mean, you would think after I'd been at the wheel for eight hours I could eat a bit of cold sausage and a slice of cheese without sufferin' for it. Damn it all, a man must eat.'

chapter fifteen

Dr Saunders was to leave them at Kanda-Meria, twin islands in the Kanda Sea, at which vessels of the Royal Netherlands Steam Packet Company called regularly. He thought it unlikely that he would have to wait long before a ship came in bound for some place to which he was not unwilling to go. The gale had forced them out of their course, and for twenty-four hours they were becalmed, so that it was not till the sixth day that, early in the morning, with but just enough wind to fill their sails, they sighted the volcano of Meria. The town was on Kanda. It was nine o'clock before they reached the entrance to the harbour, and the Sailing Directions had warned them that it was difficult. Meria was a tall conical hill covered with jungle almost to its summit, and a plume of dense smoke, like a huge umbrella pine, rose from its crater. The channel between the two islands was narrow, and tidal streams were said to run through it with great force. In one place it was barely half a cable wide, and there were shoals in the centre with very little water over them. But Captain Nichols was a fine seaman and knew it. He liked an opportunity to show off. Looking astonishingly disreputable in loud striped pyjamas, a battered topi on his head, and a week's growth of white beard, he took the *Fenton* in with style.

'Don't look so bad,' he said, as the little town was discovered.

There were warehouses to the water's edge and native houses on poles with thatched roofs. Naked children were playing about in the clear water. A Chinese in a broad-brimmed hat was fishing from a dug-out. The harbour was far from crowded: there were only two junks, three or four large prahus, a motor-boat, and a derelict schooner. Beyond the town was a hill surmounted by a flagstaff, and from it dangled limply a Dutch flag.

'I wonder if there's a hotel,' murmured the doctor.

He and Fred Blake stood on each side of Captain Nichols at the helm.

'Sure to be. Used to be a grand place in the old days. Centre

86

of the spice trade and all that. Nutmegs. Never been 'ere meself, but I been told there's marble palaces and I don't know what all.'

There were two piers. One was neat and tidy; the other, of wood, was ramshackle and badly needed a coat of paint. It was shorter than the first.

'The long 'un belongs to the Netherlands Company, I guess,' said the skipper. 'Let's go to the other.'

They reached the side. The mainsail was lowered with a clatter and they tied up.

'Well, doc, you've arrived. Luggage ready and all that?'

'You're coming ashore, aren't you?'

'What about it, Fred?'

'Yes, come on. I'm sick of being aboard this boat. And we've got to get another dinghy, anyway.'

'We'll be wantin' a new jib, too. I'll just go and doll meself up and then I'll join you.'

The skipper went down into the cabin. His toilet did not take him long, for it consisted only in changing his pyjamas for a pair of khaki trousers, putting a khaki coat on his bare back, and slipping his naked feet into old tennis shoes. They clambered by rickety steps on to the pier and walked along it. There was no one there. They reached the quay and after hesitating for a moment took what looked like the main street. It was empty and silent. They wandered down the middle of the roadway, abreast, and looked about them. It was pleasant to be able to stretch one's legs after those days on the lugger, and a relief to feel under one's feet the solid earth. The bungalows on either side of the road had very high roofs, thatched and pointed, and the roofs, jutting out, were supported by pillars, Doric and Corinthian, so as to form broad verandas. They had an air of ancient opulence, but their whitewash was stained and worn, and the little gardens in front of them were rank with tangled weeds. They came to shops and they all seemed to sell the same sort of things, cottons, sarongs and canned foods. There was no animation. Some of the shops had not even an attendant, as though no purchaser could possibly be expected. The few persons they passed, Malays or Chinese, walked quickly as though they were afraid to awaken the echo. Now and then a whiff of nutmeg assaulted the nostrils. Dr Saunders stopped a Chinese and asked him where the hotel was. He told them to go straight on, and presently they came to it. They went in. There was no one about, but they sat down at a table on the veranda and thumped on it with their fists. A native woman in a sarong came and looked at them, but vanished when the doctor addressed her. Then appeared a half-caste, buttoning up his stengah-shifter, and Dr Saunders asked if he could have a room. The man did not understand, and the doctor spoke to him in Chinese. The man answered in Dutch, but when the doctor shook his head, with a smile made signs that they were to wait and ran down the steps. They saw him cross the road.

'Gone to fetch someone, I expect,' said the skipper. 'Extraordinary thing they shouldn't speak English. They gave me to understand the place was civilized.'

The half-caste returned in a few minutes with a white man, who gave them a curious glance as his companion pointed them out to him, and then as he came up the steps politely raised his topi.

'Good morning, gentlemen,' he said. 'Can I be of any service to you? Van Ryk cannot understand what you want.'

He spoke English very correctly, but with a foreign accent. He was a young man, in the twenties, very tall, six foot three at least, and broad-shouldered, a powerful fellow, but clumsily built, so that though he gave you an impression of great strength, it was of an ungainly nature. His ducks were neat and clean. A fountain pen protruded from the pocket of his closely buttoned tunic.

'We've just come in on a sailing-boat,' said the doctor, 'and I want to know if I can have a room here till the next steamer comes in.'

'Surely. The hotel isn't as full as all that.'

He turned to the half-caste and fluently explained what the doctor wanted. After a brief conversation he returned to English.

'Yes, he can give you a nice room. Your board included, it'll come to eight gulden a day. The manager's away at Batavia, but van Ryk's looking after things, and he'll make you comfortable.'

'What about a drink?' said the skipper. 'Let's 'ave some beer.'

'Won't you join us?' asked the doctor politely.

'Thank you very much.'

The young man sat down and took off his topi. He had a broad, flat face and a flat nose, with high cheekbones and rather small black eyes; his smooth skin was sallow, and there was no colour in his cheeks; his hair, cut very short, was coal-black. He was not at all good-looking, but his great ugly face bore an expression of such good nature that you could not but be somewhat taken by him. His eyes were mild and kindly.

'Dutch?' asked the skipper.

'No, I'm a Dane. Erik Christessen. I represent a Danish company here.'

'Been here long?'

'Four years.'

'Good God!' cried Fred Blake.

Erik Christessen gave a little laugh, childlike in its simplicity, and his friendly eyes beamed with good will.

'It's a fine place. It's the most romantic spot in the East. They wanted to move me, but I begged them to let me stay on.'

A boy brought them bottled beer, and the huge Dane before drinking raised his glass.

'Your very good health, gentlemen.'

Dr Saunders did not know why the stranger so very much attracted him. It was not only his cordiality, that was common enough in the East: there was something in his personality that pleased.

'Don't look as if there was much business 'ere,' said Captain Nichols.

'The place is dead. We live on our memories. That is what gives the island its character. In the old days, you know, there was so much traffic that sometimes the harbour was full and vessels had to wait outside till the departure of a fleet gave them a chance to enter. I hope you'll stay here long enough to let me show you round. It's lovely. An unsuspected isle in far-off seas.'

The doctor pricked up his ears. He recognized it as a quotation, but could not place it.

'What does that come from?'

'That? Oh, *Pippa Passes*. Browning, you know.'

'How does it happen that you've read that?'

'I read a lot. I have plenty of time, you see. I like English poetry best of all. Ah, Shakespeare.' He looked at Fred with a soft, gracious glance, a smile on his great mouth, and began to recite:

... of one whose hand,
Like the base Indian, threw a pearl away
Richer than all his tribe; of one whose subdued eyes,
Albeit unused to the melting mood,
Drop tears as fast as the Arabian trees
Their med'cinable gum.

It sounded odd in that foreign accent, somewhat gruff and guttural, but what was odder still was that there a young Danish trader should quote Shakespeare to the shifty scoundrel Captain Nichols and to the oafish lad Fred Blake. Dr Saunders found the situation faintly humorous. The skipper gave him a wink that signified quite clearly that this was a queer fish, but Fred Blake flushed and looked shy. The Dane had no notion that he had done anything to excite surprise. He went on eagerly:

'The old Dutch merchants were so rich here in the great days of the spice trade, they didn't know what to do with their money. There was no cargo for the ships to bring out and so they used to bring marble and use it for their houses. If you're not in a hurry I'll show you mine. It used to belong to one of the perkeniers. And sometimes, in winter, they'd bring a cargo of nothing but ice. Funny, isn't it? That was the greatest luxury they could have. Just think of bringing ice all the way from Holland. It took six months, the journey. And they all had their carriages, and in the cool of the evening the smart thing was to drive along the shore and round and round the square. Someone ought to write about it. It was like a Dutch *Arabian Nights'* Tale. Did you see the Portuguese fort as you came in? I'll take you there this afternoon. If there is anything I can do for you, you must let me know. I shall be very glad.'

'I shall get my traps,' said the doctor. 'These gentlemen have very kindly given me a passage here. I don't want to put them out more than I can help.'

Erik Christessen beamed amiably on the other two. 'Ah, that is what I like in the East. Everyone is so nice. Nothing is too much trouble. You cannot imagine the kindness I've received at the hands of perfect strangers.'

The four of them got up and the Dane told the half-caste manager that Dr Saunders would be coming along in a little while with his luggage and his boy.

'You should have tiffin here. It is *reistafel* today, and they make it very well. I shall be here.'

'You two fellows had better have tiffin with me,' said the doctor.

'*Reistafel*'s death to me,' said Captain Nichols. 'But I don't mind sittin' and watch you eat it.'

Erik Christessen solemnly shook hands with the three of them.

'I'm so very glad to have met you. It's not often we get strangers on the island. And it's always a pleasure to me to meet English gentlemen.'

He gave them a bow as they separated at the bottom of the steps.

'Intelligent chap, that,' said Captain Nichols when they had walked a little. 'Knew we was gentlemen at once.'

Dr Saunders gave him a glance. There was no trace of irony in his expression.

chapter sixteen

A couple of hours later, the doctor having settled in, he and his guests off the *Fenton* were sitting on the veranda of the hotel drinking a glass of Schnapps before tiffin.

'The East ain't what it was,' said the skipper shaking his head. 'Why, when I was a young chap, at Dutch 'otels there'd be bottles of Schnapps on the table, at tiffin and dinner, and you just 'elped yourself. Free of charge it was. And when you'd finished the bottle you told the boy to bring another.'

'Must have come expensive.'

'Well, you know, that's the funny thing, it didn't. You very seldom found a chap as took advantage of it. Human nature's like that. Treat a man proper and 'e'll respond wonderfully. I believe in 'uman nature, I always 'ave.'

Erik Christessen came up the steps, took off his hat to them and was passing into the hotel.

'Come and have a drink with us,' called Fred.

'With pleasure. I'll just go in and wash first.'

He went in.

'Hulloa, what's this?' said the skipper, eyeing Fred slyly. 'I thought you didn't like strangers.'

'It depends. Seems rather a good sort to me. He never asked us who we were or what we were doing here? Generally everyone's so curious.'

'He has naturally good manners,' said the doctor.

'What'll you have?' asked Fred when the Dane rejoined them.

'The same as you.'

He dropped his ungainly bulk into a chair. They began to chat. He said nothing that was very clever or amusing, but there was a guilelessness in his conversation that made it pleasing. He filled you with confidence. He irradiated well-being. Dr Saunders did not judge hastily, and he mistrusted his instincts, but this he could not miss and, reflecting upon it, he could ascribe it to nothing but an amazing and delightful sincerity. It was quite obvious that Fred Blake was much taken with the huge Dane. Dr Saunders had never heard him talk so easily.

'Look here, you'd better know our names,' he said after a few minutes. 'Mine's Blake, Fred Blake, and the doctor's called Saunders, and this fellow is Captain Nichols.'

Somewhat absurdly Erik Christessen got up and shook hands all round.

'I'm very pleased to make your acquaintance,' he said. 'I hope you're going to stay here a few days.'

'Are you still sailing tomorrow?' asked the doctor.

'Nothing to stay for. We saw a dinghy this morning.'

They went into the dining-room. It was cool and dim. Punkahs drawn by a small boy fitfully stirred the air. There was one long table, and at one end of it were sitting a Dutchman with a half-caste wife, a stout woman in loose pale draperies, and another Dutchman with a dark enough skin to suggest that he, too, had native blood in him. Erik Christessen exchanged polite greeting with them. They gave the strangers an incurious stare. *Reistafel* was served. They piled their plates with rice and curry, fried eggs, bananas, and a dozen strange concoctions that boys kept bringing them. When everything was handed they were faced with a mountain of food. Captain Nichols looked at his with profound distaste.

'This'll be my death,' he said solemnly.

'Don't eat it, then,' said Fred.

'I must keep up me strength. Where would you be now if I 'adn't me strength when we struck that bad weather? It's not for my sake I'm eatin' it. It's for yours. I don't take a job unless I know I can do it, and not me worst enemy can say I spare meself.'

Gradually the piles of food diminished, and Captain Nichols with stubborn determination cleaned up his plate.

'God, we haven't had a meal like this for weeks,' said Fred.

He ate voraciously, with a boy's appetite, and enjoyed his food. They drank beer.

'If I don't suffer for this it'll be a miracle,' said the skipper.

They had their coffee on the veranda.

'You'd better have a sleep now,' said Erik, 'and then when it's cooler I'll come round and show you the sights. Pity you're not staying a bit longer. It's a beautiful walk up the volcano. You can see for miles. The sea and all the islands.'

'I don't see why we shouldn't stay till the doctor sails,' said Fred.

'Suits me,' said the skipper. 'After all the 'ardships of life on the ocean wave this is a bit of all right. I'm not sure if a drop of brandy wouldn't settle that *reistafel* now I come to think of it.'

'Trading, I suppose?' asked the Dane.

'We're prospectin' for shell,' said the skipper. 'Got to find some new beds. There's a fortune for anyone who's lucky.'

'D'you have any papers here?' asked Blake. 'In English, I mean.'

'Not London papers. But Frith gets a paper from Australia.'

'Frith. Who's Frith?'

'He's an Englishman. He gets a bundle of *Sydney Bulletins* every mail.'

Fred went strangely pale, but what the emotion was that blanched his cheek, who could tell?

'D'you think there's a chance of my having a squint at them?'

'Of course. I'll borrow them or I'll take you up there.'

'How old's the latest?'

'It oughtn't to be very old. A mail came in four days ago.'

chapter seventeen

Later, when the heat of the day was passed and his own work finished, Erik fetched them. Dr Saunders was sitting alone with Fred, for the skipper, suffering from a violent attack of indigestion, had announced that he didn't want to see no bloody sights and had returned to the lugger. They sauntered through the town. There were more people about than in the morning. Now and then Erik took off his hat to a sun-burned Dutchman who walked with a stout and listless wife. There were few Chinese, for they do not settle where no trade is, but a number of Arabs, some in smart tarbouches and neat suits of duck, others in white caps and sarongs; they were dark-skinned, with large shining eyes, and they had the Semitic look of the merchants of Tyre and Sidon. There were Malays, Papuans, and half-castes. It was strangely silent. The air was heavy with fatigue. The grand houses of the old perkeniers, in which dwelt now the riff-raff of the East from Baghdad to New Hebrides, had the shame-faced look of respectable citizens who could not pay their rates. They came to a long white wall, all crumbling away, and this once had been a Portuguese monastery; and then to a ruined fort of great grey stones overrun

94

with a wild jungle of trees and flowering shrubs. There was a wide space in front of it, facing the sea, where grew huge old trees, planted it was said by the Portuguese, casuarinas, kanaris, and wild figs; and here, after the heat of the day, they had been used to ramble.

Panting a little, for he was somewhat inclined to corpulence, the doctor with his companions ascended the hill on which stood the stronghold, grey and bare, which had commanded the harbour. It was surrounded by a deep moat and the only doorway was high from the ground, so that they had to climb a ladder to enter. Inside the great square walls was the keep, and in this were large and well-proportioned chambers, with windows and doorways of a style that suggested the later Renaissance. Here officers and garrison dwelt. From the upper towers was a spacious and magnificent view.

'It's like Tristan's castle,' said the doctor.

The day was softly dying, and the sea was as wine-dark as the sea on which Odysseus sailed. The islands, encircled by the smooth and shining water, had the rich green of a vestment in the treasury of a Spanish cathedral. It was a colour so bizarre and sophisticated that it seemed to belong to art rather than to nature.

'Like a green thought in a green shade,' murmured the young Dane.

'They're all right from a distance,' said Fred, 'those islands, but when you go there – my God! At first I used to want to land. They looked fine from the sea. I thought I'd like to live on one of them for the rest of my life, away from everyone, if you know what I mean, just fishing and keeping my own chickens and pigs. Nichols laughed his head off, said they were lousy, but I insisted on seeing for myself, oh, half a dozen we must have gone to before I gave it up as a bad job. When you got to one of them and went on shore, it all went – I mean, it was just trees and crabs and mosquitos. It slipped through your fingers, so to speak.'

Erik looked at him with his soft beaming eyes, and his smile was sweet with goodwill.

'I know what you mean,' he said. 'It's always a risk to put things to the test of experience. It's like the locked room in

Bluebeard's castle. One's all right so long as one keeps clear of that. You have to be prepared for a shock if you turn the key and walk in.'

Dr Saunders listened to the conversation of the two young men. He was perhaps a cynic and his withers were unwrung at many of the misfortunes that affect men, but he had a peculiar feeling for youth, perhaps because it promised so much and lasted too short a time, and it seemed to him that there was in the bitterness it experiences when reality breaks upon its illusions something more pathetic than in many graver ills. Notwithstanding the clumsy expression he understood what Fred meant and gave the boy's emotion the tribute of a sympathetic smile. As he sat there, in the mellow light, in his singlet and khaki trousers, with his hat off so that you saw his dark curling hair, he was astonishingly handsome. There was something appealing in his beauty so that Dr Saunders, who had thought him a rather dull young man, felt on a sudden kindly disposed to him. Perhaps it was his good looks that deceived him, perhaps it was due to the companionship of Erik Christessen, but at that moment he felt that there was in the lad a strain of something he had never suspected. Perhaps there was there the dim groping beginning of a soul. The thought faintly amused Dr Saunders. It gave him just that little shock of surprise that one feels when what looked like a twig on a branch suddenly opens wings and flies away.

'I come up here almost every evening to watch the sunset,' said Erik. 'To me all the East is here. Not the East of story, the East of palaces and sculptured temples and conquerors with hordes of warriors, but the East of the beginning of the world, the East of the garden of Eden, when men were very few, simple and humble and ignorant, and the world was just waiting, like an empty garden for its absent owner.'

He had a way, that hulking, plain young man, of talking in a lyrical manner that would have been disconcerting if you had not had the feeling that it was as natural to him as to talk of pearl shell and copra and *bêche de mer*. His grandiloquence was a trifle absurd, but if it made you smile it was with kindness. He was strangely ingenuous. The prospect was so lovely, the place they sat in, that gaunt, ruined Portuguese fort, so romantic, that there high strains seemed not unfitting. Erik passed his great heavy hand gently over one of the huge blocks of stone.

'These stones and what they've seen! They have one great advantage over those islands of yours, you can never discover their secret. You can only guess. And you can guess so little. No one knows anything here. Next time I go back to Europe I shall go to Lisbon and see what I can find out of the fellows who lived here.'

Of course romance was there, but it was vague, and in your ignorance you could only form pictures as blurred as ill-developed snapshots. It was on those towers that the Portuguese captains had stood, scanning the sea for the ship from Lisbon that brought them blessed news of home, or watched with apprehension the Dutch vessels that came to attack them. In your mind's eye you saw those gallant, swarthy men, in breastplate and hauberk, who carried their adventurous lives in their hands, but they were lifeless shadows, and they owed their substance only to your fancy. There were still the ruins of the little chapel where every day the miracle of transubstantiation took place and whence the priest in his vestments came, during a siege, to administer extreme unction to the soldiers who lay dying on the ramparts. The imagination was tremulous with an indistinct impression of hazard and cruelty and dauntless courage and self-sacrifice.

'Aren't you ever homesick?' asked Fred presently.

'No. I often think of the little village from which I come, with black-and-white cows in the green pastures, and of Copenhagen. The houses in Copenhagen with their flat windows are just like smooth-faced women with large, short-sighted eyes, and the palaces and the churches look as if they had come out of a fairy tale. But I see it all like a scene in a play, it is very clear, and amusing, but I don't know that I want to step on to the stage. I am quite willing to sit in my dark seat in the gallery and watch the spectacle from far away.'

'After all, one's only got one life.'

'That is what I think, too. But life is what you make it. I might have been a clerk in an office, and then it would have been more difficult, but here, with the sea and the jungle, and all the memories of the past crowding in upon you, and these people, the Malays, the Papuans, the Chinese, the stolid Dutch, with my books and as much leisure as if I were a millionaire – good heavens, what can the imagination want more?'

Fred Blake looked at him for a moment, and the effort of unaccustomed reflection made him frown. When he understood what the Dane meant, his surprise was evident in his voice.

'But that's all make-believe.'

'It's the only reality there is,' smiled Erik.

'I don't know what you mean by that. Reality's doing things, not dreaming about them. One's only young once, one must have one's fling, and everyone wants to get on. One wants to make money and have a good position and all that sort of thing.'

'Oh no. What does one do things for? Of course one has to work a certain amount to earn one's living, but after that, only to satisfy the imagination. Tell me, when you saw those islands from the sea and your heart was filled with delight, and when you landed on them and found them a dreary jungle, which was the real island? Which gave you most, and which are you going to treasure in your memory?'

Fred smiled into Erik's eager, gentle eyes.

'That's bloody rot, old boy. It's no good thinking the earth of something and when you come down to brass tacks finding out to your cost that it's a wash-out. One doesn't get much forrader by not facing facts. Where d'you expect to get to if you just take things at their face value?'

'The Kingdom of Heaven,' smiled Erik.

'And where is that?' asked Fred.

'In my own mind.'

'I do not wish to intrude upon this philosophic conversation,' said the doctor, 'but I'm bound to tell you that I'm suffering from the pangs of thirst.'

Erik, with a laugh, raised his huge body from the wall on which he had been sitting.

'The sun will be setting soon, anyhow. Let's go down and I'll give you a drink in my house.' He pointed to the volcano that stood over against the west, a bold cone that was silhouetted with exquisite precision against the darkening sky. He addressed himself to Fred. 'Would you like to come for a climb tomorrow? You get a grand view from the top.'

'I don't mind if I do.'

'We must start early, on account of the heat. I could fetch you on the lugger just before dawn, and we'd row over.'

'That'll do me.'

They strolled down the hill and soon found themselves back in the town.

Erik's house was one of those they had passed in the morning when on landing they had wandered down the street. Dutch merchants had lived in it for a hundred years, and the firm for which he worked had bought it lock, stock and barrel. It stood within a high, whitewashed wall, but the whitewash was peeling and in places green with damp. The wall enclosed a little garden, wild and overgrown, in which grew roses and fruit trees, wantoning creepers and flowering shrubs, bananas, and two or three tall palms. It was choked with weeds. In the waning light it looked desolate and mysterious. Fire-flies flitted heavily to and fro.

'I'm afraid it's very neglected,' said Erik. 'Sometimes I think I'll put a couple of coolies to clear up all the mess, but I think I like it like that. I like to think of the Dutch mynheer who used to take his ease here in the cool of the evening, smoking his china pipe, while his fat mevrou sat and fanned herself.'

They went into the parlour. It was a long room with a window at each end, but heavily curtained; a boy came and, standing on a chair, lit a hanging oil-lamp. There was a marble floor, and on the walls paintings in oil so dark that you could not see the subjects. There was a large round table in the middle, and round it a set of stiff chairs covered with green stamped velvet. A stuffy and uncomfortable room, but it had the charm of incongruity, and it brought vividly to the mind's eye a demure picture of nineteenth-century Holland. The sober merchant must have unpacked with pride the furniture that had come all the way from Amsterdam, and when it was neatly arranged he must have thought it very well became his station. The boy brought beer. Erik went over to a little table to put a record on the gramophone. He caught sight of a bundle of papers.

'Oh, here are the papers for you. I sent up for them.'

Fred rose from his chair, taking them, and sat down at the big round table under the lamp. Because of the doctor's remark while they were up in the old Portuguese fort, Erik put on the beginning of the last act of *Tristan*. The recollection gave an added poignancy to the music. The strange and subtle little tune that the shepherd played on his reed, when he scanned the wide sea and saw no sail, was melancholy with blighted hope. But it was another pang that wrung the doctor's heart. He remembered Covent Garden in the old days and himself, in evening clothes, sitting in a stall on the aisle; in the boxes were women in tiaras, with pearls round their necks; the King, obese, with great pouches under his eyes, sat in the corner of the omnibus box; on the other side, in the corner, looking over the orchestra, the Baron and the Baroness de Meyer sat together, and she catching his eye bowed. There was an air of opulence and of security. Everything in its grand manner seemed so well-ordered, the thought of change never crossed the mind. Richter conducted. How passionate that music was, how full and with what a melodious splendour it unrolled itself sonorously upon the senses! But he had not heard in it then that something shoddy, blatant, and a trifle vulgar, a sort of baronial buffet effect, that now somewhat disconcerted him. It was magnificent, of course, but a little frowsty; his ear had grown accustomed in China to complications more exquisite and harmonies less suave. He was used to a music pregnant with suggestion, illusive and nervous, and the brutal statement of facts a trifle shocked the fastidiousness of his taste. When Erik got up to turn the record over Dr Saunders glanced at Fred to see what effect those strains were having on him. Music is queer. Its power seems unrelated to the other affections of man, so that a person who is elsewise perfectly commonplace may have for it an extreme and delicate sensitiveness. And he was beginning to think that Fred Blake was not so ordinary as he had at first imagined. He had in him something, scarcely awakened and to himself unknown, like a little flower self-sown in a stone wall that pathetically sought the sun, which excited sympathy and interest. But Fred had not heard a note. He sat, unconscious of his surroundings, staring out of the window. The short twilight of the tropics had darkened into night, and in the blue sky one or two stars twinkled already, but he did not look at them, he seemed to look into some black abyss of thought. The light of the lamp under which he sat threw strange, sharp shadows on his face so that it was like a mask that you hardly recognized. But his body was relaxed, as though a tension had been suddenly withdrawn, and the muscles under his brown skin were loose. He felt the doctor's cool stare and looking at him forced his lips to a smile, but it was a painful little smile, oddly appealing and pathetic. The beer by his side was untouched.

'Anything in the paper?' asked the doctor.

Fred suddenly flushed scarlet.

'No, nothing. They've had the elections.'

'Where?'

'New South Wales. Labour's got in.'

'Are you Labour?'

Fred hesitated a little, and into his eyes came that watchful look that the doctor had seen in them once or twice before.

'I'm not interested in politics,' he said. 'I don't know anything about them.'

'You might let me have a look at the paper.'

Fred took a copy from the bundle and handed it to the doctor. But he did not take it.

'Is that the latest?'

'No, this is the latest,' answered Fred, putting his hand on the one he had just been reading.

'If you've done with it I'll read that. I don't know that I'm very keen on news when it's too stale.'

Fred hesitated for a second. The doctor held him with smiling but determined eyes. Obviously Fred could think of no plausible way to refuse the very natural request. He gave him the paper, and Dr Saunders drew forward to the light to read it. Fred did not take up any of the other copies of the *Bulletin*, though certainly there were some he could not have seen, but sat pretending to look at the table, and the doctor was conscious that he was closely watching him from the sides of his eyes. There was no doubt that Fred had read in the paper he now held in his hand something that deeply concerned him. Dr

Saunders turned over the pages. There was much election news. There was a London letter and a certain amount of cabled information from Europe and America. There was a good deal of local intelligence. He turned to the police news. The election had given rise to some disorder, and the courts had dealt with it. There had been a burglary at Newcastle. Some man had received a sentence for an insurance fraud. A stabbing affray between two Tonga Islanders was reported. Captain Nichols suspected that it was on account of murder that this disappearance of Fred had been arranged, and there were two columns about a murder that had taken place at a farmstead in the Blue Mountains, but this arose out of a quarrel between two brothers and the murderer, who had given himself up to the police, pleaded self-defence. Besides, it had taken place after Fred and Captain Nichols had sailed from Sydney. There was the report of an inquest on a woman who had hanged herself. For a moment Dr Saunders wondered whether there was anything in this. The *Bulletin* is a weekly, of literary tendencies, and it dealt with the matter, not summarily, but in a fashion natural to a paper catering to a public to whom the facts in detail had been made known by the dailies. It appeared that the woman had been under suspicion of the murder of her husband some weeks before, but the evidence against her was too slight for the authorities to take action. She had been repeatedly examined by the police, and this, together with the gossip of neighbours and the scandal, had preyed on her mind. The jury found that she had committed suicide while temporarily insane. The coroner, commenting on the case, remarked that with her death vanished the last chance the police had of solving the mystery of the murder of Patrick Hudson. The doctor read the account again, reflectively; it was odd, but it was too brief to tell him much. The woman was forty-two. It seemed unlikely that a boy of Fred's age could have had anything to do with her. And, after all, Captain Nichols had nothing to go on; it was pure guesswork; the boy was an accountant; he might just as well have taken money that did not belong to him or, pressed by financial difficulties, forged a cheque. If he was connected with some important person politically, that might have been enough to make it advisable to spirit him away for a period. Dr Saunders, putting the paper down, met Fred's eyes fixed upon him. He gave him a reassuring smile. His curiosity was disinterested, and he was not inclined to put himself to any trouble to gratify it.

'Going to dine at the hotel, Fred?' he asked.

'I'd like you both to stay and have pot-luck with me here,' said the Dane, 'but I'm going up to have supper with Frith.'

'Well, we'll be toddling.'

The doctor and Fred walked a few steps in silence along the dark street.

'I don't want any dinner,' the boy said suddenly. 'I can't face Nichols tonight. I'm going for a tramp.'

Before Dr Saunders could answer he had turned on his heel and rapidly walked away. The doctor shrugged his shoulders and continued on his unhurried way.

chapter eighteen

He was drinking a gin pahit before dinner, on the veranda of the hotel, when Captain Nichols strolled up. He had washed and shaved, he was wearing a khaki stengah-shifter, with his topi set at a rakish angle, so that he looked quite spruce. He reminded you of a gentlemanly pirate.

'Feelin' better tonight,' he remarked as he sat down, 'and quite peckish, to tell you the truth. I don't believe the wing of a chicken could do me any 'arm. Where's Fred?'

'I don't know. He's off somewhere.'

'Lookin' for a girl? I don't blame him. Though I don't know what he thinks he's goin' to find in a place like this. Risky, you know.'

The doctor ordered him a drink.

'I was a rare one for the girls when I was a young fellow. Got a way with me, you know. The mistake I made was to marry. If I 'ad my time over again ... I never tell you about my old woman, doc.'

'Enough,' said the doctor.

'That's impossible. I couldn't do that, not if I was to tell you about 'er till tomorrow morning. If ever there was a devil in 'uman form, it's my old woman. I ask you, is it fair to treat a man like that? She's directly responsible for my indigestion; I'm just as sure of that as I am that I'm sittin' and talking to you. It's 'umiliatin', that's what it is. I'm surprised I 'aven't killed her. I would 'ave, too, only I know that if I was to start anything, and she said to me: "You put that knife down, captain," I'd put it down. Now I ask you, is it natural? And then she'd just start on me. And if I was to edge towards the door, she'd say: "No you don't, you stay 'ere till I've said all I've got to say to you, and when I've finished with you, I'll tell you." '

They dined together, and the doctor lent a sympathetic ear to the recital of Captain Nichols' domestic infelicity. Then they sat again on the veranda, smoking Dutch cigars, and drank Schnapps with their coffee. Alcohol mellowed the skipper, and he grew reminiscent. He told the doctor stories of his early days on the coast of New Guinea and about the islands. He was a racy talker, with an ironic vein of humour, and it was diverting to listen to him, since false shame never tempted him to depict himself in a flattering light. It never occurred to him that anyone would hesitate to diddle another if he had the chance, and he felt just the same satisfaction in the success of a dirty trick as a chess-player might in winning a game by a bold and ingenious move. He was a scamp, but a courageous one. Dr Saunders found a peculiar savour in his conversation when he remembered the splendid self-confidence with which he had weathered the storm. It had been impossible then not to be impressed by his readiness, resource, and coolness.

Presently the doctor found occasion to slip in a question that had been for some time on the tip of his tongue.

'Did you ever know a fellow called Patrick Hudson?'

'Patrick 'udson?'

'He was a resident magistrate in New Guinea at one time. He's been dead a good many years now.'

'That's a funny coincidence. No, I didn't know 'im. There

104

was a fellow called Patrick 'udson in Sydney. Come to a sticky end.'

'Oh?'

'Yes. Not so very long before we sailed. The papers was full of it.'

'He might have been some relation of the man I mean.'

'He was what they call a rough diamond. Been a railway man, they said, and worked 'is way up. Took up politics and all that. He was member for some place. Labour, of course.'

'What happened to him?'

'Well, 'e was shot. With his own gun, if I remember right.'

'Suicide?'

'No, they said 'e couldn't 'a' done it 'imself. I don't know any more than you do what 'appened, on account of my leavin' Sydney. It made quite a sensation.'

'Was he married?'

'Yes. A lot of people thought 'is old woman done it. They couldn't prove anythin'. She'd been to the pictures, and when she come 'ome she found 'im lyin' there. There'd been a fight. The furniture was all over the shop. I never thought it was 'is old woman meself. My experience is they don't let you off so easy. They want to keep you alive as long as they can. They ain't going to lose their fun by puttin' you out of your misery.'

'Still, a lot of women have murdered their husbands,' objected the doctor.

'Pure accident. We all know that accidents will 'appen in the best regulated families. Sometimes they get careless and go too far, and then the poor bastard dies. But they don't mean it. Not them.'

chapter nineteen

Dr Saunders was fortunate in this that, notwithstanding the several deplorable habits he had, and in some parts of the world they would certainly have been accounted vices (*vérité au delà des Alpes, erreur ici*), he awoke in the morning with a clean

105

tongue and in a happy frame of mind. He seldom stretched himself in bed, drinking his cup of fragrant China tea and smoking the first delicious cigarette, without looking forward with pleasure to the coming day. Breakfast in the little hotels in the islands of the Dutch East Indies is served at a very early hour. It never varies. Papaia, *œufs sur le plat*, cold meat, and Edam cheese. However punctually you appear, the eggs are cold; they stare at you, two large round yellow eyes on a thin surface of white, and they look as if they had been scooped out of the face of an obscene monster of the deep. The coffee is an essence to which you add Nestlé's Swiss Milk brought to a proper consistency with hot water. The toast is dry, sodden, and burnt. Such was the breakfast served in the dining-room of the hotel at Kanda and hurriedly eaten by silent Dutchmen, who had their offices to go to.

But Dr Saunders got up late next morning, and Ah Kay brought him his breakfast out on the veranda. He enjoyed his papaia, he enjoyed his eggs, that moment out of the frying-pan, and he enjoyed his scented tea. He reflected that to live was a very enjoyable affair. He wanted nothing. He envied no man. He had no regrets. The morning was still fresh and in the clean, pale light the outline of things was sharp-edged. A huge banana just below the terrace with a haughty and complacent disdain flaunted its splendid foliage to the sun's fierce heat. Dr Saunders was tempted to philosophize: he said that the value of life lay not in its moments of excitement but in its placid intervals when, untroubled, the human spirit in tranquillity undisturbed by the recollection of emotion could survey its being with the same detachment as the Buddha contemplated his navel. Plenty of pepper on the eggs, plenty of salt and a little Worcester sauce, and then when they were finished a piece of bread to soak up the buttery remains, and that was the best mouthful of all. He was intent on this when Fred Blake and Erik Christessen came swinging down the street. They leaped up the steps and, throwing themselves on chairs at the doctor's table, shouted for the boy. They had started for their walk up the volcano before dawn, and were now ravenous. The boy hurried out with papaia and a dish of cold meats, and they finished this before he brought them eggs. They were in great spirits. The enthusiasm of youth had ripened the acquaintance made the day before into friendship, and they called one another Fred and Erik. It was a stiff climb and the violent exercise had excited them. They talked nonsense and laughed at nothing. They were like a couple of boys. The doctor had never seen Fred so gay. He was evidently much taken with Erik, and the companionship of someone only a little older than himself had loosened his constraint so that he seemed to flower with a new adolescence. He looked so young that you could hardly believe he was a grown man, and his deep, ringing voice sounded almost comic.

'D'you know, he's as strong as an ox, this blighter,' said he, with a glance of admiration at Erik. 'We had one rather nasty little bit of climbing to do, a branch broke and I slipped. I might have taken a nasty toss, broken my leg or something. Erik caught hold of me with one arm, damned if I know how he did it, and lifted me right up and set me on my feet again. And I weigh a good eleven stone.'

'I've always been strong,' smiled Erik.

'Put your hand up.'

Fred placed his elbow on the table and Erik did the same. They put palm to palm and Fred tried to force Erik's arm down. He put all his strength into the effort. He could not move it. Then with a little smile the Dane pressed back and gradually Fred's arm was forced to the table.

'I'm like a kid beside you,' he laughed. 'Gosh, a fellow wouldn't stand much chance if you hit him. Ever been in a fight?'

'No. Why should I?'

He finished eating and lit a cheroot.

'I must go to my office,' he said. 'Frith says, will you all go up there this afternoon? He wants us to have supper with him.'

'Suits me all right,' said the doctor.

'And the captain, too. I'll come for you about four.'

Fred watched him go.

'Perfect loon,' he said, turning to the doctor, with a smile. 'My belief is he isn't all there.'

'Oh, why?'

'The way he talked.'

'What did he say?'

'Oh, I don't know. Crazy. He asked me about Shakespeare. A fat lot I know about Shakespeare. I told him I'd read Henry V when I was at school (we took it one term), and he began spouting one of the speeches. Then he started talking about *Hamlet* and *Othello* and heaven knows what. He knows yards of them by heart. I can't tell you all he said about them. I never heard anyone talk in that way before. And the funny thing was that, although it was all a lot of bunk, you didn't want to tell him to shut up.'

A smile lingered in his candid blue eyes, but his face was serious.

'You've never been in Sydney, have you?'

'No.'

'We have quite a literary and artistic set there. Not much in my line, but sometimes I couldn't help myself. Women chiefly, you know. They'd talk a lot of tosh about books and then, before you knew where you were, they'd be wanting to pop into bed with you.'

'The Philistine dots his i's and crosses his t's with a definiteness that is unbecoming,' reflected the doctor, 'and when he sees a nail he hits it on the head.'

'You get rather leery of them. But, I don't know how to explain it exactly, when Erik talked about all that it was different. He wasn't showing off and he wasn't trying to impress me. He just talked like that because he couldn't help it. He didn't mind if I was bored or not. He was so keen on it all it never struck him, perhaps, I didn't care a damn about it. I didn't understand the half of what he said, you know, but somehow, I don't know, it was as good as a play, if you understand what I mean.'

Fred threw out his observations like stones that you dig up in a garden to prepare the ground for planting and cast in a heap one after the other. In his perplexity he vigorously scratched his head. Dr Saunders watched him with cool, shrewd eyes. The boy was tongue-tied, and it was diverting in his confused remarks to discover the emotion he was trying to put in words. Critics divide writers into those who have something to say and do not know how to say it, and those who know how to say it and have nothing to say. Often it is the same with men, with Anglo-Saxons at all events, to whom words come difficultly. When a man is fluent it is sometimes because he has said a thing so often that it has lost its meaning, and his speech is most significant when he has to fashion it laboriously from thoughts to which he can see no clear outline.

Fred gave the doctor a puckish glance that made him look like a mischievous boy.

'D'you know, he's lending me *Othello*. I don't exactly know why, but I said I wouldn't mind reading it. You've read it, I suppose.'

'Thirty years ago.'

'Of course I may be mistaken, but when Erik was spouting great chunks of it, it sounded quite exciting. I don't know what it is, but when you're with a chap like that everything seems different. I daresay he's crazy, but I wish there were a few more like him.'

'You've taken quite a fancy to him, haven't you?'

'Well, you can hardly help it,' answered Fred, with a sudden attack of shyness. 'You'd be a perfect damn fool not to see he's as straight as a die. I'd trust him with every penny I had in the world. He couldn't do anyone down. And you know, the funny thing is, though he's such a big hulking fellow and as strong as an ox, you have a sort of feeling you want to take care of him. I know it sounds silly, but you can't help feeling he oughtn't to be allowed about by himself; someone ought to be there to see that he doesn't get into trouble.'

The doctor, with his cynical detachment, translated in his own mind the young Australian's awkward phrases into sense. He was surprised and a trifle touched by the emotion that with this shy clumsiness fought for expression. For what emerged from those hackneyed words was the shock of admiration the lad had received when he was confronted with the realization of something quite startling. Through the oddness of the huge, ungainly Dane, lighting up his complete sincerity, giving body to his idealism and charm to his extravagant enthusiasm, shone, with a warm, all-embracing glow, pure goodness. Fred Blake's youth made him mystically able to see it, and he was amazed by it and baffled. It touched him and made him feel very shy. It shook his self-confidence and humbled him. At that moment the rather ordinary, handsome boy was conscious of something he had never imagined, spiritual beauty.

'Who would have thought it possible?' reflected the doctor.

His own feelings towards Erik Christessen, naturally enough, were more detached. He was interested in him because he was a little unusual. It was amusing, to begin with, in an island of the Malay Archipelago, to come across a trader who knew Shakespeare well enough to say long passages by heart. The doctor could not but look on it as a somewhat tiresome accomplishment. He wondered idly if Erik was a good business man. He was not very fond of idealists. It was difficult for them in this workaday world to reconcile their professions with the exigencies of life, and it was disconcerting how often they managed to combine exalted notions with a keen eye to the main chance. The doctor had often found here cause for amusement. They were apt to look down upon those who were occupied with practical matters but not averse from profiting by their industry. Like the lilies of the field they neither toiled nor spun, but took it as a right that others should perform for them these menial offices.

'Who is this fellow Frith that we're going up to this afternoon?' asked the doctor.

'He's got a plantation. He grows nutmeg and cloves. He's a widower. He lives there with his daughter.'

chapter twenty

It was about three miles to Frith's house, and they drove out in an old Ford. On each side of the road grew densely huge trees, and there was a heavy undergrowth of ferns and creepers. The jungle began at the outskirts of the town. Here and there were miserable huts. Ragged Malays lay about the verandas and listless children played among the pigs under the piles. It was humid and sultry. The estate had once belonged to a perkenier, and it had a stucco gateway, massive but crumbling, of pleasing design. Over the archway on a tablet was the old burgher's name and the date of erection. They turned down an earth road and bumped along over ruts, hillocks and holes till they came to the bungalow. It was a large, square building not on piles, but on a foundation of masonry, covered with an attap roof and surrounded by a neglected garden. They drove up, the Malay driver sounding his horn with energy, and a man came out of the house and waved to them. It was Frith. He waited for them at the top of the steps that led down from the veranda, and as they came up and Erik mentioned their names, shook hands with them one by one.

'Delighted to see you. I haven't seen any Britishers for a year. Come in and have a drink.'

He was quite a big man, but fat, with grey hair and a small grey moustache. He was growing bald and his forehead was imposing. His red face, shining with sweat, was unlined and round, so that at the first glance he looked almost boyish. He had a long yellow tooth in the middle of his mouth, which hung loosely, giving you the impression that with a sharp pull it would come out. He wore khaki shorts and a tennis shirt open at the neck. He walked with a pronounced limp. He led them into a very large room, which served at once as parlour and dining-room; the walls were adorned with Malay weapons, antlers of deer, and horns of sladang. On the floor were tiger skins that looked a trifle mouldy and moth-eaten.

When they entered a tiny little old man got up from a chair and without taking a step towards them stood and looked at them. He was wrinkled, battered and bowed. He seemed very old.

'This is Swan,' said Frith, with a casual nod of his head. 'He's by way of being my father-in-law.'

The little old man had very pale blue eyes with red-rimmed, hairless lids, but they were full of cunning, and his glance was darting and mischievous like a monkey's. He shook hands with the three strangers without speaking and then, opening a toothless mouth, addressed Erik in a language the others did not understand.

'Mr Swan is a Swede,' said Erik in explanation.

111

The old man eyed them one after the other, and in his gaze was a certain suspicion and at the same time, hardly concealed, something of mockery.

'I came out fifty years ago. I was mate of a sailing vessel. I never been back. Maybe I go next year.'

'I'm a seafarin' man meself, sir,' said Captain Nichols.

But Mr Swan was not in the least interested in him.

'I been pretty well most things in my day,' he went on. 'I been captain of a schooner in the slave trade.'

'Blackbirding,' interrupted Captain Nichols. 'There was a nice little bit of money to be picked up that way in the old days.'

'I been a blacksmith. I been a trader. I been a planter. I don't know what I haven't been. They tried to kill me over and over again. I got a hernia on my chest, I have. That come from a wound I got in a scrap with the natives in the Solomons. Left me for dead, they did. I've had a lot of money in my time. Haven't I, George?'

'So I've always heard.'

'Ruined by the great hurricane, I was. Destroyed my store. Lost everything. I didn't care. Got nothing left now but this plantation. Never mind, it gives us enough to live on and that's all that matters. I've had four wives and more children than you can count.'

He talked in a high cracked voice with a strong Swedish accent, so that you had to listen intently to understand what he said. He spoke very quickly, almost as though he were reciting a lesson, and he finished with a little cackle of senile laughter. It seemed to say that he had been through everything and it was all stuff and nonsense. He surveyed human kind and its activities from a great distance, but from no Olympian height, from behind a tree, slyly, and hopping from one foot to another with amusement.

A Malay brought in a bottle of whisky and a syphon, and Frith poured out the drinks.

'A drop of Scotch for you, Swan?' he suggested to the old man.

'Why do you ask me that, George?' he quavered. 'You know very well I can't abide it. Give me some rum and water.

Scotch has been the ruin of the Pacific. When I first come from Sweden nobody drunk Scotch. Rum. If they'd stuck to rum and stuck to sail things wouldn't be what they are now, not by a long way.'

'We ran into some pretty rough weather on the way 'ere,' Captain Nichols remarked, by way of making conversation with a fellow-seaman.

'Rough weather? You don't have rough weather nowadays. You should have seen the weather you had when I was a boy. I remember on one of the schooners I had, I was taking a parcel of labour to Samoa, from the New Hebrides, and we got caught in a hurricane. I told them savages to pop over the side pretty damn quick, and I put out to sea, and for three days I never closed my eyes. Lost our sails, lost our mainmast, lost our boats. Rough weather! Don't talk to me about rough weather, young fellow.'

'No offence meant,' said Captain Nichols, with a grin that showed his broken, decayed little teeth.

'And no offence taken,' cackled old Swan. 'Give him a tot of rum, George. If he's a sailor-man he don't want that stinking whisky of yours.'

Presently Erik suggested that the strangers would like to walk round the plantation.

'They've never seen a nutmeg estate.'

'Take 'em over, George. Twenty-seven acres. Best land on the island,' said the old man. 'Bought it thirty years ago for a parcel of pearls.'

They got up, leaving him, like a little strange bald bird, hunched up over his rum and water, and walked out into the garden. It ended casually and the plantation began. In the cool of the evening the air was limpid. The kanari trees, in the shade of which grew the portly and profitable nutmeg trees, were enormously tall. They towered like the columns of a mosque in the *Arabian Nights*. Underfoot was no tangle of undergrowth but a carpet of decaying leaves. You heard the boom of great pigeons and saw them flying about with a heavy whirr of wings. Little green parrots in flocks flitted swiftly over the nutmeg trees, screeching, and they were like living jewels darting through the softly sparkling air. Dr Saunders had a sense of extreme well-being. He felt like a disembodied spirit and his imagination was pleasantly, but not exhaustingly, occupied with image after image. He walked with Frith and the skipper. Frith was explaining the details of the nutmeg trade. He did not listen. There was an idle sensuousness in the air that was almost material, so that it reminded you of the feel of a soft, rich fabric. Erik and Fred were walking a step behind. The declining sun had found a way under the branches of the lofty kanaries and shone on the foliage of the nutmeg trees so that their dense opulent green glistened like burnished copper.

They strolled along a winding path, made by the accident of people having long followed it, and all at once saw a girl coming towards them. She was walking with eyes cast down, as though absorbed in thought, and it was not till she heard voices that she looked up. She stopped.

'There is my daughter,' said Frith.

You might have fancied she had stopped in a momentary embarrassment at the sight of strangers; but she did not move on, she stayed still, watching with a singular calm the men who advanced towards her; and then you received an impression, not exactly of self-assurance, but of tranquil unconcern. She wore nothing but a sarong of Javanese batik, with a little white pattern on a brown ground; it was attached tightly just over her breasts and came down to her knees. She was barefoot. Beside the little smile that hovered on her lips, the only sign she gave that she noticed the approach of strangers was a little shake of the head, almost involuntary, to loosen her hair and an instinctive gesture of the hand through it, for it was long and hung down her back. It spread in a cloud over her neck and shoulders, very thick, and of a fairness so ashy pale that, but for its radiance, it would have looked white. She waited with composure. The sarong tightly wrapped round her concealed nothing of her form; she was very slim, with the narrow hips of a boy, long-legged, and at first sight tall. She was burned by the sun to a rich honey colour. The doctor was not as a rule captivated by feminine beauty; he could not but think the manner in which a woman's frame was made for obvious physiological purposes much detracted from its aesthetic appeal. Just as a table should be solid, of a convenient height and roomy, so a woman should be large-breasted and broad in the beam; but in both cases beauty could only be an adjunct to utility. You might say that a table which was solid, roomy, and of a convenient height was beautiful, but the doctor preferred to say that it was solid, roomy, and of a convenient height. The girl standing there in an attitude of indolent beauty reminded him of some statue he had seen in a museum of a goddess attaching her peplum; he could not remember it very exactly. Greco-Roman, he thought. She had the same ambiguous slenderness as the little Chinese girls in the flowerboats at Canton, in whose company in his younger days he had on occasion passed moments of somewhat detached amusement. She had the same flower-like grace, and her fairness in that tropic scene gave the exotic sensation that made them so charming. She recalled to his mind the pale, profuse, delicate flowers of the plumbago.

'These are Christessen's friends,' said her father as they came up to her.

She did not hold out her hand, but slightly and graciously inclined her head as first the doctor and then Captain Nichols were introduced to her. She gave them both a cool survey in which was inquiry and then swift appraisement. Dr Saunders noticed that her brown hands were long and slender. Her eyes were blue. He features were fine and very regular. She was an extremely pretty young woman.

'I've just been having a bathe in the pool,' she said.

Her glance travelled to Erik, and she gave him a very sweet and friendly smile.

'This is Fred Blake,' he said.

She turned her head a little to look at him, and for an appreciable time her eyes rested on him. The smile died away on her lips.

'Pleased to meet you,' said Fred, holding out his hand.

She continued to look at him, not with pertness or brazenly, but as though she were a little surprised. You might have thought she had seen him before and was trying to remember where. But the incident lasted no more than a minute, and no one would have been conscious of a pause before she took the proffered hand.

'I was just going back to the house to dress,' she said.

'I'll come with you,' said Erik.

Now that he stood beside her you saw that she was not really very tall; it was only her straightness of limb, her slenderness, and her carriage, that gave the impression of more than common height.

They sauntered back towards the house.

'Who is that boy?' she asked.

'I don't know,' answered Erik. 'He's in partnership with the thin, grey one. They're looking for pearl-shell. They're trying to find some new beds.'

'He's good-looking.'

'I thought you'd like him. He's got a nice nature.'

The others continued their tour of the estate.

chapter twenty-one

When they came in they found Erik sitting alone with Swan. The old man was telling an interminable story, in an odd mixture of Swedish and English, of some adventure he had had in New Guinea.

'Where's Louise?' asked Frith.

'I've been helping her to lay the table. She's been doing something in the kitchen and now she's gone to change.'

They sat down and had another drink. They talked somewhat desultorily, as people do when they don't know one another. Old Swan was tired, and when the strangers appeared lapsed into silence, but he watched them, with his sharp rheumy eyes, as though they filled him with suspicion. Captain Nichols told Frith that he was a martyr to dyspepsia.

'I've never known what it is to have a pain in my tummy,' said Frith. 'Rheumatism's my trouble.'

'I've known men as was martyrs to it. A friend of mine at

Brisbane, one of the best pilots in the business, was just crippled by it. Had to go about on crutches.'

'One has to have something,' said Frith.

'You can't 'ave anythin' worse than dyspepsia, you take my word for it. I'd be a rich man now if it 'adn't been for my dyspepsia.'

'Money's not everything,' said Frith.

'I'm not sayin' it is. I'm sayin' I'd 'ave been a rich man today if it 'adn't been for my dyspepsia.'

'Money's never meant anything very much to me. So long as I have a roof over my head and three meals a day I'm content. Leisure's the important thing.'

Dr Saunders listened to the conversation. He could not quite place Frith. He spoke like an educated man. Though fat and gross, shabbily dressed and in want of a shave, he gave the impression, scarcely of distinction, but of being accustomed to the society of decent people. He certainly did not belong to the same class as old Swan and Captain Nichols. His manners were easy. He had welcomed them with courtesy and treated them not with the fussy politeness an ill-bred person thinks it necessary to use towards strange guests, but naturally, as though he knew the ways of the world. Dr Saunders supposed that he was what in the England of his youth they would have called a gentleman. He wondered how he had found his way to that distant island. He got up from his chair and wandered about the room. A number of framed photographs hung on the wall over a long book-case. He was surprised to find that they were of rowing eights of a Cambridge college, among which, though only by the name underneath, G. P. Frith, he recognized his host; others were groups of native boys at Perak in the Malay States, and at Kuching in Sarawak, with Frith, a much younger man than now, sitting in the middle. It looked as though on leaving Cambridge he had come to the East as a schoolmaster. The book-case was untidily stacked with books, all stained with damp and the ravages of the white ant, and these, with idle curiosity, taking out one here, one there, he glanced at. There was a number of prizes bound in leather from which he learned that Frith had been at one of the smaller public schools, and had been an industrious and even

117

brilliant boy. There were the text-books that he had used at Cambridge, a good many novels, and a few volumes of poetry which gave the impression that they had been much read, but long ago. They were well-thumbed and many passages were marked in pencil or underlined, but they had a musty smell as though they had for years remained unopened. But what surprised him most was to see two shelves filled with works on Indian religion and Indian philosophy. There were translations of the *Rig-Veda* and of certain of the *Upanishads*, and there were paper-bound books published in Calcutta or Bombay by authors with names odd to him and with titles that had a mystical sound. It was an unusual collection to find in the house of a planter in the Far East, and Dr Saunders, trying to make something of the indications they afforded, asked himself what sort of man they suggested. He was turning the pages of a book by one Srinivasa Iyengar called *Outlines of Indian Philosophy*, when Frith somewhat heavily limped up to him.

'Having a look at my library?'

'Yes.'

He glanced at the volume the doctor was holding.

'Interesting. Those Hindus, they're marvellous; they have a natural instinct for philosophy. They make all our philosophers look cheap and obvious. Their subtlety is so amazing. Plotinus is the only fellow I know to compare with them.' He replaced the book on a shelf. 'Of course, Brahma is the only religion that a reasonable man can accept without misgiving.'

The doctor gave him a sidelong glance. With his red, round face, and that long yellow tooth hanging loose in his jaw, his baldish head, he had none of the look of a man with spiritual leanings. It was surprising to hear him talk in this strain.

'When I consider the universe, those innumerable worlds and the vast distances of interstellar space, I cannot think it the work of a creator, and if it were, then I am forced to ask who or what created the creator. The *Vedanta* teaches that in the beginning was the existent, for how could the existent be born from the non-existent? And this existent was Atman, the supreme spirit, from whom emanated maya, the illusion of the phenomenal world. And when you ask those wise men of the East why the supreme spirit should have sent forth this phantasmagory they will tell you it was for his diversion. For being complete and perfect, he could not be actuated by aim or motive. Aim and motive imply desire and he that is perfect and complete needs neither change nor addition. Therefore the activity of the eternal spirit has no purpose, but like the frolic of princes or the play of children, is spontaneous and exultant. He sports in the world, he sports in the soul.'

'That is an explanation of things that does not entirely displease me,' the doctor murmured, smiling. 'There is a futility about it that gratifies the sense of irony.'

But he was watchful and suspicious. He was conscious that he would have attached more significance to what Frith said had he been of ascetic appearance, and his face, instead of shining with sweat, shone with the travail of urgent thought. But does the outer man represent the man within? The face of a scholar or a saint may well mask a vulgar and a trivial soul. Socrates, with his flattened nose and protruding eyes, his thick lips and unwieldy belly, looked like Silenus, and yet was full of admirable temperance and wisdom.

Frith gave a little sigh.

'For a time I was attracted by Yoga, but after all it's only a schismatic branch of Sankhya, and its materialism is unreasonable. All that mortification of the senses is inane. The goal is perfect knowledge of the soul's nature, and apathy and abstraction and rigidity of posture will not enable you to attain that any more than rites and ceremonies. I've got masses of notes. When I have time I shall get some sort of order in my material and write a book. I've had it in mind for twenty years.'

'I should have thought you had time to burn here,' said the doctor dryly.

'Not enough for all I have to do. I've been spending the last four years doing a metrical translation of *The Lusiads*. Camoens, you know. I should like to read you one or two cantos. There's no one here who has any critical discernment. Christessen is a Dane, and I can't trust his ear.'

'But hasn't it been translated before?'

'Yes. By Burton, among others. Poor Burton was no poet. His version is intolerable. Every generation must retranslate the great works of the world for itself. My aim is not only to render the sense, but also to preserve the rhythm and music and lyrical quality of the original.'

'What made you think of it?'

'It's the last of the great epics. After all, my book on the *Vedanta* can only hope to appeal to a small and special public. I felt I owed it to my daughter to undertake a work of more popular character. I have nothing. This estate belongs to old Swan. My translation of *The Lusiads* shall be her dowry. I am going to give her every penny I make out of it. But that is not all; money isn't very important. I want her to be proud of me; I don't think my name will be very easily forgotten: my fame also shall be her dowry.'

Dr Saunders kept silence. It seemed to him fantastic that this man should expect to get money and fame by translating a Portuguese poem that not a hundred people had any wish to read. He shrugged a tolerant shoulder.

'It is strange how things happen,' Frith continued, his face heavy and serious. 'It's hard for me to believe that it is only by accident that I have undertaken this task. You know, of course, that Camoens, a soldier of fortune as well as a poet, came to this island, and he must often have watched the sea from the fort as I have watched it. Why should I have come here? I was a schoolmaster. When I left Cambridge I had an opportunity to come to the East, and I jumped at it. I'd longed to ever since I was a child. But the routine of school-work was too much for me. I couldn't bear the people I had to mix with. I was in the Malay States, and then I thought I'd try Borneo. It was no better. At last I couldn't stand it any more. I resigned. For some time I was in an office in Calcutta. Then I started a book-shop in Singapore. But it didn't pay. I ran a hotel in Bali, but I was before my time, and I couldn't make both ends meet. At last I drifted down here. It's strange that my wife should have been called Catherine, because that was the name of the only woman Camoens loved. It was for her he wrote his perfect lyrics. Of course, if there's anything that seems to me proved beyond all doubt it's the doctrine of transmigration which the Hindus call Samsara. Sometimes I've asked myself if perhaps the spark that issued from the fire and formed the spirit of Camoens is not the self-same spark that now forms mine. So often when I'm reading *The Lusiads* I come across a line that I seem to remember so distinctly that I can't believe I'm reading it for the first time. You know that Pedro de Alcaçova said that *The Lusiads* had only one fault. They were not short enough to learn by heart and not long enough to have no ending.'

He gave a deprecating smile as a man might to whom an extravagant compliment was addressed.

'Ah, here's Louise,' he said. 'That looks as if supper was nearly ready.'

Dr Saunders turned to look at her. She was wearing a sarong of green silk in which was woven an elaborate pattern in gold thread. It had a sleek and glowing splendour. It was Javanese, and such as the ladies of the Sultan's harem at Djokjakarta wore on occasions of state. It fitted her slim body like a sheath, tight over her young nipples and tight over her narrow hips. Her bosom and her legs were bare. She wore high-heeled green shoes, and they added to her graceful stature. That ashy blonde hair of hers was done high on her head, but very simply, and the sober brilliance of the green-and-gold sarong enhanced its astonishing fairness. Her beauty took the breath away. The sarong had been kept with sweet-smelling essences or she had scented herself; when she joined them they were conscious of a faint and unknown perfume. It was languorous and illusive, and it was pleasant to surmise that it was made from a secret recipe in the palace of one of the rajahs of the islands.

'What's the meaning of this fancy dress?' asked Frith, with a smile in his pale eyes and a waggle of his long tooth.

'Erik gave me this sarong the other day, I thought it would be a good opportunity to wear it.'

She gave the Dane a friendly little smile that thanked him again.

'It's an old one,' said Frith. 'It must have cost you a small fortune, Christessen. You'll spoil the child.'

'I got it for a bad debt. I couldn't resist it. I know Louise likes green.'

A Malay servant brought in a great bowl of soup and set it down on the table.

'Will you take Dr Saunders on your right, Louise, and Captain Nichols on your left?' said Frith, with a certain stateliness.

'What does she want to sit between those two old men for?' cackled the ancient Swan suddenly. 'Let her sit between Erik and the kid.'

'I see no reason not to conform to the usages of polite society,' said Frith in a very dignified manner.

'Want to show off?'

'Then will you sit beside me, doctor?' said Frith, taking no notice of this. 'And perhaps Captain Nichols wouldn't mind sitting on my left.'

Old Swan, with a funny quick crawl, took what was evidently his accustomed place. Frith ladled out the soup.

'Pair of crooks they look to me,' said the little old man, shooting a sharp glance from the doctor to Nichols. 'Where'd you fish 'em from, Erik?'

'You're ginny, Mr Swan,' said Frith, handing him gravely a plate of soup to be passed down the table.

'No offence meant,' said Mr Swan.

'And no offence taken,' answered Captain Nichols, graciously. 'I'd ever so much sooner somebody said I looked like a crook than I looked like a fool. And I'm sure the doctor'll say the same as me. What does a fellow mean when 'e says you're a crook? Well, 'e means you're cleverer than 'im, that's all; I ask you, am I right or am I wrong?'

'I know a crook when I see one,' said old Swan. 'I've known too many in my time not to. Been a bit of a crook meself at times.'

He gave a little cackling laugh.

'And who hasn't?' said Captain Nichols, wiping his mouth, for he ate soup somewhat untidily. 'What I always say is, you must take the world as you find it. Compromise, that's the thing. Ask anybody and they'll tell you what made the British Empire what it is, is compromise.'

With a deft movement of his lower lip Frith sucked the remains of his soup off his little grey moustache.

'It's a matter of temperament, I suppose. Compromise has never appealed to me. I have had other fish to fry.'

'Someone else caught 'em for you, I bet,' said old Swan, with a little snicker of senile glee. 'Bone-idle, that's what you are, George. Had a dozen jobs in your time and never kept one of them.'

Frith gave Dr Saunders an indulgent smile. It said as clearly as if he had spoken that it was mightily absurd to hurl such charges at a man who had spent twenty years in the study of the highly metaphysical thought of the Hindus and in whom in all probability dwelt the spirit of a celebrated Portuguese poet.

'My life has been a journey in search of truth and there can be no compromise with truth. The Europeans ask what is the use of truth, but for the tinkers of India it is not a means but an end. Truth is the goal of life. Years ago I used sometimes to hanker for the world I had left behind me. I would go down to the Dutch club and look at the illustrated papers, and when I saw pictures of London my heart ached. But now I know that it is only the recluse who enjoys the civilization of cities to the full. At long last I have learnt that it is we exiles from life who get most value from it. For the way of knowledge is the true way and that way passes every door.'

But at that moment, three chickens, the scrawny, pallid, tasteless chickens of the East, were set before him. He rose from his chair and seized a carving knife.

'Ah, the duties and ceremonies of the householder,' he said cheerfully.

Old Swan had been sitting silent, hunched up in his chair like a little gnome. He ate his soup greedily. Suddenly, in his thin cracked voice, he began to speak:

'I spent seven years in New Guinea, I did. I spoke every language they spoke in New Guinea. You go to Port Moresby and ask 'em about Jack Swan. They remember me. I was the first white man ever walked across the island. Moreton did it afterwards, unarmed, with a walking stick, but he had his police with him. I did it by myself. Everyone thought I was dead, and when I walked into town they thought I was a ghost. Been shooting birds of paradise, we had, my mate and me, a New Zealander he was, been a bank-manager and got into some mess-up, we had our own cutter and we sailed along the coast

123

from Merauke. Got a lot of birds. Worth a mint of money they was then. We was very friendly with the natives, used to give them a drink now and then, and a stick of tobacco. One day I'd been out shooting by myself and I was coming back to the cutter, I was just going to give my mate a shout to come and fetch me in the dinghy when I see some natives on it. We never allowed them to come on board, and I thought something was up. So I just hid myself and I stood there looking. I didn't half like the look of it. I crept along very quiet and I saw the dinghy pulled up on the beach. I thought my mate had come ashore and some of them natives had swum out to the cutter. I thought I wouldn't half give them what for. And then I bumped against something. My God, it did give me a turn. D'you know what it was? It was my mate's body, with the head cut off, and all a mass of blood from the wounds in his back. I didn't wait to see no more. I knew I'd go the same way if they caught me. They was waiting for me on the cutter, that's what they was doing. I'd got to get away and I'd got to get away damned quick. Rare time I had getting across. The things that happened to me! You could write a book about it. One old fellow, chief of a big village he was, took quite a fancy to me, wanted to adopt me and give me a couple of wives, said I'd be chief after him. I was nippy with my hands when I was a young fellow, having been a sailor and all that. I knew a lot. Nothing I couldn't do. Three months I stayed there. If I hadn't been a young fool I'd have stayed for good. Powerful chief he was. I might have been a king, I might. King of the Cannibal Islands.'

He ended with his high-pitched cackle and relapsed into silence; but it was a strange silence, for he seemed to notice everything that was going on around him, and yet live his own life apart. The sudden burst of reminiscence, which had no connexion with anything that had been said, had a sort of automatic effect as though a machine controlled by an unseen clock at intervals uncannily shot forth a stream of patter. Dr Saunders was puzzled by Frith. What he said was on occasion not without interest; to the doctor, indeed, sometimes striking; and yet his manner and appearance predisposed you to listen to him warily. He seemed sincere, his attitude had even nobility, but there was something in him that the doctor found disconcerting. It was odd that these two men, old Swan and Frith, the man of action and the man who had devoted his life to speculation, should have ended up there, together, on this lonely island. It looked as though it all came to very much the same in the end. The end of all the adventurer's hazards, like the end of the philosopher's high thoughts, was a comfortable respectability.

Frith, having to his satisfaction divided three birds among seven people, sat down again and helped himself to boiled potatoes.

'I have always been attracted by the idea of the Brahmans, that a man should devote his youth to study,' he said, turning to Dr Saunders, 'his maturity to the duties and ceremonies of a householder, and his age to abstract thought and meditation of the Absolute.'

He glanced at old Swan, hunched up in his chair and laboriously gnawing a drumstick, and then at Louise.

'It will not be very long now before I am liberated from the obligations of my maturity. Then I shall take my staff and journey out into the world in search of the knowledge which passeth all understanding.'

The doctor's eyes had followed Frith's, and they rested for a while on Louise. She sat at the end of the table between the two young men. Fred, as a rule tongue-tied, was talking nineteen to the dozen. He had lost the slight sulkiness of expression that his features bore in repose and looked frank, carefree and boyish. His face was lit up by the play of his words and his desire to please lent a soft and engaging lustre to his fine eyes. Dr Saunders, smiling, saw how taking was his charm. He was not shy with women. He knew how to amuse them and you had only to see the girl's easy gaiety, and her animation, to know that she was happy and interested. The doctor caught snatches of his conversation; it was about the races at Randwick, bathing at Manly Beach, the cinema, the amusements of Sydney; the sort of things that young people talk to one another about and because all experience is fresh to them find so absorbing. Erik, with his great clumsy size and his massive square head, a kindly smile on his pleasantly ugly face, sat watching Fred quietly. You could see that he was glad the boy he had brought to the house was going down well. It gave him a little warm feeling of self-satisfaction that he was so charming.

When dinner was finished, Louise went up to old Swan and put her hand on his shoulder.

'Now, grandpa, you must go to bed.'

'Not before I've had me tot of rum, Louise.'

'Well, drink it up quick.'

She poured him out the considerable amount he wanted, while he watched the glass with cunning rheumy eyes, and added a little water.

'Put a tune on the gramophone, Erik,' she said.

The Dane did as he was bid.

'Can you dance, Fred?' he asked.

'Can't you?'

'No.'

Fred rose to his feet, and looking at Louise outlined a gesture of invitation. She smiled. He took her hand and put his arm round her waist. They began to dance. They made a lovely couple. Dr Saunders, standing with Erik by the gramophone, saw to his surprise that Fred was an exquisite dancer. He had an unimaginable grace. He made his partner, not more than competent, appear to dance as well as he did. He had the gift of being able to absorb her movements into his so that she was instinctively responsive to the notions as they formed themselves in his brain. He made the foxtrot they danced a thing of the most delicate beauty.

'You're a pretty good dancer, young fellow,' said Dr Saunders, when the record came to an end.

'It's the only thing I can do,' answered the boy, with a smile.

He was so well aware of his amiable gift that he took it as a matter of course and compliments upon it meant nothing to him. Louise looked down at the floor with a serious look on her face. Suddenly she seemed to rouse herself.

'I must go and put grandfather to bed.'

She went over to the old man, still hugging his empty glass, and leaning over him, tenderly cajoled him to come with her.

He took her arm and toddled, a foot shorter than she, out of the room beside her.

'What about a game of bridge?' said Frith. 'Do you gentlemen play?'

'I do,' said the skipper. 'I don't know about the doctor and Fred.'

'I'll make up a four,' said Dr Saunders.

'Christessen plays a very good game.'

'I don't play,' said Fred.

'That's all right,' said Frith. 'We can manage without you.'

Erik brought forward a bridge table, its green baize patched and worn, and Frith produced two packs of greasy cards. They brought up chairs and cut for partners. Fred stood beside the gramophone, alert, as though his body were on springs, and with little movements kept time to an inaudible tune. When Louise came back he did not move, but in his eyes was a smile of goodwill. It had a familiarity that was not offensive and it gave her the feeling that she had known him all her life.

'Shall I put on the gramophone?' he asked.

'No, they'll have a fit.'

'We must have another dance.'

'Dad and Erik take their bridge very seriously.'

She walked over to the table and he accompanied her. He stood behind Captain Nichols for a few minutes. The skipper gave him one or two uneasy glances and then, having made a bad play, turned round irascibly.

'I can't do a thing with someone lookin' over me 'and,' he said. 'Nothin' puts me off like that.'

'Sorry, old man.'

'Let's go outside,' said Louise.

The living-room of the bungalow opened on to a veranda, and they stepped out. Beyond the little garden you saw in the starlight the towering kanari-trees and below them, thick and dark, the massy verdure of the nutmegs. At the bottom of the steps, on one side, grew a large bush and it was alight with fire-flies. There was a multitude of them and they sparkled softly. It was like the radiance of a soul at peace. They stood side by side for a little while looking at the night. Then he took her

127

hand and led her down the steps. They walked along the pathway till they came to the plantation and she let her hand rest in his as though it were such a natural thing for him to hold it that she paid no attention.

'Don't you play bridge?' she asked.

'Yes, of course.'

'Why aren't you playing, then?'

'I didn't want to.'

It was very dark under the nutmeg-trees. The great white pigeons that roosted in their branches were asleep, and the only sound that broke the silence was when one of them for some reason rustled its wings. There was not a breath of wind and the air, vaguely aromatic, had a warm softness so that it surrounded them sensible to the nerves of touch like water to the swimmer. Fire-flies hovered across the path with a sort of swaying movement that made you think of drunken men staggering down an empty street. They walked a little without saying a word. Then he stopped and took her gently in his arms and kissed her on the mouth. She did not start. She did not stiffen, with surprise, or modesty; she made no instinctive movement of withdrawal; she accepted his embrace as though it were in the order of things. She was soft in his arms, but not weak, yielding, but yielding with a sort of tender willingness. They were accustomed to the darkness now, and when he looked into her eyes they had lost their blue and were dark and unfathomable. He had his hand round her waist and an arm round her neck. She rested her head against it comfortably.

'You are lovely,' he said.

'You're awfully good-looking,' she answered.

He kissed her again. He kissed her eyelids.

'Kiss *me*,' he whispered.

She smiled. She took his face in her two hands and pressed her lips to his. He placed his hands on her two small breasts. She sighed.

'We must go in.'

She took his hand and side by side they walked back slowly to the house.

'I love you,' he whispered.

She did not answer, but tightly pressed his hand. They came

into the light from the house, and when they went into the room for an instant were dazzled. Erik looked up as they entered and gave Louise a smile.

'Been down to the pool?'

'No, it was too dark.'

She sat down and, taking up an illustrated Dutch paper, began to look at the pictures. Then putting it down she let her gaze rest on Fred. She stared at him thoughtfully, without expression on her face, as though he were not a man but an inanimate object. Now and then Eric glanced across at her and when he caught her eye, she gave him a tiny little smile. Then she got up.

'I shall go to bed,' she said.

She bade them all good night. Fred sat down behind the doctor and watched them play. Presently, having finished a rubber, they stopped. The old Ford had come back for them and the four men piled in. When they reached the town it drew up to put the doctor and Erik down at the hotel and then drove on to the harbour with the others.

chapter twenty-two

'Are you sleepy?' asked Erik.

'No, it's early yet,' replied the doctor.

'Come over to my place and have a night-cap.'

'All right.'

The doctor had not smoked for a night or two and intended to do so that evening, but he did not mind waiting a little. To delay the pleasure was to increase it. He accompanied Erik along the deserted street. People went to bed early at Kanda and there was not a soul about. The doctor walked with a little quick trip and he took two steps to Erik's one. With his short legs and somewhat prominent belly he cut a comic figure beside the striding giant. It was not more than two hundred yards to the Dane's house, but he was a little out of breath when they arrived. The door was unlocked, there was not much fear of thieves on that island where people could neither escape nor dispose of stolen property, and Erik, opening the door, walked in ahead to light the lamp. The doctor threw himself in the most comfortable of the chairs and waited while Erik fetched glasses, ice, whisky, and soda. In the uncertain light of a paraffin lamp, with his short grey hair, snub nose, and the bright colour on his high cheek-bones, he reminded you of an elderly chimpanzee, and his little bright eyes had the monkey's scintillating sharpness. It would have been a foolish man who thought they would not see through pretence, but perhaps it would have been a wise one who discerned that, however clumsily an awkward address concealed it, they would recognize sincerity. He was not likely to take at its face value what a man said, however plausible, though no more than the shadow of a mischievous smile betrayed his thoughts, but honesty, however naïve, and true feeling, however incongruous, he could repay with a sympathy somewhat ironical and amused, but patient and kindly.

Erik poured out a drink for his guest and a drink for himself.

'What about Mrs Frith?' asked the doctor. 'Is she dead?'

'Yes, she died last year. Heart disease. She was a fine woman. Her mother came from New Zealand, but to look at her you would have said she was pure Swedish. The real Scandinavian type, tall and big and fair, like one of the goddesses in the *Rheingold*. Old Swan used to say that when she was a girl she was better-looking than Louise.'

'A very pretty young woman,' said the doctor.

'She was like a mother to me. You can't imagine how kind she was. I used to spend all my spare time up there, and if I didn't go for a few days because I was afraid of abusing their hospitality she'd come down and fetch me herself. We Danes, you know, we think the Dutch are rather dull and heavy, and it was a godsend for me to have that house to go to. Old Swan used to like talking Swedish to me.' Erik gave a little laugh. 'He'd forgotten most of it, he talks half Swedish, half English, and Malay words thrown in and bits of Japanese; at first I had a job to understand. Funny how a man can forget his native language. I've always liked the English. It was fine for me to have long talks with Frith. You wouldn't expect to find a man with that education in a place like this.'

'I was wondering how he ever found his way here.'

'He'd read about it in some old travel book. He's told me he wanted to come ever since he was a kid. It's a funny thing, he'd got it into his head that it was the one place in the world he wanted to live in. And I'll tell you what's strange, he'd forgotten the name of it; he could never find again the book in which he'd read about it; he just knew there was an island all by itself in a little group somewhere between Celebes and New Guinea, where the sea was scented with spices and there were great marble palaces.'

'It sounds more like the sort of thing you read about in *The Arabian Nights* than in a book of travel.'

'That's what a good many people expect to find in the East.'

'Sometimes they do,' murmured the doctor.

He thought of the noble bridge that spanned the river at Fuchou. There was a press of traffic on the Min, great junks with eyes painted on their prows so that they could see the way to go, wupans with their rattan hoods, frail sampans and chugging motor-boats. On the barges dwelt the turbulent river-folk. In midstream on a raft two men, wearing nothing but a loin cloth, fished with cormorants. It was a sight you could watch for an hour at a time. The fisherman sent his bird into the water; it dived, it caught; as it rose to the surface he drew it in by a string tied to its leg; then, while it struggled angrily flapping its wings, he seized it by the throat and made it disgorge the fish it had seized. After all it was just such a fisherman, fishing in his different Arab way, to whom a casual chance brought such amazing adventures.

The Dane continued:

'He came out East when he was twenty-four. It took him twelve years to get here. He asked everyone he met if they'd heard of the island, but you know, in the F.M.S. and in Borneo they don't know much about these parts. He was a bit of a rolling-stone when he was a young chap and he wandered from place to place. You heard what old Swan said to him and I guess it was true. He never kept a job very long. He got here at last. The skipper of a Dutch ship told him about it. It didn't sound very much like the place he was looking for, but it was the only island in the Archipelago that answered to the description at all, and he thought he'd come and look at it. When he landed he hadn't much beside his books and the clothes he stood up in. At first he couldn't believe it was the right place; you've seen the marble palaces, you're sitting in one of them now.' Erik looked round the room and laughed. 'You see, he'd pictured them to himself all those years like the palaces on the Grand Canal. Anyhow if it wasn't the place he was looking for it was the only place he could find. He shifted his standpoint, if you understand what I mean, and forced the reality to tally with his fancy. He came to the conclusion that it was all right. Because they've got marble floors and stucco columns he really thinks they are marble palaces.'

'You make him out a wiser man than I thought he was.'

'He got a job here, there was more trade then than there is now; after that, he fell in love with old Swan's daughter and married her.'

'Were they happy together?'

'Yes. Swan didn't like him much. He was pretty active in those days and he was always concocting some scheme or other. He could never get Frith to get a move on. But she worshipped him. She thought he was wonderful. When Swan got too old, she ran the estate and looked after things and made both ends meet. You know, some women are like that. It gave her a sort of satisfaction to think of Frith sitting in his den with his books, reading and writing and making notes. She thought him a genius. She thought everything she did for him was only his due. She was a fine woman.'

The doctor reflected on what Erik told him. What a picture of a strange life this offered to the fancy! The shabby bungalow in the nutmeg plantation, with the immensely tall kanari-trees; that old pirate of a Swede, ruthless and crotchety, brave adventurer in the soulless deserts of hard fact; the dreamy, unpractical schoolmaster, lured by the mirage of the East, who like – like a coster's donkey let loose on a common, wandered aimlessly in the pleasant lands of the spirit, browsing at random; and then, the great blonde woman, like a goddess of the Vikings, with her efficiency, her love, her honesty of mind, and

132

surely her charitable sense of humour, who held things together, managed, guided, and protected those two incompatible men.

'When she knew she was dying she made Louise promise to look after them. The plantation belongs to Swan. Even now it brings in enough to keep them all. She was afraid that after she was gone the old man would turn Frith out.' Erik hesitated a little. 'And she made me promise to look after Louise. It hasn't been very easy for her, poor child. Swan is like a cunning old monkey. He's up to any mischief. His brain in a way is as active as ever it was, and he'll lie and plot and intrigue just to play some silly little trick on you. He dotes on Louise. She's the only person who can do anything with him. Once, just for fun, he tore some of Frith's manuscripts into tiny fragments. When they found him he was surrounded by a snow-fall of little bits of paper.'

'No great loss to the world, I daresay,' smiled the doctor, 'but exasperating to a struggling author.'

'You don't think much of Frith?'

'I haven't made my mind up about him.'

'He's taught me so much. I shall always be grateful to him. I was only a kid when I first came here. I'd been to the university at Copenhagen, and at home we'd always cared for culture; my father was a friend of George Brandes, and Holger Drachmann, the poet, used often to come to our house; it was Brandes who first made me read Shakespeare, but I was very ignorant and narrow. It was Frith who made me understand the magic of the East. You know, people come out here and they see nothing. Is that all? they say. And they go home again. That fort I took you to see yesterday, just a few old grey walls overgrown with weeds. I shall never forget the first time *he* took me there. His words built up the ruined walls and put ordnance on the battlements. When he told me how the governor had paced them week after week in sickening anxiety, for the natives, in the strange way they have in the East of knowing things before they can possibly be known, were whispering of a terrible disaster to the Portuguese, and he waited desperately for the ship that would bring news; and at last it came, and he read the letter which told him that King Sebastian, with his splendid train of nobles and courtiers, had been annihilated at the battle of Alcacer, and the tears ran down his old cheeks, not only because his king had met a cruel death, but because he foresaw that the defeat must cost his country her freedom; and that rich world they had discovered and conquered, those innumerable islands a handful of brave men had seized for the power of Portugal, must pass under the dominion of foreigners – then, believe me or not, I felt a lump in my throat, and for a little while I couldn't see because my eyes were blurred with tears. And not only this. He talked to me of Goa the Golden, rich with the plunder of Asia, the great capital of the East, and of the Malabar Coast and Macao, and Ormuz and Bassora. He made that old life so plain and vivid that I've never since been able to see the East but with the past still present today. And I've thought what a privilege it was that I, a poor Danish country boy, should see all these wonders with my own eyes. And I think it's grand to be a man when I think of those little swarthy chaps from a country no bigger than my own Denmark who, by their dauntless courage, their gallantry, their ardent imagination, held half the world in fee. It's all gone now and they say that Goa the Golden is no more than a poverty-stricken village; but if it's true that the only reality is spirit, then somehow that dream of empire, that dauntless courage, that gallantry, live on.'

'It was strong wine for a young head that our Mr Frith gave you to drink,' murmured the doctor.

'It intoxicated me,' smiled Erik, 'but that intoxication causes no headache in the morning.'

The doctor did not reply. He was inclined to think that its effects, more lasting, might be a great deal more pernicious. Erik took a sip of whisky.

'I was brought up a Lutheran, but when I went to the university I became an atheist. It was the fashion, and I was very young. I just shrugged my shoulders when Frith began to talk to me of Brahma. Oh, we've spent hours sitting on the veranda, up at the plantation, Frith, his wife Catherine, and me. He'd talk. She never said much, but she listened, looking at him with adoring eyes, and he and I would argue. It was all vague and difficult to understand, but you know, he was very persuasive, and what he believed had a sort of grandeur and beauty; it seemed to fit in with the tropical, moonlit nights and the distant stars and the murmur of the sea. I've often wondered if there isn't something in it. And if you know what I mean, it fits in too with Wagner and Shakespeare's plays and those lyrics of Camoens. Sometimes I've grown impatient and said to myself, the man's an empty windbag. You see, it bothered me that he should drink more than was good for him, and be so fond of his food, and when there was a job of work to do always have an excuse for not doing it. But Catherine believed in him. She was no fool. If he'd been a fake she couldn't have lived with him for twenty years and not found it out. It was funny that he should be so gross and yet be capable of such lofty thoughts. I've heard him say things that I shall never forget. Sometimes he could soar into mystical regions of the spirit – d'you know what I mean? – when you couldn't follow him, but just watched dizzily from the ground and yet were filled with rapture. And you know, he could do surprising things. That day that old Swan tore up his manuscript, a year's work, two whole cantos of *The Lusiads*, when they saw what had happened Catherine burst out crying, but he just sighed and went out for a walk. When he came in he brought the old man, delighted with his mischief, but a little scared all the same, a bottle of rum. It's true he'd bought it with Swan's money, but that doesn't matter. "Never mind, old man," he said, "you've only torn up a few dozen sheets of paper; they were merely an illusion and it would be foolish to give them a second thought; the reality remains, for the reality is indestructible." And next day he set to work to do it all over again.'

'He said he was going to give me some passages to read,' said Dr Saunders. 'I suppose he forgot.'

'He'll remember,' said Erik, with a smile in which there was a good-natured grimness.

Dr Saunders liked him. The Dane was genuine, at all events; an idealist, of course, but his idealism was tempered with humour. He gave you the impression that his strength of character was greater even than the strength of his mighty frame.

Perhaps he was not very clever, but he was immensely reliable, and the charm of his simple, honest nature pleasantly complemented the charm of his ungainly person. It occurred to the doctor that a woman might very well fall deeply in love with him and his next remark was not entirely void of guile.'

'And that girl we saw, is that the only child they had?'

'Catherine was a widow when Frith married her. She had a son by her first husband, and a son by Frith, too, but they both died when Louise was a child.'

'And has she looked after everything since her mother's death?'

'Yes.'

'She's very young.'

'Eighteen. She was only a kid when I first came to the island. They sent her to the missionary school here, and then her mother thought she ought to go to Auckland. But when Catherine fell ill they sent for her. It's funny what a year'll do for girls; when she went away she was a child who used to sit on my knee, and when she came back she was a young woman.' He gave the doctor his small, diffident smile. 'I'll tell you in confidence that we're engaged.'

'Oh?'

'Not officially, so I'd sooner you didn't mention it. Old Swan's willing enough, but her father says she's too young. I suppose she is, but that's not his real reason for objecting. I'm afraid he doesn't think me good enough. He's got an idea that one of these days some rich English lord will come along in his yacht and fall madly in love with her. The nearest approach so far is young Fred in a pearling lugger.'

He chuckled.

'I don't mind waiting. I know she's young. That's why I didn't ask her to marry me before. You see, it took me some time to get it into my head that she wasn't a little girl any more. When you love anyone like I love Louise a few months, a year or two – well, they don't matter. We've got all life before us. It won't be quite the same when we're married. I know it's going to be perfect happiness, but we shall have it, we shan't be looking forward to it any more. We've got something now that we shall lose. D'you think that's stupid?'

'No.'

'Of course, you've only just seen her, you don't know her. She's beautiful, isn't she?'

'Very.'

'Well, her beauty's the least of her qualities. She's got a head on her shoulders, she's got the same practical spirit that her mother had. It makes me laugh sometimes to see this lovely child – after all, she is hardly more than a kid – manage the labour on the estate with so much common-sense. The Malays know it's useless to try any tricks with her. Of course, having lived practically all her life here, she has all sorts of knowledge in her bones. It's amazing how shrewd she is. And the tact she shows with those two men, her grandfather and Frith. She knows them inside out; she knows all their faults, but she doesn't mind them; she's awfully fond of them, of course, and she takes them as they are, as though they were just like everybody else. I've never seen her even impatient with either of them. And you know, one wants one's patience when old Swan rambles on with some story you've heard fifty times already.'

'I guessed that it was she who made things run smooth.'

'I suppose one would. But what one wouldn't guess is that her beauty, and her cleverness, and the goodness of her heart mask a spirit of the most subtle and exquisite delicacy. Mask isn't the right word. Mask suggests disguise and disguise suggests deceit. Louise doesn't know what disguise and deceit mean. She is beautiful, and she is kind, and she is clever; all that's she; but there's someone else there too, a sort of illusive spirit that somehow I think no one but her mother who is dead and I have ever suspected. I don't know how to explain it. It's like a wraith within the body; it's like a soul within the spirit, if you can imagine it; it's like the essential flame of the individual of which all the qualities that the world sees are only emanations.'

The doctor raised his eyebrows. It seemed to him that Erik Christessen was getting a bit out of his depth. Still, he listened to him without displeasure. He was very much in love and Dr Saunders had a half cynical tenderness for young things in that condition.

'Have you ever read Hans Andersen's *Little Mermaid*?' asked Erik.

'A hundred years ago.'

'That lovely flame-like spirit not my eyes but my soul has felt in Louise seems to me just like that little mermaid. It's not quite at home in the haunts of men. It has always a vague nostalgia for the sea. It's not quite human; she's so sweet, she's so gentle, she's so tender, and yet there is a sort of aloofness in her that keeps you at a distance. It seems to me very rare and beautiful. I'm not jealous of it. I'm not afraid of it. It's a priceless possession and I love her so much that I almost regret that she cannot always keep it. I feel that she will lose it when she becomes a wife and a mother, and whatever beauty of soul she has then it will be different. It's something apart and independent. It's the self which is part of the universal self; perhaps we've all got it; but what is so wonderful in her is that it's almost sensible, and you feel that if only your eyes were a little more piercing you could see it plain. I'm so ashamed that I shall not go to her as pure as she will come to me.'

'Don't be so silly,' said the doctor.

'Why is it silly? When you love someone like Louise it's horrible to think that you've lain in strange arms and that you've kissed bought and painted mouths. I feel unworthy enough of her as it is. I might at least have brought her a clean and decent body.'

'Oh, my dear boy.'

Dr Saunders thought the young man was talking nonsense, but he felt no inclination to argue with him. It was getting late and his own concerns called him. He finished his drink.

'I have never had any sympathy with the ascetic attitude. The wise man combines the pleasures of the senses and the pleasures of the spirit in such a way as to increase the satisfaction he gets from both. The most valuable thing I have learnt from life is to regret nothing. Life is short, nature is hostile, and man is ridiculous; but oddly enough most misfortunes have their compensations and with a certain humour and a good deal of horse-sense one can make a fairly good job of what is after all a matter of very small consequence.'

With that he got up and left.

chapter twenty-three

Next morning, comfortably seated on the veranda of the hotel, with his legs up, Dr Saunders was reading a book. He had just learnt from the steamship office that news had been received of the arrival of a ship on the following day but one. It stopped at Bali, which would give him the opportunity of seeing that attractive island, and from there it would be easy to get to Surabaya. He was enjoying his holiday. He had forgotten that it was so pleasant to have nothing in the world to do.

'A man of leisure,' he murmured to himself. 'By God, I might almost pass for a gentleman.'

Presently Fred Blake strolled along the road, nodded and joined him.

'You haven't received a cable, have you?' he asked.

'No, that's the last thing I expect.'

'I was in the post-office a minute ago. The man asked me if my name was Saunders.'

'That's funny. No one has the least notion I'm here; nor do I know anyone in the world who wants to communicate with me urgently enough to waste money on a cablegram.'

But a surprise was in store for him. Barely an hour had passed when a youth rode up to the hotel on a bicycle and the manager shortly afterwards came out with him on to the veranda and asked Dr Saunders to sign for a cable that had just arrived for him.

'What an extraordinary thing!' he cried. 'Old Kim Ching is the only man who can even suspect that I'm here.'

But when he opened the cablegram he was more astonished still.

'That's a damned idiotic thing,' he said. 'It's in code. Who in God's name can have done such a silly thing as that? How can I be expected to make head or tail of it?'

'May I have a look?' asked Fred. 'If it's one of the well-known codes I might be able to tell you. One's sure to be able to get all the usual code-books here.'

The doctor handed him the slip of paper. It was a numeral code. The words, or phrases, were represented by groups of numbers and the termination of each group was clearly indicated by a zero.

'The commercial codes use made-up words,' said Fred.

'I know as much as that.'

'I've made rather a study of codes. Been a hobby of mine. D'you mind if I have a shot at deciphering it?'

'Not a bit.'

'They say it's only a question of time before you can find the secret of any code. There's one fellow in the British service, they say, who can solve the most complicated code anyone can invent in twenty-four hours.'

'Go right ahead.'

'I'll go inside. I must have pens and paper.'

Dr Saunders suddenly remembered. He reached out.

'Let me just see that cable again.'

Fred handed it to him and he looked for the place of despatch. Melbourne. He did not give it back.

'Is it for you by any chance?'

Fred hesitated for an instant. Then he smiled. When he wanted to cajole anyone he could be very ingratiating.

'Well, it is, as a matter of fact.'

'Why did you have it addressed to me?'

'Well, I thought that me living on the *Fenton* and all that, perhaps they wouldn't deliver it, or they might want proof of identity or something. I thought it would save a lot of trouble if I had it sent to you.'

'You've got your nerve with you.'

'I knew you were a sport.'

'And that little realistic detail about your being asked at the post-office if your name was Saunders?'

'Pure invention, old man,' Fred answered airily.

Dr Saunders chuckled.

'What would you have done if I hadn't been able to make head or tail of it and torn it up?'

'I knew it couldn't arrive till today. They only got the address yesterday.'

'Who's "they"?'

'The people who sent the cable,' replied Fred, with a smile.

'Then it's not entirely for the pleasure of my society that you have been giving me your company this morning?'

'Not entirely.'

The doctor gave him back the flimsy.

'You've got the cheek of the devil. Take it. I suppose you've got the key in your pocket.'

'In my head.'

He went into the hotel. Dr Saunders began to read again. But he read with divided attention. He could not entirely dismiss from his head the incident that had just occurred. It amused him not a little and he wondered again what was the mystery in which the boy was involved. He was discreet. He had never so much as dropped a hint upon which an agile intelligence might work. There was nothing to go upon. The doctor shrugged his shoulders. After all, the matter was no business of his. He sought to dissipate his baffled curiosity by pretending to himself that he didn't care a damn and made a resolute effort to attend to what he was reading. But after an interval Fred came back on to the veranda.

'Have a drink, doctor?' he said.

His eyes were shining, his face was flushed, but at the same time he bore an air of some bewilderment. He was excited. He wanted to burst out laughing, but since he could give no reason for hilarity plainly was trying to control himself.

'Had good news?' asked the doctor.

Suddenly Fred could restrain himself no longer. He burst into a peal of laughter.

'As good as all that?'

'I don't know if it's good or bad. It's awfully funny. I wish I could tell you. It's strange. It makes me feel rather queer. I don't quite know what to make of it. I must have a bit of time to get used to it. I don't quite know if I'm standing on my head or my heels.'

Dr Saunders looked at him reflectively. The boy seemed to have gained vitality. There had always been something hangdog in his expression that took away from his unusual good looks. Now he looked candid and open. You would have thought a load had been lifted from his shoulders. The drinks came.

'I want you to drink to the memory of a deceased friend of mine,' he said, seizing his glass.

'By name?'

'Smith.'

He emptied the glass in a draught.

'I must ask Erik if we can go somewhere this afternoon. I feel like walking my legs off. A bit of exercise would do me good.'

'When are you sailing?'

'Oh, I don't know. I like it here. I wouldn't mind staying for a bit. I wish you could have seen the view from the top of that volcano Erik and I went up yesterday. Pretty, I can tell you. The world's not a bad old place, is it?'

A buggy drawn by a small shabby horse came trundling shakily down the road, raising a cloud of dust, and stopped at the hotel. Louise was driving and her father sat by her side. He got out and walked up the steps. He had in his hand a flat brown-paper parcel.

'I forgot to give you the manuscripts last night that I promised to let you see, so I've brought them down.'

'That's very kind of you.'

Frith untied the string and disclosed a small pile of typewritten sheets.

'Of course, I want an absolutely candid opinion.' He gave the doctor a doubtful look. 'If you have nothing very much to do at the moment I might read you a few pages myself. I always think poetry should be read aloud and it's only the author who can do justice to it.'

The doctor sighed. He was weak. He could think of no excuse that would turn Frith from his purpose.

'D'you think your daughter ought to wait in the sun?' he hazarded.

'Oh, she has things to do. She can go upon her errands and come back for me.'

'Would you like me to go with her, sir?' said Fred Blake. 'I've got nothing to do.'

'I think she'd be very glad.'

He went down and spoke to Louise. The doctor saw her look at him gravely, then smile a little and say something. She was wearing this morning a dress of white cotton and a large straw hat of native make. Under it her face had a golden coolness. Fred swung himself up beside her and she drove off.

'I'd like to read you the third canto,' said Frith. 'It has a lyrical quality that suits me. I think it's about the best thing I've done. Do you know Portuguese?'

'No, I don't.'

'That's a pity. It's almost a word-for-word translation. It would have amused you to see how closely I've managed to reproduce the rhythm and music, the feeling, in fact, everything that makes it a great poem. Of course you won't hesitate to criticize, I'm only too willing to listen to anything you have to say, but I have no doubt in my own mind that this is the definitive translation. I can't honestly believe that it will ever be superseded.'

He began to read. His voice had a pleasing quality. The poem was in *ottava rima*, and Frith laid an emphasis on the metre that was not ineffective. Dr Saunders listened attentively. The version seemed fluent and easy, but he could not be sure how much this was due to the measured and stately elocution. Frith's delivery was dramatic, but he put the drama into the sound, rather than the sense, so that the meaning of what he read tended to escape you. He stressed the rhyme so that it reminded Dr Saunders of a slow train jogging over an ill-laid rail and his body felt a slight jolt as the expected sound at regular intervals fell upon his ear. He found his attention wandering. The rich monotonous voice hammered on and he began to feel a little drowsy. He stared hard at the reader, but his eyes closed involuntarily; he opened them with a slight effort and frowned with the violence of his concentration. He gave a start, for his head fell suddenly towards his chest, and he realized that for a moment he had dozed. Frith read of gallant deeds and the great men that had made Portugal an empire. His voice rose when he read of high heroical things and trembled and fell when he read of death and untoward fate. Suddenly Dr Saunders was conscious of silence. He opened his eyes. Frith was no longer there. Fred Blake was sitting in front of him, a roguish smile on his handsome face.

'Had a nice nap?'

'I haven't been asleep.'

'You've been snoring your head off.'

'Where's Frith?'

'He's gone. We came back in the buggy and they've gone home to dinner. He said I wasn't to disturb you.'

'I know what's wrong with him now,' said the doctor. 'He had a dream and it's come true. What gives an ideal beauty is that it's unattainable. The gods laugh when men get what they want.'

'I don't know what you're talking about,' said Fred, 'You're half asleep still.'

'Let's have a glass of beer. That at all events is real.'

chapter twenty-four

Round about ten o'clock that night the doctor and Captain Nichols were playing piquet in the sitting-room of the hotel. They had been driven indoors by the flying ants which the lamp on the veranda attracted. Erik Christessen came in.

'Where have you been all day?' asked the doctor.

'I had to visit a plantation we've got over at the other end of the island. I thought I'd be back earlier, but the manager's just had a son and he was giving a feast. I had to stay for it.'

'Fred was looking for you. He wanted to go for a walk.'

'I wish I'd known. I'd have taken him with me.' He threw himself into a chair and called for beer. 'I've had the best part of ten miles to walk and then we had to row back half-way round the island.'

'Like to play *chouette*?' asked the skipper, giving him his sharp, foxy look.

'No, I'm tired. Where's Fred?'

'Courtin', I expect.'

'Not much chance of that here,' said Erik, good naturedly.

'Don't you be too sure. Good-lookin' young fellow, you know. The girls fall for 'im. At Merauke I 'ad a rare job keepin' 'em away from 'im. Between you and me and the gate-post I should 'ave said 'e clicked good and proper last night.'

'Who with?'

'That girl up there.'

'Louise?'

Erik smiled. The idea was quite preposterous to him.

'Well, I don't know. She come and 'ad a look at the boat with 'im this mornin'. And I know 'e dolled 'imself up somethin' fierce tonight. Shaved 'imself. Brushed 'is 'air. Put on a clean suit. I ask 'im what it was all about and 'e tell me to mind me own bloody business.'

'Frith was down here this morning,' said Dr Saunders. 'It may be he asked Fred to go and have supper there again tonight.'

'He 'ad supper on the *Fenton*,' said Nichols.

He dealt the cards. The players went on with their game. Erik smoking a big Dutch cigar watched them and sipped his beer. Now and again the skipper gave him that sidelong glance of his in which there was something so unpleasant that it sent a shiver down your spine. His little close-set eyes glittered with malicious amusement. After a while Erik looked at his watch.

'I'll go down to the *Fenton*. Maybe Fred'd like to come fishing with me tomorrow morning.'

'You won't find 'im,' said the skipper.

'Why not? He wouldn't be at Swan's as late as this.'

'Don't you be too sure.'

'They go to bed at ten and it's past eleven now.'

'Maybe 'e's gone to bed, too.'

'Rot.'

'Well, if you ask me I think that girl looked as though she knew a thing or two. It wouldn't surprise me if they was comfortably tucked up together at this very minute. And very nice too. I wish I was in 'is place.'

Erik was standing up. With his great height he towered over the two men seated at the table. His face grew pale, and he clenched his fists. For a moment it looked as though he would hit the skipper. He gave an inarticulate cry of rage. The skipper looked up at him and grinned. Dr Saunders could not but see that he was not in the least frightened. A blow from that great fist would certainly have knocked him out. He was a mean skunk, but he had pluck. The doctor saw with what a tremendous effort Erik controlled himself.

'It's not a bad plan to judge others by oneself,' he said, his voice trembling, 'but not if one's a mangy cur.'

''Ave I said anythin' to offend you?' asked the skipper. 'I didn't know the lady was a friend of yours.'

Erik stared at him for a moment. His face showed the disgust he felt for the man, and his withering contempt. He turned on his heel and walked heavily out of the hotel.

'Wanting to commit suicide, skipper?' asked the doctor dryly.

'Known a lot of them big fellows. Sentimental, that's what they are. Never 'it a chap smaller than yourself. Their minds don't work quick, you know. A bit stupid, generally.'

The doctor chuckled. It diverted him to think of that rascal making shrewd use of the decent feelings of others to go his crooked, nasty way.

'You took a risk. If he hadn't had himself well in hand he might have hit you before he knew what he was doing.'

'What was 'e upset about? Sweet on the girl 'imself?'

Dr Saunders thought it unnecessary to tell him that Erik was engaged to Louise Frith.

'There are men who object to hearing their girl friends spoken of in that way,' he answered.

'Come off it, doc. Don't pull that stuff on me. It don't go with you at all. If a girl's easy a chap likes to know. If someone else 'as been there, well, there's a chance for 'im, ain't there? Stands to reason.'

'You know, you're one of the dirtiest tykes I've ever met, skipper,' said the doctor in his detached manner.

'That's a compliment in its way, ain't it? Funny part is, you don't like me any the less if I am. Seems to me to prove you ain't exactly a saint yourself. And I don't mind tellin' you I've 'eard as much in various quarters.'

Dr Saunders' eyes twinkled.

'Digestion troubling you tonight, skipper?'

'I ain't exactly comfortable, and it would be a lie if I said I was. I don't say I'm in pain, mind you, but I just ain't comfortable.'

'It's a long business. You can't expect to be able to digest a pound of lead after a week's treatment.'

'I don't want to digest a pound of lead, doc, and I don't pretend for a minute I do. Mind you, I ain't complaining. I don't say you ain't done me good. You 'ave. But I got a long way to go yet.'

'Well, I've told you, have your teeth out. They're no use to you, and God knows, they don't add to your beauty.'

'I will. I give you me word of honour. The minute I'm through with the cruise. I don't see why we can't pop over to Singapore. Sure to be a good American dentist there. The kid wants to go to Batavia now.'

'Does he?'

'Yes, 'e got a cable this mornin'. I don't know what it was all about, but 'e's all for stoppin' on 'ere a bit and then goin' to Batavia.'

'How d'you know he got a cable?'

'I found it in the pocket of 'is pants. He put on a clean suit to go ashore in, and 'e left his pants lyin' about. Untidy little blighter. That shows you 'e's not a sailor. A sailor-man's always tidy. Has to be. It was all Greek to me. The cable, I mean. In cypher.'

'I suppose you didn't notice that it was addressed to me?'

'You? No, I can't say I did.'

'Well, have another look at it. I just gave it to Fred to decode.'

The doctor found it highly diverting thus to throw Captain Nichols off the scent.

'Then what's the reason of all this changin' around? He was always for keepin' away from big places. Naturally, I thought it was on account of the cops. Anyhow, I mean to get to Singapore or sink the ruddy boat in the attempt.' Captain Nichols leaned over impressively and looked with deep emotion into the doctor's eyes. 'I wonder if you realize what it means to a chap not to 'ave 'ad a beefsteak and kidney puddin' for ten years. Talk of girls. You can 'ave all the girls in the world you like. There's not one I wouldn't give if I could only eat a suet puddin' with plenty of treacle and a good wallop of cream all over it. That's my idea of 'eaven and you can put your golden 'arps where the monkey put the nuts.'

chapter twenty-five

Erik, with his deliberate stride that seemed to measure the earth as a man might measure a cricket pitch, walked down to the beach. He was unmoved. He dismissed the skipper's shameless innuendo from his mind. It had left a nasty taste in his mouth and as though he had drunk a nauseous draught, he spat. But he was not devoid of humour and he gave a little low chuckle as he thought of the innuendo's absurdity. Fred was just a boy. He could not imagine that any woman would look at him twice; and he knew Louise much too well to suppose even for an instant that she could give him even a thought.

The beach was deserted. Everyone slept. He walked along the pier and hailed the *Fenton*. She was anchored a hundred yards out. Her light shone like a little steady eye on the smooth surface of the water. He shouted again. There was no answer. But a muffled, sleepy voice rose from below him. It was the blackfellow in the dinghy waiting for Captain Nichols. Erik went down the steps and found it tied to the bottom rung of the rail. The man was still half asleep. He yawned noisily as he stirred himself.

'Is that the *Fenton*'s dinghy?'

'Ye'. What you want?'

The blackfellow thought it might be the skipper or Fred Blake, but seeing his mistake was irritable and suspicious.

'Just row me on board. I want to see Fred Blake.'

'He ain't on board.'

'Sure?'

'If he ain't swum.'

'Oh, all right. Good night.'

The man gave a discontented grunt and settled down again to sleep. Erik walked back along the silent road. He thought that Fred had gone to the bungalow and Frith had kept him talking. He smiled as he wondered what the boy would make of the Englishman's mystical discourse. Something. He had taken to Fred. Beneath his pretence of worldly wisdom, and behind all that idle chatter about racing and cricketing, dancing and prize-fighting, you could not but be conscious of a pleasant and simple nature. Erik was not altogether unaware of the lad's feelings towards himself. Hero-worship. Oh, well, there was no great harm in that. It would pass. He was a decent kid. One might make something of him if one had the chance. It was nice to talk to him and feel that, even if it was all strange to him, he was trying to understand. It might be that if you cast a seed on that grateful soil a fair plant would spring up. Erik tramped on, hoping to meet Fred; they would walk back together, they might go on to his house, and they could rout themselves out some cheese and biscuits and have a bottle of beer. He did not feel at all sleepy. He had not many people to talk to on the island; with Frith and old Swan he had mostly to listen. It was good to talk deep into the night.

'Had tired the sun with talking,' he quoted to himself, 'and sent him down the sky.'

Erik was reticent about his private affairs, but he made up his mind to tell Fred of his engagement to Louise. He would like him to know. He had a great desire to talk about her that night. Sometimes love so possessed him that he felt if he did not tell somebody about it his heart would break. The doctor was old and could not understand; he could say things to Fred that it would have embarrassed him to say to a grown man.

It was three miles to the plantation, but his thoughts so absorbed him that he did not notice the distance. He was quite surprised when he arrived. It was funny that he had not met Fred. Then it occurred to him that Fred must have gone in to the hotel during the time he had gone down to the beach. How stupid of him not to think of that! Oh, well, there was nothing to be done about it. Now that he was there he might just as well go in and sit down for a bit. Of course, they'd all be asleep, but he wouldn't disturb anyone. He often did that; went up to the bungalow after they'd gone to bed and sat there thinking. There was a chair in the garden, below the veranda, in which old Swan sometimes rested in the cool of the evening. It was in front of Louise's room and it reposed him strangely to sit there quite quietly and look at her window and think of her sleeping so peacefully under her mosquito curtains. Her lovely ash-blonde hair was spread on the pillow and she lay on her side, her young breast rising and falling softly in deep slumber. The emotion that filled his heart when he thus pictured her was angel-pure. Sometimes he was a little sad when he thought that this virginal grace must perish and that slim and lovely body at last lie still in death. It was dreadful that a being so beautiful should die. He sat there sometimes till a faint chill in the balmy air, the rustle of the pigeons in the trees, warned him that day was at hand. They were hours of peace and of enchanting serenity. Once he had seen the shutter softly open, and Louise stepped out. Perhaps the heat oppressed her or a dream had awakened her and she wanted a breath of air. On her bare feet she walked across the veranda and with her hands on the rail stood looking at the starry night. She wore a sarong round her loins, but the upper part of her body was naked. She raised her hands and shook out her pale hair over her shoulders. Her body was silhouetted in wan silver against the darkness of the house. She did not look a woman of flesh and blood. She was like a spirit-maiden and Erik, his mind full of the old Danish stories, almost expected her to change into a lovely white bird and fly away to the fabled lands of the sunrise. He sat very still. He was hidden by the darkness. It was so silent that when she gave a little sigh he heard it as though he held her in his arms and her heart were pressed to his. She turned round and went back into her room. She drew the shutter to.

Erik walked up the earth road that led to the house and sat down in the chair that faced Louise's room. The house was dark. It was wrapped in a silence so profound that you might have thought its inmates were not asleep but dead. But there was no fear in the silence. It had an exquisite peace. It reassured you. It was comfortable, like the feel of a girl's smooth skin. Erik gave a little sigh of content. A sadness, but a sadness in which there was anguish no longer, befell him because dear Catherine Frith was there no more. He hoped that he would never forget the kindness she had shown him when, a shy and callow boy, he had first come to the island. He had worshipped her. She was then a woman of forty-five, but neither hard work nor child-bearing had had any effect on her powerful physique. She was tall and full-breasted, with magnificent golden hair, and she held herself proudly. You would have thought she would live to be a hundred. She took the place for him of the mother, a woman of character and of courage too, that he had left in a farmhouse in Denmark, and she loved in him the sons that had been born to her years before and of whom death had robbed her. But he felt that the relation between them was more intimate than it ever could have been if they had been mother and son. They could never have talked to one another so openly. Perhaps it could never have been such a tranquil satisfaction just to be in one another's company. He loved her and admired her and it made him very happy to be so sure that she loved him. Even then he had an inkling that the love he might one day feel for a girl would never have exactly the restful and comforting quality that he found in his very pure affection for Catherine Frith. She was a woman who had never read much, but she had a vast fund of knowledge, lying there like an unworked mine, gathered, you would have said, through innumerable generations out of the timeless experience of the race, so that she could cope with your book-learning and meet you on level terms. She was one of those persons who made you feel as though you were saying wonderful things, and when you talked to her thoughts came to you that you had never dreamt you were capable of. She was of a practical turn and she had a canny sense of humour; she was quick to ridicule absurdity, but the kindness of her heart was such that if she laughed at you, it was so tenderly that you loved her for it. It seemed to Erik that her most wonderful trait was a sincerity so perfect that it glowed all about her with a light that shone into the heart of all that had communication with her.

It filled Erik with a warm and grateful feeling to think that her life for so long had been as happy as she deserved it to be. Her marriage with George Frith had been an idyll. She had been a widow for some time when he first came to that distant and beautiful island. Her first husband was a New Zealander, skipper of a schooner engaged in the island trade, and he was drowned at sea in the great hurricane that ruined her father. Swan, owing to the wound in his chest unable to do any hard work, was broken by the accident that swept away almost all his life's savings, and together they came to that plantation which with his shrewd Scandinavian sense he had kept for years as a refuge should all else fail. She had had a son by the New Zealander, but he had died of diphtheria when still a baby. She had never known anyone like George Frith. She had never heard anyone talk as he did. He was thirty-six, with an untidy mop of dark hair and a haggard, romantic look. She loved him. It was as though her practical sense, her nobly terrestrial instincts, sought their compensation in this mysterious waif who spoke so greatly of such high things. She loved him not as she had loved her rough downright sailor husband, but with a half-amused tenderness that wanted to protect and guard. She felt that he was infinitely above her. She stood in awe of his subtle and aspiring intelligence. She never ceased to believe in his goodness and his genius. Erik thought that, notwithstanding Frith's tiresomeness, he would always feel kindly towards him because she had so devotedly loved him and he for so many years had given her happiness.

It was Catherine who had first said that she would like him to marry Louise. She was then a child.

'She'll never be as lovely as you, my dear,' he smiled.

'Oh, much more. You can't tell yet. I can. She'll be like me, but quite different, and she'll be better-looking than I ever was.'

'I would only marry her if she was exactly like you. I don't want her different.'

'Wait till she's grown-up and then you'll be very pleased she isn't a fat old woman.'

It amused him now to think of that conversation. The darkness of the house was paling and for a moment he thought with a start that it must be the dawn that was breaking, but then, looking round, he saw that a lopsided moon was floating up over the tops of the trees, like an empty barrel drifting with the tide, and its light, dim still, shone on the sleeping bungalow.

He gave the moon a friendly little wave of the hand.

When that strong, muscular, and vigorous woman was inexplicably attacked by a disease of the heart, and violent spasms of agonizing pain warned her that death at any moment might overtake her, she spoke to Erik again of her wish. Louise, at school in Auckland, had been sent for, but she could only get home by a round-about route, and it would take her a month to arrive.

'She'll be seventeen in a few days. I think she's got a head on her shoulders, but she'll be very young to take full charge of everything here.'

'What makes you think she'll want to marry me?' asked Erik.

'She adored you when she was a child. She used to follow you about like a dog.'

'Oh, that's just a school-girl's *Schwärmerei*.'

'You'll be practically the only man she's ever known.'

'But, Catherine, you wouldn't wish me to marry her if I didn't love her.'

She gave him her sweet, humorous smile.

'No, but I can't help thinking that you will love her.' She was silent for a moment. Then she said something that he did not quite understand. 'I think I'm just as glad that I shan't be here.'

'Oh, don't say that. Why?'

She did not answer. She just patted his hand and chuckled.

It touched him with a sort of sad emotion to reflect how right she had been and he was inclined to attribute her prescience to the strange presentiment of the dying. He was staggered when he saw Louise on her return. She was grown into a lovely girl. She had lost her childish worship of him, but also her shyness; she was perfectly at ease with him. She was, of course, very fond of him; he couldn't doubt that, she was so sweet, friendly and affectionate; but he had the impression, not exactly that she criticized him, but that she coolly appraised him. It did not embarrass him, but it made him feel a little self-conscious. She had acquired the quizzical, humorous look in the eyes that he knew so well in her mother, but whereas in her it warmed your heart because it was so rich with love, with

Louise it slightly disconcerted you; you were not sure that she did not find you a trifle absurd. Erik discovered that he had to start with her from the beginning, for it was not only her body that had changed, it was her spirit too. She was as companionable as ever, as jolly, and they took the same long walks together as in the old days, bathed and fished; they talked and laughed together as freely as when he was twenty-two and she fourteen; but he was vaguely conscious that there was in her a new aloofness. Her soul had been transparent as glass; now it was mysteriously veiled, and he was aware that its depths held something he did not know.

Catherine died quite suddenly. She had an attack of angina, and when the half-caste doctor reached the bungalow she was beyond his aid. Louise broke down completely. The years, with the early maturity they had brought, fell away from her, and she was a little girl again. She did not know how to cope with her grief. She was shattered. For long hours she lay in Erik's arms on his lap, weeping, like a child who cannot realize that sorrow will pass, and would not be comforted. The situation was more than she could deal with, and she did meekly what he told her. Frith went all to pieces and no sense could be got from him. He spent his time drinking whisky and water and crying. Old Swan talked of all the children he had had and how they had died one after the other. They'd all treated him very badly. There was not one of them left now to look after a poor old man. Some of them had run away and some had robbed him, and some had married he didn't know whom, and the rest had died. One would have thought one of them would have had the decency to stay and look after his father now he wanted looking after.

Erik did everything that had to be done.

'You are angelic,' Louise said to him.

He saw the light of love in her eyes, but he contented himself with patting her hand and telling her not to be silly; he did not want to take advantage of her emotion, of the sense of helplessness and of being deserted that just then overwhelmed her, to ask her to marry him. She was so young. It would be unfair to take this advantage over her. He loved her madly. But no sooner had he said this to himself than he corrected it;

he loved her sanely. He loved her with all the energy of his solid intelligence, with all the power of his mighty limbs, with all the vigour of his honest character; he loved her not only for the beauty of her virginal body, but for the firm outlines of her growing personality and for the purity of her virginal soul. His love increased his sense of his own strength. He felt there was nothing he could not achieve. And yet, when he considered her perfection, so much more than the healthy mind in the healthy body, the subtle, sensitive soul that so wonderfully corresponded with the lovely form, he felt abject and humble.

And now it was all settled. Frith's hesitations were not serious; he could be induced, if not to listen to reason, at least to yield to persuasion. But Swan was very old. He was failing fast. It might be necessary to await his death before they married. Erik was efficient. The company would not leave him indefinitely on that island. Sooner or later they would move him to Rangoon, Bangkok, or Calcutta. Eventually they would need him at Copenhagen. He could never be satisfied, like Frith, to spend his life on the plantation and make a bare living by selling cloves and nutmegs. Nor had Louise the placidity that had enabled her mother to make a lovely idyll of her life on that beautiful island. There was nothing he had admired in Catherine so much as that out of these simple elements, the common round of every day, the immemorial labours of husbandry, peace, quiet, humour, and a contented mind, she had been able to make a pattern of such an exquisite and completed beauty. Louise was highstrung as her mother had never been. Though she accepted her circumstances with serenity, her vagrant spirit roved. Sometimes, when they sat on the ramparts of the old Portuguese fort and looked at the sea together, he felt that there was an activity in her soul that craved exercise.

They had often spoken of their wedding journey. He wanted to arrive in Denmark in the spring when all the trees after the long cruel winter were bursting into leaf. The green of that northern country had a fresh tenderness that the tropics never knew. The meadows with their black-and-white cows and the farmsteads nestling among trees had a sweet and tidy beauty that did not amaze you, but made you feel at home. Then there

155

was Copenhagen, with its wide, busy streets, the prim, dignified houses with so many windows you were quite surprised, and its churches and the red palaces King Christian had built that looked as though they belonged to a fairy story. He wanted to take her to Elsinore. It was on its battlements that his father's ghost had appeared to the Danish prince. It was grand on the Sound in summer, the calm sea grey or milk-blue; life there was very pleasant, then, with music and laughter; and all through the long northern twilight the cheerful talk flowed. But they must go to England. There was London, with the National Gallery and the British Museum. Neither of them had ever been to England. They would go to Stratford-on-Avon and see Shakespeare's tomb. Paris, of course. It was the centre of civilization. She would go shopping at the Louvre, and they would drive in the Bois de Boulogne. They would walk hand in hand in the Forest of Fontainebleau. Italy and the Grand Canal by moonlight in a gondola! For Frith's sake they must go to Lisbon. It would be wonderful to see the country from which those old Portuguese had sallied to found an empire of which, besides a few ruined forts and here and there a moribund station, nothing remained but a little deathless poetry and an imperishable renown. To see all these lovely places with the person who is all the world to you, what could life offer more perfect? At that moment Erik understood what Frith meant when he said that the Primal Spirit, who you can call God if you will, was not apart from the world but in it. That great spirit was in the stone on the mountain side, in the beast of the field, in man, and in the thunder that rolled down the vault of heaven.

The late moon now flooded the house with white light. It gave its neat lines an airy distinction and its substantial mass a fragile and charming unreality. Suddenly the shutter of Louise's room was slowly pushed open. Erik held his breath. If he had been asked what he wanted most in the world, he would have said just for one moment to be allowed to see her. She came out on the veranda. She was wearing nothing but the sarong in which she slept.

In the moonlight she looked like a wraith. The night seemed on a sudden to stand still and the silence was like a living thing that listened. She took a step or two and looked up and down the veranda. She wanted to see that no one was about. Erik expected her to come to the rail as she had done before and stand there for a while. In that light he thought he could almost see the colour of her eyes. She turned round towards the window of her room and beckoned. A man came out. He stopped for an instant as though to take her hand, but she shook her head and pointed to the rail. He went up to it and quickly stepped over. He looked down at the ground, six feet below him, and leapt lightly down. Louise slipped back into her room and closed the shutter behind her.

For a moment Erik was so astonished, so bewildered, that he could not understand. He did not believe his eyes. He sat where he was, in old Swan's chair, stockstill, and stared and stared. The man landed on his feet and then sat down on the ground. He appeared to be putting on his shoes. Suddenly Erik found the use of his limbs. He sprang forwards, the man was only a few yards away, and with a bound seized him by the collar of his coat and dragged him to his feet. The man, startled, opened his mouth to cry out, but Erik put his great heavy hand over it. Then he slowly dropped his hand till it encircled the man's throat. The man was so taken aback that he did not struggle. He stood there stupidly, staring at Erik, powerless in that mighty grasp. Then Erik looked at him. It was Fred Blake.

chapter twenty-six

An hour later Dr Saunders, lying awake in bed, heard steps in the passage and then a scratching on the door. He did not answer and the handle was tried. The door was locked.

'Who is it?' he called out.

The reply came on the top of his cry, quickly, in a low, agitated voice.

'Doctor. It's me, Fred. I want to see you.'

The doctor had smoked half a dozen pipes after Captain

Nichols had left him to go back on board the *Fenton*, and when he had been smoking he hated to be disturbed. Thoughts as clear as the geometrical designs in a child's drawing-book, squares, oblongs, circles, triangles, flowed through his mind in an orderly procession. The delight he felt in their lucidity was part and parcel of the indolent pleasure of his body. He raised his mosquito curtains and padded across the bare floor to the door. When he opened it he saw the night watchman, hooded with a blanket against the noxious air of the night, holding a lantern, and just behind him Fred Blake.

'Let me in, doctor. It's frightfully important.'

'Wait till I light the lamp.'

By the light of the watchman's lantern he found the matches and lit the lamp. Ah Kay, who slept on a mat on the veranda outside the doctor's room, awoke at the disturbance and raising himself on his seat rubbed his dark, sloe-like eyes. Fred gave the watchman a tip and he went away.

'Go to sleep, Ah Kay,' said the doctor. 'There's nothing for you to get up for.'

'Look here, you must come to Erik's at once,' said Fred. 'There's been an accident.'

'What d'you mean?'

He looked at Fred and saw that he was as white as a sheet. He was trembling in every limb.

'He's shot himself.'

'Good God! How d'you know?'

'I've just come from there. He's dead.'

At Fred's first words the doctor had instinctively begun to busy himself, but at this he stopped short.

'Are you sure?'

'Oh, quite.'

'If he's dead, what's the good of my going?'

'He can't be left like that. Come and see. Oh, my God.' His voice broke as though he were going to cry. 'Perhaps you can do something.'

'Who's there?'

'Nobody. He's lying there alone. I can't bear it. You must do something. For Christ's sake come.'

'What's that on your hand?'

Fred looked at it. It was smeared with blood. By a natural instinct he was about to wipe it on his duck trousers.

'Don't do that,' cried the doctor, catching hold of his wrist. 'Come and wash it off.'

Still holding him by the wrist, with the lamp in his other hand, he led him into the bath-house. This was a little dark, square chamber with a concrete floor; there was a huge tub in the corner and you bathed yourself by sluicing water over your body with a small tin pan which you filled from the tub. The doctor gave a pan full of water and a piece of soap to Fred and told him to wash.

'Have you got any on your clothes?'

He held up the lamp to look.

'I don't think so.'

The doctor poured the blood-stained water away and they went back to the bedroom. The sight of the blood had startled Fred and he sought to master his hysterical agitation. He was whiter than ever and though he held his hands clenched, Dr Saunders saw that he could not control their violent trembling.

'Better have a drink. Ah Kay, give the gentleman some whisky. No water.'

Ah Kay got up and brought a glass into which he poured the neat spirit. Fred tossed it off. The doctor watched him closely.

'Look here, my boy, we're in a foreign country. We don't want to run up against the Dutch authorities. I don't believe they're very easy people to deal with.'

'We can't leave him lying there in a pool of blood.'

'Isn't it a fact that something happened in Sydney that made you leave in a hurry? The police here are going to ask you a lot of questions. D'you want them to cable to Sydney?'

'I don't care. I'm fed up with the whole thing.'

'Don't be a fool. If he's dead you can do no good and neither can I. We'd better keep out of it. The best thing you can do is get away from the island as soon as you can. Did anyone see you there?'

'Where?'

'At his house,' said the doctor impatiently.

'No, I was only there a minute. I rushed straight round here.'

'What about his boys?'

'I suppose they were asleep. They live at the back.'

'I know. The night watchman's the only person who's seen you. Why did you rouse him?'

'I couldn't get in. The door was locked. I had to get hold of you.'

'Oh, well, it doesn't matter. There are plenty of reasons why you should rout me out in the middle of the night. What made you go to Erik's?'

'I had to. I had something to say to him that couldn't wait.'

'I suppose he did shoot himself. You didn't shoot him, did you?'

'Me?' The boy gasped with horror and surprise. 'Why, he's ... I wouldn't have hurt a hair of his head. If he'd been my brother I couldn't have thought more of him. The best pal a chap ever had.'

The doctor frowned with faint distaste of the language Fred used, but his feeling for Erik was very clear, and the shock the doctor's question caused him was plain enough proof that he spoke the truth.

'Then what does it all mean?'

'Oh, my God, I don't know. He must have gone crazy. How the hell should I know he was going to do a thing like that?'

'Spit it out, sonny. You needn't be afraid I shall give you away.'

'It's that girl up at old Swan's. Louise.'

The doctor sharpened his look, but did not interrupt him.

'I had a bit of fun with her tonight.'

'You? But you only saw her for the first time yesterday.'

'I know. What's that got to do with it? She took a fancy to me the first moment she saw me. I knew that. I took a fancy to her, too. I haven't had a thing since I left Sydney. Somehow, I can't stick these natives. When I had that dance with her I knew it was all right. I could have had her then. We went out in the garden when you were playing bridge. I kissed her. She was just aching for it. When a girl's like that you don't want to give her time to think twice about it. I was in a bit of a state myself. I've never seen anyone to touch her. If she'd told me to go and throw myself over a cliff I'd have done it. When she came this morning with her old man I asked her if we couldn't meet. She said, No. I said, Couldn't I come up after they'd all gone to bed and we could have a bathe in the pool together? She said, No, but she wouldn't say why not. I told her I was crazy about her. And I was too. My God, she's a peach. I took her down to the ketch and showed her over. I kissed her there. That damned old Nichols wouldn't leave us alone for more than a minute. I said I'd go up to the plantation tonight. She said she wouldn't come, but I knew she would, she wanted me just as much as I wanted her; and sure enough when I got there, she was waiting for me. It was lovely there, in the dark, except for the mosquitoes; they were biting like mad, it was more than flesh and blood could stand, and I said, Couldn't we go to her room? and she said she was afraid, but I told her it was all right, and at last she said Yes.'

Fred stopped. The doctor looked at him from under his heavy eyelids. His pupils, from the opium he had smoked, were like pin-points. He listened and pondered over what he heard.

'At last she said I'd better get a move on. I put on my clothes, all but my shoes, so that I shouldn't make a row on the veranda. She went out first to see the coast was clear. Sometimes when he couldn't sleep old Swan wandered up and down there as if it was the deck of a ship. Then I slipped out and hopped over the veranda. I sat down on the ground and started to put on my shoes and before I knew what had happened someone grabbed me and pulled me up. Erik. He's got the strength of an ox, he lifted me up as if I was a bit of a kid, and he put his hand over my mouth, but I was so startled I couldn't have shouted if I'd wanted to. Then he put his hand round my throat and I thought he was going to choke the life out of me. I don't know, I was paralysed, I couldn't even struggle. I couldn't see his face. I heard him breathing; by God, I thought I was done for, and then suddenly he let me go; he gave me a great clout over the side of the head, with the back of his hand, I think it was, and I just fell like a log. He stood over me for a bit; I didn't move; I thought if I moved he'd kill me, and then suddenly he turned round and walked away at about a hundred miles an hour. I got up in a minute and looked at the house. Louise hadn't heard a thing. I thought: should I go and tell her? but I didn't dare, I was afraid someone would hear me knocking on the shutter. I didn't want to frighten her. I didn't know what to do. I started to walk, and then I found I hadn't put my shoes on, I had to go back for them. I was in a panic because just at first I couldn't find them. I drew a long breath when I got back on the road. I was wondering if Erik was waiting for me. It's no joke walking along a road at night, with not a soul about, and knowing that a great hulking fellow may step out at any minute and give you a hiding. He could wring my neck like a chicken's, and I shouldn't be able to do a thing about it. I didn't walk very quick and I kept my eyes peeled. I thought if I saw him first I'd make a dash for it. I mean, it's no good standing up to a chap when you haven't got a chance, and I knew I could run a lot faster than him. I expect it was only nerves. After I'd walked about a mile I wasn't in a funk any more. And then, you know, I felt I must see him at any price. If it had been anybody else I shouldn't have cared a damn, but, somehow, I couldn't stand him thinking me just a damned swine. You can't understand, but I've never met anyone like him, he's so straight himself, you can't bear he shouldn't think you straight, too. Most people you know – well, they're no better than you are; but Erik was different. I mean, you'd have to be a perfect damned fool not to see that he was one in a thousand. See what I mean?'

The doctor gave his thin, derisive smile, and his lips were drawn back from his long yellow teeth so that you thought of the snarl of a gorilla.

'Goodness. I know, it's shattering. One doesn't know what to do about it. It knocks human relations endways. Damned shame, isn't it?'

'Christ, why can't you talk like everybody else?'

'Go on.'

'Well, I just felt I had to have it out with him. I wanted to tell him the whole thing. I was quite ready to marry the girl. I just couldn't help myself with her, I mean. After all, it was only human nature. You're old, you don't know what it is. It's all very well when you're fifty. I knew I shouldn't have a moment's rest till I put myself right with him. When I got to his

162

house I stood outside for I don't know how long, screwing up my courage; it wanted some nerve to go in, you know, but I just forced myself. I couldn't help thinking that if he hadn't killed me then he wouldn't kill me now. I knew he didn't lock the door. That first time we went there he just turned the handle and walked in. But, my God, my heart was thumping when I got in the passage. It was pitch-black when I shut the door. I called his name, but he didn't answer. I knew where his room was and I went along and I knocked at the door. Somehow, I didn't believe he was asleep. I knocked again and then I shouted, "Erik, Erik." At least I tried to shout, but my throat was so dry my voice was as hoarse as a raven's. I couldn't make out why he didn't answer. I thought he was just waiting in there, listening. I was in a blue funk, I had half a mind to cut and run, but I didn't. I tried the latch, the door wasn't locked, and I opened it. I couldn't see a thing. I called again and I said: "For God's sake speak to me, Erik." Then I struck a match and I gave a great jump. I almost jumped out of my skin, he was lying on the floor, at my feet, and if I'd taken a step more I should have tumbled over him. I dropped the match and I couldn't see a thing. I screamed at him. I thought he'd fainted or was dead drunk or something. I tried to strike another match, but the damned thing wouldn't light, and then, when it did, I held it over him and my God, the whole side of his head was shot away. The match went out and I lit another. I saw the lamp and I lit that. I knelt down and felt his hand. It was quite warm. He had a revolver clenched in the other hand. I touched his face to see if he was alive. There was blood all over the place. My God, you never saw such a wound; and then I just came round here as quick as I could. I shall never forget that sight as long as I live.'

He hid his face with his hands and in his misery rocked to and fro. Then a sob broke from him and, throwing himself back in the chair, he turned his face away and wept. Dr Saunders let him cry. He reached out for a cigarette, lit it and deeply inhaled the smoke.

'Did you leave the lamp burning?' he said at last.

'Oh, damn the lamp,' cried Fred impatiently. 'Don't be such a bloody fool.'

'It doesn't matter. He could just as well have shot himself with the lamp burning as in the darkness. Funny none of the boys should have heard anything. I suppose they would have thought it was a Chinaman letting off a cracker.'

Fred put aside all that the doctor said. Nothing of that was of any consequence.

'What in God's name made him do it?' he cried desperately.

'He was engaged to Louise.'

The effect of the doctor's remark was startling. Fred sprang to his feet with a bound, and his face grew livid. His eyes almost started out of his head with horror.

'Erik? He never told me.'

'I suppose he thought it was none of your damned business.'

'She didn't tell me. She never said a word. Oh, God. If I'd known I wouldn't have touched her with the fag-end of a barge-pole. You're just saying that. It can't be true. It can't.'

'He told me so himself.'

'Was he awfully in love with her?'

'Awfully.'

'Then why didn't he kill me or her instead of himself?'

Dr Saunders gave a laugh.

'Curious, isn't it?'

'For God's sake don't laugh. I'm so miserable. I thought nothing worse could happen to me than what has. But this ... She meant nothing to me, really. If I'd only known I wouldn't have thought of fooling about with her. He was the best pal a chap ever had. I wouldn't have hurt him for anything in the world. What a beast he must have thought me! He'd been so awfully decent to me.'

Tears filled his eyes and flowed slowly down his cheeks. He cried bitterly.

'Isn't life foul? You start a thing and you don't think twice about it, and then there's hell to pay. I think there's a curse on me.'

He looked at the doctor, his mouth trembling and his fine eyes heavy with woe. Dr Saunders examined his own feelings. He did not quite approve of the faint satisfaction he felt in the young man's grief. He had a tendency to feel that what he was suffering served him right. At the same time he was unreasonably sorry to see him unhappy. He looked so young and woe-begone he could not help being touched.

'You'll get over it, you know,' he said. 'There's nothing one doesn't get over.'

'I wish I was dead. My old man said I was no damned good and I bet he was right. I make trouble wherever I go. I swear it's not all my fault. The lousy bitch. Why didn't she leave me alone? Can you imagine that a girl who was engaged to a chap like Erik should go to bed with the first man she sees. Well, there's one thing, he was well rid of her.'

'You're talking rubbish.'

'I may be a stinking bad lot, but, by God, I'm not as bad as she is. I thought I was going to get another chance and now it's all gone to hell.'

He hesitated a moment.

'You remember that cable I got this morning? It told me something I didn't know. It was so extraordinary, I couldn't make it out at first. There's a letter for me at Batavia. It's all right for me to go there now. It was rather a shock at first. I didn't know whether to laugh or what. The cable says I died of scarlet fever at the Fever Hospital just outside Sydney. I saw what it meant after a bit. Father's rather important in New South Wales. There was a bad epidemic. They rushed someone to the hospital under my name; they had to explain why I didn't go to the office and all that, and when the chap died I died too. If I know my old man he was damned glad to get rid of me. Well, there's someone who'll lie nice and cosy in the family grave. Father's a wonderful organizer. It's him that's kept the party in power so long. He wasn't going to take a risk if he could help it, and I expect as long as I was above ground he never could feel quite safe. The government got in again at the election. Did you see that? A thumping majority. I can see him with a black band round his arm.'

He gave a mirthless chuckle. Dr Saunders shot a question at him, abruptly.

'What did you do?'

Fred looked away. He answered in a low, choked voice.

'I killed a chap.'

'I wouldn't tell too many people if I were you,' said the doctor.

'You seem to take it pretty calm. Have you ever killed anyone?'

'Only professionally.'

Fred looked up quickly and a smile was wrung from his tortured lips.

'You're a queer fellow, doc. Blest if I can make you out. When one's talking to you, somehow nothing seems to matter a damn. Isn't there anything that makes a difference to you? Isn't there anything you believe in?'

'Why did you kill him? For fun?'

'A damned lot of fun I got out of it. What I've gone through! I wonder it hasn't turned my hair grey. You see, I brooded over it. I could never forget it. I'd be feeling all merry and bright and having a good time and then suddenly I'd remember. I was afraid to go to sleep sometimes. I used to dream I was being pinioned and just going to be hanged. Half a dozen times I've been on the point of slipping overboard one night when nobody was looking, and just swimming till I drowned or a shark got me. If you only knew what a relief it was when I got that cable and understood what it meant! My God, it was a weight off my mind. I was safe. You know, I never felt really safe on the lugger and when we landed anywhere I was always looking for someone to nab me. The first time I saw you, I thought you were a detective and you were on my track. D'you know the first thing I thought this morning? "Now I shall be able to sleep sound." And then this had got to happen. I tell you there's a curse on me.'

'Don't talk such rot.'

'What am I to do? Where am I to go? Tonight, while that girl and I were lying in one another's arms, I thought: why shouldn't I marry her and settle down here? The boat'll be damned useful. Nichols could have gone back on the same ship that you're taking. You could have got my letter that's waiting in Batavia. I expect it's got a bit of money in it. Mother would have made the old man send something. I thought me and Erik, we could have gone into partnership.'

'You can't do that, but you can still marry Louise.'

'Me?' cried Fred. 'After what's happened? I couldn't stick the sight of her. I hope to God I never see her again. I'll never forgive her. Never. Never.'

'What are you going to do, then?'

'God knows. I don't. I can't go home. I'm dead and buried in the family grave. I should like to see Sydney again, George Street, you know, and Manly Bay. I haven't got anyone in the world now. I'm a pretty good accountant, I suppose. I can get a job as book-keeper in some store. I don't know where to go. I'm like a lost dog.'

'If I were you the first thing I'd do is go back to the *Fenton* and try and get a little sleep. You're all in. You'll be able to think better in the morning.'

'I can't go back to the boat. I hate it. If you knew how often I've woken up in a cold sweat, with my heart beating, because those men opened the door of my cell, and I knew the rope was waiting for me! And now Erik's lying there with half his head blown away. My God, how can I sleep?'

'Well, curl up on that chair. I'm going to bed.'

'Thanks. Go ahead. Will it disturb you if I smoke?'

'I'll give you a little something. There's no object in your lying awake.'

The doctor got out his hypodermic needle and gave the boy a shot of morphine. Then he put out the lamp and slipped under his mosquito curtain.

chapter twenty-seven

The doctor awoke when Ah Kay brought him a cup of tea. Ah Kay drew back the mosquito curtains and raised the jalousie to let in the day. The doctor's room looked on the garden, tangled and neglected, with its palm trees, its clumps of ba-nanas, their immense flat leaves still shining with the night, its bedraggled but splendid cassias; and the light filtered through cool and green. The doctor smoked a cigarette. Fred lay on the long chair, sleeping still, and his unlined boyish face, so calm, had an innocence in which the doctor, with a suspicion of sardonic humour, found a certain beauty.

'Shall I wake him?' asked Ah Kay.

'Not yet.'

While he slept he was at peace. He must awake to grief. An odd boy. Who would have thought that he could be so susceptible to goodness? For, though he didn't know it, though he put what he felt in clumsy and stupid words, there was no doubt about it, what had knocked him off his feet in the Dane, what had excited his embarrassed admiration and made him feel that here was a man of a different sort, was the plain, simple goodness that shone in him with so clear and steadfast a light. You might have thought Erik a trifle absurd, you might have asked yourself uneasily whether his head were quite equal to his heart, but there was no doubt about it, he had, heaven only knew by what accident of nature, a real and simple goodness. It was specific. It was absolute. It had an aesthetic quality, and that common-place lad, insensible to beauty in its usual forms, had been moved to ecstasy by it as a mystic might be moved by the sudden overwhelming sense of union with the Godhead. It was a queer trait that Erik had possessed.

'It leads to no good,' said the doctor, with a grim smile as he got out of bed.

He went over to the mirror and stared at himself. He looked at his grey hair all disarranged after the night and his stubble of white beard that had grown since he had shaved the day before. He bared his teeth to look at his long yellow fangs. There were heavy pouches under his eyes. His cheeks had an unsightly purple. He was seized with disgust. He wondered why it was that of all creatures man was the only one that age so hideously disfigured. It was pitiful to think that Ah Kay, with his slender ivory beauty, must become nothing but a little shrivelled, wizened Chinaman, and that Fred Blake, so slim, upright, and square-shouldered, would be just a red-faced old man with bald head and a belly. The doctor shaved and had his bath. Then he awakened Fred.

'Come along, young fellow. Ah Kay's just gone to see about our breakfast.'

Fred opened his eyes, immediately alert, eager in his youth

to welcome another day, but then, looking about him, he remembered where he was, and everything else. His face all of a sudden grew sullen.

'Oh, buck up,' said the doctor impatiently. 'Go and have a wash down.'

Ten minutes later they were seated at breakfast, and the doctor noticed without surprise that Fred ate with a hearty appetite. He did not talk. Dr Saunders congratulated himself. After so disturbed a night he felt none too well. His reflections upon life, then, were acid, and he preferred to keep them to himself.

When they were finishing the manager came up to them and addressed himself to Dr Saunders in voluble Dutch. He knew the doctor did not understand, but talked nevertheless, and his signs and gestures would have made him comprehensible even if his manner, agitated and distressed, had not made what he was saying quite clear. Dr Saunders shrugged his shoulders. He pretended he had no notion what the half-caste was talking about, and presently, in exasperation, the little man left them.

'They've found out,' said the doctor.

'How?'

'I don't know. I suppose his house-boy went in to take him his tea.'

'Isn't there anybody who can interpret?'

'We shall hear soon enough. Don't forget, we neither of us know anything about it.'

They relapsed into silence. A few minutes later the manager returned with a Dutch official, in a white uniform with brass buttons; he clicked his heels together, and mentioned an incomprehensible name. He spoke English with a very strong accent.

'I'm sorry to tell you that a Danish trader called Christessen has shot himself.'

'Christessen?' cried the doctor. 'That tall fellow?'

He watched Fred out of the corner of his eye.

'He was found by his boys an hour ago. I am in charge of the inquiry. There can be no doubt that it is a case of suicide. Mr van Ryk,' he motioned to the half-caste manager, 'informs me that he was here last night to visit you.'

'That's quite true.'

'How long did he stay?'

'Ten minutes or a quarter of an hour.'

'Was he sober?'

'Quite.'

'I never saw him drunk myself. Did he say anything that suggested he had the intention of doing away with himself?'

'No. He was quite cheerful. I didn't know him very well, you know. I only arrived three days ago, and I'm waiting for the *Princess Juliana.*'

'Yes, I know. Then you can give no explanation of the tragedy?'

'I'm afraid not.'

'That is all I wanted to know. If I have any need of anything more from you I will let you know. Perhaps you will not mind coming to my office.' He glanced at Fred. 'And this gentleman can tell us nothing?'

'Nothing,' said the doctor. 'He was not here. I was playing cards with the skipper of the ketch in the harbour just now.'

'I've seen her. I'm sorry for the poor fellow. He was very quiet and never gave any trouble. You could not help liking him. I'm afraid it's the old story. It's a mistake to live alone in a place like this. They brood. They get homesick. The heat is killing. And then one day they can't stand it any more, and they just put a bullet through their heads. I've seen it before, more than once. Much better to have a little girl to live with you, and it makes hardly any difference to your expenses. Well, gentlemen, I am much obliged to you. I won't take up any more of your time. You have not been to the *Gesellschaft* yet, I believe? We shall be very glad to see you there. You will find all the most important people of the island there from six or seven till nine. It is a jolly place. Quite a social centre. Well, good morning, gentlemen.'

He clicked his heels, shook hands with the doctor and Fred, and stumped somewhat heavily away.

chapter twenty-eight

In that hot country not much time was permitted to pass between a person's death and his burial, but in this case the examination had to be conducted, and it was not till latish in the afternoon that the funeral took place. It was attended by a few Dutch friends of Erik, Frith and Dr Saunders, Fred Blake and Captain Nichols. This was an occasion after the skipper's heart. He had managed to borrow a black suit from an acquaintance he had made on the island. It did not fit very well, since it belonged to a man both taller and stouter than he, and he was obliged to turn up the trousers and the sleeves, but in contrast with the others, clad in nondescript fashion, it produced a satisfactory effect of respectability. The service was conducted in Dutch, which seemed to Captain Nichols a little out of place, and he could not take part in it, but there was much unction in his deportment; and when it was over he shook hands with the Lutheran pastor and the two or three Dutch officials present as though they had rendered him a personal service, so that they thought for a moment he must be a near relative of the deceased. Fred wept.

The four Britishers walked back together. They came to the harbour.

'If you gentlemen will come on board the *Fenton*,' said the skipper, 'I'll open a bottle of port for you. I 'appened to see it in the store this mornin', and I always think a bottle of port's the right thing after a funeral. I mean, it's not like beer and whisky. There's somethin' serious about port.'

'I never thought of it before,' said Frith, 'but I quite see what you mean.'

'I'm not coming,' said Fred. 'I've got a hump. Can I go along with you, doctor?'

'If you like.'

'We've all got a 'ump,' said Captain Nichols. 'That's why I vote we 'ave a bottle of port. It won't take the 'ump away. Not by any manner of means. It'll make it worse if anythin', at least that's my experience, but it means you can enjoy it, if you follow me, you get something out of it, and it's not wasted.'

'Go to hell,' said Fred.

'Come on, Frith. If you're the man I take you for, you and me can drink a bottle of port without strainin' ourselves.'

'We live in degenerate days,' said Frith. 'Two-bottle men, three-bottle men, they're as extinct as the dodo.'

'An Australian bird,' said Captain Nichols.

'If two grown men can't drink one bottle of port between them I despair of the human race. Babylon is fallen, is fallen.'

'Exactly,' replied Captain Nichols.

They got into the dinghy and a blackfellow rowed them out to the *Fenton*. The doctor and Fred walked slowly on. When they reached the hotel they went in.

'Let's go to your room,' said Fred.

The doctor poured himself out a whisky and soda and gave one to Fred.

'We're sailing at dawn,' said the boy.

'Are you? Have you seen Louise?'

'No.'

'Aren't you going to?'

'No.'

Dr Saunders shrugged his shoulders. It was no business of his. For a while they drank and smoked in silence.

'I've told you so much,' the boy said at last, 'I may as well tell you the rest.'

'I'm not curious.'

'I've wanted to tell someone badly. Sometimes I could hardly prevent myself from telling Nichols. Thank God, I wasn't such a fool as that. Grand opportunity for blackmail it would have been for him.'

'He isn't the sort of man I'd choose to confide a secret to.'

Fred gave a little derisive chuckle.

'It wasn't my fault, really. It was just rotten luck. It is bloody that your life should be ruined by an accident like that. It's so damned unfair. My people are in a very good position. I was in one of the best firms in Sydney. Eventually, my old man was going to buy me a partnership. He's got a lot of influence and he could have thrown business in my way. I could have made plenty of money and sooner or later of course I should have married and settled down. I expect I should have gone into

172

politics like father did. If ever anyone had a chance I had. And look at me now. No home, no name, no prospects, a couple of hundred pounds in my belt and whatever the old man's sent to Batavia. Not a friend in the world.'

'You've got youth. You've got some education. And you're not bad-looking.'

'That's what makes me laugh. If I'd had a squint in my eye or a hump-back I'd have been all right. I'd be in Sydney now. You're no beauty, doctor.'

'I am conscious of the fact and resigned to it.'

'Resigned to it! Thank your lucky stars every day of your life.'

Dr Saunders smiled.

'I'm not prepared to go as far as that.'

But the foolish boy was desperately serious.

'I don't want you to think I'm conceited. God knows I've got nothing to be conceited about. But you know, I've always been able to get any girl I wanted to. Oh, almost since I was a kid. I thought it rather a lark. After all, you're only young once. I didn't see why I shouldn't have all the fun I could get. D'you blame me?'

'No. The only people who would are those who never had your opportunities.'

'I never went out of my way to get them. But when they practically asked for it – well, I should have been a fool not to take what I could get. It used to make me laugh sometimes to see them all in a dither and often I'd pretend I didn't notice. They'd get furious with me. Girls are funny, you know, nothing makes them so mad as a chap standing off. Of course, I never let it interfere with my work; I'm not a fool, you know, in any sense of the word, and I wanted to get on.'

'An only child, were you?'

'No. I've got a brother. He went into the business with father. He's married. And I've got a married sister, too.

'Well, one Sunday last year, a chap brought his wife to spend the day up at our house. His name was Hudson. He was a Roman Catholic, and he'd got a lot of influence with the Irish and the Italians. Father said he could make all the difference at the election, and he told mother she was to do them proud. They came up to dinner, the Premier came and brought his wife, and mother gave them enough to eat to feed a regiment. After dinner father took them into his den to talk business and the rest of us went and sat in the garden. I'd wanted to go fishing, but father said I'd got to stay and make myself civil. Mother and Mrs Darnes had been at school together.'

'Who was Mrs Darnes?'

'Mr Darnes is the Premier. He's the biggest man in Australia.'

'I'm sorry. I didn't know.'

'They always had a lot to talk about. They tried to be polite to Mrs Hudson, but I could see they didn't much like her. She was doing her best to be nice to them, admiring everything and buttering them up, but the more she laid it on the less they liked it. At last, mother asked me if I wouldn't show her round the garden. We strolled off and the first thing she said was: "For God's sake give me a cigarette." She gave me a look when I lit it for her and she said: "You're a very good-looking boy." "D'you think so?" I said. "I suppose you've been told that before?" she said. "Only by mother," I said, "and I thought perhaps she was prejudiced." She asked me if I was fond of dancing and I said I was, so she said she was having tea at the Australia next day and if I liked to come in after the office we could have a dance together. I wasn't keen on it, so I said I couldn't; then she said: "What about Tuesday or Wednesday?" I couldn't very well say I was engaged both days, so I said Tuesday would suit me all right; and when they'd gone away I told father and mother. She didn't much like the idea, but father was all for it. He said it wouldn't suit his book at all to have us stand-offish. "I didn't like the way she kept on looking at him," said mother, but father told her not to be silly. "Why, she's old enough to be his mother," he said. "How old is she?" Mother said: "She'll never see forty again."

'She was nothing to look at. Thin as a rail. Her neck was absolutely scraggy. Tallish. She had a long thin face, with hollow cheeks, and a brown skin, all one colour, rather leathery, if you know what I mean; and she never seemed to take any trouble with her hair, it always looked as though it would come down in a minute; and she'd have a wisp hanging down in front of her ear or over her forehead. I do like a woman to have a neat head, don't you? It was black, rather like a gipsy's, and she had enormous black eyes. They made her face. When you talked to her you didn't really see anything else. She didn't look British, she looked like a foreigner, a Hungarian or something like that. There was nothing attractive about her.

'Well, I went on the Tuesday. She knew how to dance, you couldn't deny that. You know, I'm rather keen on dancing. I enjoyed myself more than I expected. She had a lot to say for herself. I shouldn't have had a bad time if there hadn't been some of my pals there: I knew they'd rot my head off for dancing the whole afternoon with an old geyser like that. There are ways *and* ways of dancing. It didn't take me long to see what she was up to. I couldn't help laughing. Poor old cow, I thought, if it gives her any pleasure, well, let her have it. She asked me to go to the pictures with her one night when her husband had to go to a meeting. I said I didn't mind, and we made a date. I held her hand at the pictures. I thought it'd please her and it didn't do me any harm, and afterwards she said, Couldn't we walk a bit. We were pretty friendly by then; she was interested in my work, and she wanted to know all about my home. We talked about racing, I told her there was nothing I'd like to do more than ride in a big race myself. In the dark she wasn't so bad, and I kissed her. Well, the end of it was that we went to a place I knew and we had a bit of a rough and tumble. I did it more out of politeness than anything else. I thought that would be the finish. Not a bit of it. She went crazy about me. She said she'd fallen in love with me the first time she saw me. I don't mind telling you that just at first I was a bit flattered. She had something. Those great flashing eyes, sometimes they made me feel all funny, and that gipsy look, I don't know, it was so unusual, it seemed to take you right away and you couldn't believe you were in good old Sydney; it was like living in a story about Nihilists and Grand Dukes and I don't know what all. By God, she was hot stuff. I thought I knew a thing or two about all that, but when she took me in hand I found I didn't know a thing. I'm not particular, but really, sometimes she almost disgusted me. She was proud of it. She used to say that after a chap had loved her, other women were duller than cold roast mutton.

'I couldn't help liking it in a way, but you know, I didn't feel easy about it. You don't like a woman to be absolutely shameless. There was no satisfying her either. She made me see her every day, and she'd ring me up at the office and ring me up at home. I told her for God's sake to be careful; after all she had a husband to think of, and there was father and mother, father was quite capable of packing me off to a sheep-station for a year if he had the smallest suspicion that things weren't going right, but she said she didn't care. She said if I was packed off to a sheep-station she'd come with me. She didn't seem to mind what risks she took, and if it hadn't been for me it would have been all over Sydney in a week. She'd telephone to mother and ask if I couldn't go to supper at her place and make a four at bridge, and when I was there she'd make love to me under her husband's nose. When she saw I was scared she laughed her head off. It excited her. Pat Hudson just treated me like a boy; he never took much notice of me, he fancied himself at bridge, and got a lot of fun out of telling me all about it. I didn't dislike him. He was a bit of a rough-neck, and he could put his liquor away rather, but he was a smart fellow in his way. He was ambitious, and he liked having me there because I was father's son. He was quite ready to come in with father, but he wanted to get something pretty substantial for himself out of it.

'I was getting a bit fed up with it all. I couldn't call my soul my own. And she was as jealous as hell. If we were anywhere and I happened to look at a girl it would be: "Who's that? Why d'you look at her like that? Have you had her?" And if I said I hadn't ever spoken to her even, she'd say I was a damned liar. I thought I'd slack off a bit. I didn't want to chuck her too suddenly in case she got her knife in me. She could turn Hudson round her little finger, and I knew father wouldn't be very pleased if he did the dirty on us at the election. I began to say I was busy at the office or had to stay at home, when she wanted me to go out with her. I told her mother was getting suspicious and that we must be careful. She was as sharp as a knife. She wouldn't believe a word I said. She made me the most awful scenes. To tell you the truth I began

176

to get rather scared. I'd never known anyone like that. With most of the girls I'd played about with – well, they'd known it was just a lark, same as I did, and it just ended naturally, without any fuss or bother. You'd have thought, when she guessed I'd had enough, her pride would prevent her from clinging to me. But no. Quite the contrary. D'you know, she actually wanted me to run away with her, to America or somewhere, so that we could get married. It never seemed to occur to her that she was twenty years older than me. I mean, it was too ridiculous. I had to pretend that it was out of the question, on account of the election, you know, and because we shouldn't have anything to live on. She was absolutely unreasonable. She said, what did we care about the election, and anyone could make a living in America, she said; she'd been on the stage and she was sure she could get a part. She seemed to think she was a girl. She asked me if I'd marry her if it wasn't for her husband and I had to say I would. The scenes she made got me so nervous I was ready to say anything. You don't know what a life she led me. I wished to God I'd never set eyes on her. I was so worried I didn't know what to do. I had half a mind to tell mother, but I knew it would upset her so frightfully. She never left me alone for a minute. She came up to the office once. I had to be polite to her and pretend it was all right, because I knew she was capable of making a scene before everybody, but afterwards I told her if she ever did it again I wouldn't have anything more to do with her. Then she started waiting for me in the street outside. My God, I could have wrung her neck. Father used to go home in a car and I always walked to his office to fetch him, and she insisted on walking there with me. At last things got to such a pitch that I just couldn't stick it any more; I didn't care what happened. I told her I was sick and tired of the whole thing and it had got to stop.

'I made up my mind that I was going to say it and I did. My God, it was awful. It was at her place, they had a little jerry-built house, overlooking the harbour, on a cliff, rather far out, and I'd got off from the office in the middle of the afternoon on purpose. She screamed and she cried. She said she loved me and she couldn't live without me and I don't know what all.

She said she'd do anything I liked and she wouldn't bother me in future and she'd be quite different. She promised every sort of thing. God knows what she didn't say. Then she flew into a rage and cursed me and swore at me and called me every name under the sun. She went for me, and I had to hold her hands to prevent her from scratching my eyes out. She was like a mad woman. Then she said she was going to commit suicide, and tried to run out of the house. I thought she'd throw herself over the cliff or something, and I held her back by main force. She kicked and struggled. And then she threw herself on her knees and tried to kiss my hands, and when I pushed her away she fell on the ground and started sobbing and sobbing. I seized the opportunity and made a bolt for it.

'I'd hardly got home before she rang me up. I wouldn't speak to her and rang off. She rang again and again, fortunately mother was out, and I just didn't answer. There was a letter waiting for me at the office next morning, ten pages of it, you know the sort of thing; I took no notice of it; I certainly wasn't going to answer. When I went out for lunch at one o'clock she was standing in the doorway waiting for me, but I walked right past her, as quick as I could, and got away in the crowd. I thought she might be there when I came back, so I walked along with one of the chaps at the office, who had his dinner the same place that I had lunch. She was there right enough, but I pretended I didn't see her, and she was afraid to speak. I found another chap to walk out with in the evening. She was still there. I suppose she'd been waiting all the time so that I shouldn't slip out. D'you know, she had the nerve to come straight up to me. She put on a society manner.

' "How d'you do, Fred?" she said. "What a bit of luck meeting you. I've got a message for your father."

'The chap walked on before I could stop him, and I was caught.

' "What d'you want?" I said.

'I was in a flaming passion.

' "Oh, my God, don't talk to me like that," she said. "Have pity on me. I'm so unhappy. I can't see straight."

' "I'm very sorry," I said. "I can't help it."

'Then she began to cry, right there in the middle of the

street, with people passing all the time. I could have killed her.

' "Fred, it's no good," she said, "you can't throw me over. You're everything in the world to me."

' "Oh, don't be so silly," I said. "You're an old woman and I'm hardly more than a kid. You ought to be ashamed of yourself."

' "What does that matter?" she said. "I love you with all my heart."

' "Well, I don't love you," I said. "I can't bear the sight of you. I tell you it's finished. For God's sake leave me alone."

' "Isn't there anything I can do to make you love me?" she said.

' "Nothing," I said. "I'm fed up with you."

' "Then I shall kill myself," she said.

' "That's your trouble," I said, and I walked away quickly before she could stop me.

'But although I said it just like that, as if I didn't care a damn, I wasn't easy about it. They say people who threaten to commit suicide never do, but she wasn't like other people. The fact is, she was a madwoman. She was capable of anything. She was capable of coming up to the house and shooting herself in the garden. She was capable of swallowing poison and leaving some awful letter behind. She might accuse me of anything. You see, I hadn't only myself to think of, I had to think of father, too. If I was mixed up in something it might have done him an awful lot of harm, especially just then. And he isn't the sort of man to let you off easy, if you've made a fool of yourself. I can tell you I didn't sleep much that night. I worried myself sick. I should have been furious if I'd found her hanging about the street outside the office in the morning, but in a way I'd have been rather relieved. She wasn't there. There was no letter for me either. I began to get a bit scared, and I had a job to prevent myself ringing up to see if she was all right. When the evening paper came out I just made a grab at it. Pat Hudson was pretty prominent, and if something had happened to her there'd sure to be a lot about it. But there wasn't a thing. That day there was nothing, no sign of her, no telephone message, no letter, nothing in the paper, and the day after, and the

179

day after that it was just the same. I began to think it was all right and I was rid of her. I came to the conclusion it was all a bluff. Oh, my God, how thankful I was! But I'd had my lesson. I made up my mind to be damned careful in future. No more middle-aged women for me. I'd got all nervous and wrought-up. You can't think what a relief it was to me. I don't want to make myself out any better than I am, but I have some sense of decency, and really that woman was the limit. I know it sounds silly, but sometimes she just horrified me. I'm all for having a bit of fun, but damn it all, I don't want to make a beast of myself.'

Dr Saunders did not reply. He understood pretty well what the boy meant. Careless and hot-blooded, with the callousness of youth, he took his pleasure where he found it, but youth is not only callous, it is modest, and his instinct was outraged by the unbridled passion of the experienced woman.

'Then about ten days later I got a letter from her. The envelope was typewritten or I shouldn't have opened it. But it was quite sensible. It started, "Dear Fred." She said she was awfully sorry she'd made me all those scenes, and she thought she must have been rather crazy, but she'd had time to calm down and she didn't want to be a nuisance to me. She said it was her nerves, and she'd taken me much too seriously. Everything was all right now, and she didn't bear me any ill will. She said I mustn't blame her, because it was partly my fault for being so absurdly good-looking. Then she said she was starting for New Zealand next day, and was going to be away for three months. She'd got a doctor to say she needed a complete change. Then she said Pat was going to Newcastle that night, and would I come in for a few minutes to say good-bye to her. She gave me her solemn word of honour that she wouldn't be troublesome, all that was over and done with, but somehow or other Pat had got wind of something, it was nothing important, but it was just as well I told the same story as her if by any chance he asked me any questions. She hoped I'd come, because though it couldn't matter to me and I was absolutely safe, things might be a little awkward for her and she certainly didn't want to get into any trouble if she could help it.

'I knew it was true about Hudson going to Newcastle because my old man had said something about it at breakfast that morning. The letter was absolutely normal. Sometimes she wrote in a scrawl that you could hardly read, but she could write very well when she wanted to, and I could see that when she'd written this she'd been absolutely calm. I was a little anxious about what she'd said about Pat. She had insisted on taking the most awful risks, though I'd warned her over and over again. If he'd heard anything it did seem better that we should tell the same lie, and forewarned is forearmed, isn't it? So I rang her up and said I'd be there about six. She was so casual over the telephone that I was almost surprised. It sounded as though she didn't much care if I came or not.

'When I got there she shook hands with me as if we were just friends. She asked me if I'd like some tea, I said I'd had it before I came. She said she wouldn't keep me a minute because she was going to the pictures. She was all dressed up. I asked her what was the matter with Pat, and she said it wasn't really very serious, only he'd heard that I'd been at the pictures with her, and he didn't much like it. She'd said it was just an accident. Once I'd seen her sitting by herself and come over and sat by her, and another time we'd met in the vestibule, and as she was alone I'd paid for her seat and we'd gone in together. She said she didn't think Pat would mention it, but if he did, she wanted me to back her up. Of course I said I would. She mentioned the two times he was asking about, so that I should know, and then she began talking about her journey. She knew New Zealand well and she started talking about it. I'd never been there. It sounded fine. She was going to stay with friends and she made me laugh telling me about them. She could be jolly nice when she liked. She was awfully good company when she was in a good temper, I must admit that, and I never realized that time was passing. She was just like what she was when I first knew her. At last she got up and said she'd better be going. I suppose I'd been there about half an hour, maybe three-quarters. She gave me her hand and she looked at me half laughing.

' "It wouldn't really hurt you to kiss me good-bye, would it?" she said.

'She said it chaffingly, and I laughed.

181

' "No, I don't suppose it would," I said.

'I bent down and kissed her. Or rather she kissed me. She put her arms round my neck and when I tried to break away she wouldn't let me go. She just clung to me like a vine. And then she said, as she was going away tomorrow, wouldn't I have her just once more. I said she'd promised she wouldn't make a nuisance of herself, and she said she didn't mean to, but seeing me, she couldn't help herself, and she swore it would be the last time. After all, she was going away, and it couldn't matter just once. And all the time she was kissing me and stroking my face. She said she didn't blame me for anything, and she was just a foolish woman and wouldn't I be kind to her? Well, it had all gone off so well and I was so relieved that she seemed to accept the situation; I didn't want to be a brute. If she'd been staying I'd have refused at any price, but as she was going away I thought I might just as well send her away happy.

' "All right," I said, "let's go upstairs."

'It was a little two-storey house, and the bedroom and spare-room were on the first floor. They've been building a lot of them round Sydney lately.

' "No," she said. "The whole place is in a mess."

'She drew me towards the sofa. It was one of those Chester-fields, and there was lots of room to cuddle up in it.

' "I love you, I love you," she kept on saying.

'Suddenly the door opened. I sprang up and there was Hudson. For a minute he was just as startled as I was. Then he shouted at me, I don't know what he said, and jumped. He let out his fist, but I dodged it; I'm pretty quick on my feet, and I've done a bit of boxing; and then he just chucked himself at me. We grappled. He was a big, powerful chap, bigger than me, but I'm pretty strong. He was trying to get me down, but I wasn't going to let him do that if I could help it. We were struggling all over the room. He hit me when he could, and I hit him back. Once I got away from him, but he charged me like a bull and I staggered. We knocked down chairs and tables. We had a hell of a fight. I tried to get away from him again, but I couldn't. He wanted to trip me up. It didn't take me long to find out he was a lot stronger than me. But I was more active. He'd got his coat on and I hadn't got anything but my undies. Then he got me down; I don't know if I slipped, or if he just forced me, but we were rolling over on the floor like a couple of madmen. He got on top of me and began hitting my face; there was nothing I could do then, and I just tried to protect it with my arm. Suddenly I thought he was going to kill me. God, I was scared. I made a hell of an effort and slipped away, but he was on me again like a flash of lightning. I felt my strength giving out; he put his knee on my windpipe and I knew I'd choke. I tried to shout, but I couldn't. I threw out my right arm and suddenly I felt a revolver put in my hand; I swear I didn't know what I was doing, it all happened in a second, I twisted my arm and fired. He gave a cry and started back. I fired again. He gave a great groan and rolled off me on to the floor. I slid away and jumped to my feet.

'I was trembling like a leaf.'

Fred threw himself back in his chair and closed his eyes, so that Dr Saunders thought he was going to faint. He was as white as a sheet, and great beads of sweat stood on his forehead. He took a long breath.

'I was in a sort of daze. I saw Florrie kneel down, and though you wouldn't believe it I noticed that she was careful about it so that she shouldn't get any blood on her. She felt his pulse and she pulled down his eyelid. She got up.

' "I think it's all right," she said. "He's dead." She gave me a funny look. "It wouldn't have been very nice if we'd had to polish him off."

'I was horror-struck. I suppose I couldn't have been all there or I wouldn't have said anything so stupid as I did.

' "I thought he was at Newcastle," I said.

' "No, he didn't go," she said. "He had a telephone message."

' "What telephone message?" I said. Somehow I couldn't understand what she was talking about. "Who sent it?"

'D'you know that she almost laughed.

' "I did," she said.

' "What for?" I said. Then it suddenly flashed across me. "You don't mean to say it was a put-up job?"

' "Don't be silly," she said. "What you've got to do now is

to keep your head. You go home and have supper quite quietly with the family. I'm going to the pictures like I said I would."

' "You're crazy," I said.

' "No, I'm not," she said. "I know what I'm doing. You'll be all right if you do what I say. You just behave as if nothing had happened and leave it all to me. Don't forget that if it comes out you'll hang."

'I expect I nearly jumped out of my skin when she said that, because she laughed. My God, the nerve that woman had got!

' "You've got nothing to be afraid of," she said. "I won't let them touch a hair of your head. You're my property, and I know how to look after what belongs to me. I love you and I want you, and when it's all over and forgotten we'll be married. What a fool you were to think I was ever going to give you up."

'I swear to you that I felt my blood run icy in my veins. I was in a trap and there was no getting out of it. I stared at her and I hadn't a thing to say. I shall never forget the look on her face. Suddenly she looked at my undervest. I hadn't got anything on but that and my drawers.

' "Oh, look!" she said.

'I looked at myself and saw that on one side it was just dripping with blood. I was just going to touch it, I don't know why, when she caught hold of my hand.

' "Don't do that," she said. "Wait a minute."

'She got a newspaper and began rubbing it.

' "Hold your head down," she said. "I'll take it off."

'I bent my head and she skinned me.

' "Have you got any blood anywhere else?" she said. "Damned lucky for you you hadn't got your trousers on."

'My drawers were all right. I dressed myself as quick as I could. She took the vest.

' "I'll burn it and I'll burn the paper," she said, "I've got a fire in the kitchen. It's my washing day."

'I looked at Hudson. He was dead all right. It made me feel rather sick to look at him. There was a great pool of blood on the carpet.

' "Are you ready?" she said.

' "Yes," I said.

184

'She came out in the passage with me and just before she opened the door she put her arms round my neck and kissed me as if she wanted to eat me alive.

' "My darling," she said, "Darling. Darling."

'She opened the door and I slipped out. It was pitch dark.

'I seemed to walk in a dream. I walked pretty quick. As a matter of fact, I had all I could do not to run. I had my hat as far down as it would go and my collar turned up, but I hardly passed anybody and no one could have recognized me. I went a long way round, as she'd said I was to, and took the tram from right away in the neighbourhood of Chester Avenue.

'They were just going to sit down to dinner when I got home. We always had late dinner and I ran upstairs to wash my hands. I looked at myself in the glass, and d'you know, I was absolutely astonished because I looked just the same as usual. But when I sat down and mother said, "Tired, Fred? You're looking very white," I went as red as a turkey-cock. I didn't manage to eat very much. Luckily I didn't have to talk, we never talked much when we were alone, and after dinner father started to read some reports and mother looked at the evening paper. I was feeling awful.'

'Half a minute,' said the doctor. 'You said you suddenly felt a revolver in your hand. I don't quite understand.'

'Florrie put it there.'

'How did she get it?'

'How should I know? She took it out of Pat's pocket when he was on the top of me or else she had it there. I only fired in self-defence.'

'Go on.'

'Suddenly mother said, "What's the matter, Fred?" It came so unexpectedly and her voice was so – gentle, it just broke me. I tried to control myself; I couldn't, I just burst out crying. "Hullo, what's this?" said father. Mother put her arms round me and rocked me as if I was a baby. She kept on asking me what was the matter, and at first I wouldn't say. At last I had to. I pulled myself together. I made a clean breast of the whole thing. Mother was frightfully upset, and started weeping, but father shut her up. She began reproaching me, but he wouldn't let her do that either. "All that doesn't matter now," he said.

185

His face was like thunder. If the earth could have opened and swallowed me on a word of his, he'd have said the word. I told them everything. Father had always said the only chance a criminal has is to be absolutely frank with his lawyer, and that a lawyer couldn't do a thing unless he knew every single fact.

'I finished. Mother and I looked at father. He'd stared at me all the time I was speaking, but now he looked down. You could see he was thinking like hell. You know, in some ways father's an extraordinary man. He's always been very keen on culture. He's one of the trustees of the Art Gallery and he's on the committee that gets up the symphony concerts and all that. He's gentlemanly and rather quiet. Mother used to say he looked very distinguished. He was always very mild and amiable and polite. You'd have thought he wouldn't hurt a fly. He was everything he seemed, but there was a lot more in him than that. After all, he'd got the biggest lawyer's business in Sydney, and there was nothing he didn't know about people. Of course he was highly respected, but everyone knew it wasn't much good trying on any hanky-panky with him. And it was the same in politics. He ran the party and old Darnes never did a thing without consulting him. He could have been premier himself if he'd wanted to, but he didn't, he was quite satisfied just to be in the government and manage the whole shooting match behind the scenes.

' "You mustn't blame the boy too much, Jim," mother said.

'He made a sort of impatient movement with his hand. I almost thought he wasn't thinking about me at all. It sent a chill down my spine. He spoke at last.

' "It looks very much like a put-up job between those two," he said. "Hudson has been rather difficult lately. I shouldn't be surprised if there was blackmail behind it. And she double-crossed him."

' "What's Fred to do?" said mother.

'Father looked at me. You know, he looked just as mild as always and his voice had the same rather pleasant note in it. "If he's caught, he'll hang," he said. Mother gave a shriek and father frowned a little. "Oh, I'm not going to let him hang," he said. "Don't be afraid. He can escape that by going out now and shooting himself." "Jim, d'you want to kill me?" said mother. "Unfortunately that wouldn't help us much," he said. "What?" I asked. "Your shooting yourself," he said. "The thing's got to be hushed up. We can't afford a scandal. We're going to have a stiff fight at the election, and with me out of it and all this we shouldn't have much chance." "Father, I'm so awfully sorry," I said. "I don't doubt that," he said. "Fools and blackguards generally are when they have to take the consequences of their actions."

'We were all silent for a bit and then I said, "I'm not sure if it wouldn't be the best thing if I went and shot myself." "Don't be so stupid," he said; "that would only make things worse. D'you think the newspapers are such fools that they wouldn't put two and two together? Don't talk. Let me think." We sat like mutes. Mother was holding my hand. "There's the woman to deal with, too," he said at last. "We're in her clutches all right. Nice to have her as a daughter-in-law." Mother didn't dare say a word. Father leaned back in his chair and crossed his legs. A little smile came into his eyes. "Fortunately we live in the most democratic country in the world," he said. "Nobody is above corruption." He liked saying that. He looked at us for a minute or two. He had a way of thrusting out his jaw when he'd made up his mind to do something and meant to put it through that I knew as well as mother did. "I suppose it'll be in the paper tomorrow," he said, "I'll go and see Mrs Hudson. I think I know what she's going to say. If she sticks to her story, barring accidents I don't think anyone can prove anything. It looks to me as if she'd worked it all out pretty thoroughly. The police will question her, but I'll see they don't interview her without my being present." "And what about Fred?" said mother. Father smiled again. You'd have sworn butter couldn't melt in his mouth. "Fred'll go to bed and stay there," he said. "By a merciful interposition of providence there's a lot of scarlet fever about, an epidemic practically; tomorrow or the next day we'll rush him off to the fever hospital." "But why?" asked mother. "What's the use of that?" "My dear," said father, "it's the best way I know of keeping someone out of the way for a few weeks with perfect security." "But supposing he catches it?" said mother. "He'd be acting natural," he said.

'In the morning father rang up my boss and said I'd got a temperature and he didn't half like the look of it. He was keeping me in bed and had sent for the doctor. The doctor came all right. He was my uncle, mother's brother, and he'd attended me since I was born. He said he couldn't say for certain, it looked like scarlet fever, but he wouldn't send me to the hospital till the symptoms declared themselves. Mother told the cook and the maid that they weren't to come near me, and she'd look after me herself.

'The evening paper was full of the murder. Mrs Hudson had gone to the pictures by herself, and when she came home and went into the sitting-room she had found the body of her husband. They didn't keep a servant. You don't know Sydney, but the house was a sort of little villa in a quarter they'd been developing; it stood in its own ground, and the next house was twenty or thirty yards away. Florrie didn't know the people who lived in it, but she ran there and battered on the door till they opened it. They were in bed and asleep. She told them her husband had been murdered and asked them to come quickly; they ran along, and there he was lying all heaped up on the floor. The man from the other house remembered after a while that he'd better call up the police. Mrs Hudson was hysterical. She threw herself on her husband, screaming and crying, and they had to drag her away.

'Then there were all the details that the reporters had managed to pick up. The police doctor thought the man had been dead two or three hours. Strangely enough, he'd been shot with his own revolver, but the possibility of suicide was dismissed at once. When Mrs Hudson had collected herself a bit she told the police that she'd spent the evening at a picture palace. She had a part of the ticket still in her bag, and she'd spoken while there to two people she knew. She explained that she'd decided to go to the pictures that evening because her husband had arranged to go to Newcastle. He'd come home shortly before six and told her he wasn't going. She said she'd stay at home with him and get him his supper, but he told her to go as she'd intended. Someone was coming to see him on important business, and he wanted to be alone. She went out and that was the last she saw of him alive. There were signs of a terrific struggle in the room. Hudson had evidently fought desperately for his life. Nothing had been stolen from the house, and the police and the reporters at once jumped to the conclusion that the crime had a political motive. Passions run pretty high politically in Sydney, and Pat Hudson was known to be mixed up with some very rough characters. He had a lot of enemies. The police were prosecuting their inquiries, and the public were asked to inform them if they had seen a suspicious-looking person, possibly an Italian, in the neighbourhood or in a tram coming away from there who bore signs of having been engaged in a fight. A couple of nights later an ambulance came to our house and I was taken to the hospital. They kept me there for three or four days, and then I was slipped out and brought to the place where the *Fenton* was waiting for me.'

'But that cable,' said the doctor. 'How did they manage to get the death certificate?'

'I know no more than you do. I've been trying to puzzle it out. I didn't enter the hospital as myself, I was told to call myself Blake. I've been asking myself if someone else didn't go in as me. They'd done all they could in the papers to pretend there wasn't an epidemic, but there was, and the hospital was crowded. The nurses were just run off their feet, and there was a lot of confusion. It's pretty clear that someone died and was buried in my place. Father's clever, you know, and he wouldn't stick at much.'

'I think I should like to meet your father,' said Dr Saunders.

'It's struck me that perhaps people got suspicious. After all we must have been seen about together, and they may have started asking questions. I expect the police went into it all pretty thoroughly. I daresay father thought it safer to have me die. I expect he got a lot of sympathy.'

'It may be that's why she hanged herself,' said the doctor.

Fred started violently.

'How did you know that?'

'I read it in the paper Erik Christessen brought the other night from Frith's.'

'Did you know it was anything to do with me?'

'No, not till you began to tell me. Then I remembered the name.'

'It gave me an awful turn when I read it.'

'Why d'you think she did it?'

'It said in the paper she'd been worried by malicious gossip. I don't think father would be satisfied till he got even with her. D'you know, I think the thing that made him see red was that she'd wanted to marry into his family. He must have got a lot of pleasure when he told her I was dead. She was horrible, and I hated her, but, by God, she must have loved me to do that.' Fred hesitated for a moment reflectively. 'Father knew the whole story. I shouldn't put it past him to tell her that I'd confessed before my death and the police were going to arrest her.'

Dr Saunders slowly nodded. It seemed to him a pretty device. He only wondered that the woman had adopted such an unpleasant means of death as hanging. Of course it looked as though she were in a hurry to do what she intended. Fred's supposition seemed very plausible.

'Anyway, she's out of it,' said Fred. 'And I've got to go on.'

'You surely don't regret her?'

'Regret her? She's ruined my life. And the rotten thing is that the whole thing happened by the merest chance. I never intended to have an affair with her. I wouldn't have touched her if I'd known she was going to take it seriously. If father had let me go out fishing that Sunday, I shouldn't even have met her. I don't know what to make of anything. And except for that I should never have come to this blasted island. I seem to bring misfortune wherever I go.'

'You should put a little vitriol on your handsome face,' said the doctor. 'You are certainly a public danger.'

'Oh, don't sneer at me. I'm so awfully unhappy. I've never cared for a chap like I cared for Erik. I shall never forgive myself for his death.'

'Don't think he killed himself on your account. You had very little to do with that. Unless I'm greatly mistaken, he killed himself because he couldn't survive the shock of finding out that the person whom he'd endowed with every quality and every virtue was, after all, but human. It was madness on his part. That's the worst of being an idealist; you won't accept people as they are. Wasn't it Christ who said, "Forgive them, for they know not what they do?"'

Fred stared at him with perplexed and haggard eyes.

'But you're not a religious man, are you?'

'Sensible men are all of the same religion. And what is that? Sensible men never tell.'

'My father wouldn't say that. He'd say that sensible men don't go out of their way to give offence. He'd say, it looks well to go to church and you must respect the prejudices of your neighbours. He'd say, what is the good of getting off the fence when you can sit on it very comfortably? Nichols and I have talked about it all. You wouldn't believe it, but he can talk about religion by the hour. It's funny, I've never met a meaner crook, or a man who had less idea of decency, and yet he honestly believes in God. And hell, too. But it never strikes him that he may go there. Other people are going to suffer for their sins and serve 'em damn well right. But he's a stout fellow, he's all right, and when he does the dirty on a friend it isn't of any importance; it's what anyone would do under the circumstances, and God isn't going to hold that up against him. At first I thought he was just a hypocrite. But he isn't. That's the odd thing about it.'

'It shouldn't make you angry. The contrast between a man's profession and his actions is one of the most diverting spectacles that life offers.'

'You look at it from the outside and you can laugh, but I look at it from the in, and I'm a ship that's lost its bearings. What does it all mean? Why are we here? Where are we going? What can we do?'

'My dear boy, you don't expect me to answer, do you? Ever since men picked up a glimmer of intelligence in the primeval forests, they've been asking those questions.'

'What do *you* believe?'

'Do you really want to know? I believe in nothing but myself and my experience. The world consists of me and my thoughts and my feelings; and everything else is mere fancy. Life is a dream in which I create the objects that come before me. Everything knowable, every object of experience, is an idea in my mind, and without my mind it does not exist. There is

191

no possibility and no necessity to postulate anything outside myself. Dream and reality are one. Life is a connected and consistent dream, and when I cease to dream, the world, with its beauty, its pain and sorrow, its unimaginable variety, will cease to be.'

'But that's quite incredible,' cried Fred.

'That is no reason for me to hesitate to believe it,' smiled the doctor.

'Well, I'm not prepared to be made a fool of. If life won't fulfil the demands I make on it, then I have no use for it. It's dull and stupid play, and it's only waste of time to sit it out.'

The doctor's eyes twinkled and a grin puckered his ugly little face.

'Oh, my dear boy, what perfect nonsense you talk. Youth, youth! You're a stranger in the world yet. Presently, like a man on a desert island, you'll learn to do without what you can't get and make the most of what you can. A little common sense, a little tolerance, a little good humour, and you don't know how comfortable you can make yourself on this planet.'

'By giving up all that makes life worth while. Like you. I want life to be fair. I want life to be brave and honest. I want men to be decent and things to come right in the end. Surely that's not asking too much, is it?'

'I don't know. It's asking more than life can give.'

'Don't you mind?'

'Not much.'

'You're content to wallow in the gutter.'

'I get a certain amount of fun from watching the antics of the other creatures that dwell there.'

Fred gave his shoulder an angry shrug and a sigh was rung from him.

'You believe nothing. You respect nobody. You expect man to be vile. You're a cripple chained to a bath-chair and you think it's just stuff and nonsense that anyone should walk or run.'

'I'm afraid you don't very much approve of me,' the doctor suggested mildly.

'You've lost heart, hope, faith, and awe. What in God's name have you got left?'

'Resignation.'

The young man jumped to his feet.

'Resignation? That's the refuge of the beaten. Keep your resignation. I don't want it. I'm not willing to accept evil and ugliness and injustice. I'm not willing to stand by while the good are punished and the wicked go scot-free. If life means that virtue is trampled on and honesty is mocked and beauty is fouled, then to hell with life.'

'My dear boy, you must take life as you find it.'

'I'm fed up with life as I find it. It fills me with horror. I'll either have it on my own terms or not at all.'

Rhodomontade. The boy was nervous and upset. It was very natural. Dr Saunders had little doubt that in a day or two he would be more sensible, and his reply was designed to check this extravagance.

'Have you ever read that laughter is the only gift the gods have vouchsafed to man that he does not share with the beasts?'

'What do you mean by that?' asked Fred sullenly.

'I have acquired resignation by the help of an unfailing sense of the ridiculous.'

'Laugh, then. Laugh your head off.'

'So long as I can,' returned the doctor, looking at him with his tolerant humour, 'the gods may destroy me, but I remain unvanquished.'

Rhodomontade? Perhaps.

The conversation might have proceeded indefinitely if at that moment there had not come a knock on the door.

'Who the devil is that?' cried Fred irascibly.

A boy who spoke a little English came in to say that someone wished to see Fred, but they could not understand who it was. Fred, shrugging his shoulders, was about to go when an idea struck him and he stopped.

'Is it a man or a woman?'

He had to repeat the question in two or three different ways before the boy caught his meaning. Then with a smile brightened by the appreciation of his own cleverness, he answered that it was a woman.

'Louise.' Fred shook his head with decision. 'You say, Tuan sick, no can come.'

The boy understood this and withdrew.

'You'd better see her,' said the doctor.

'Never. Erik was worth ten of her. He meant all the world to me. I loathe the thought of her. I only want to get away. I want to forget. How could she trample on that noble heart!'

Dr Saunders raised his eyebrows. Language of that sort chilled his sympathy.

'Perhaps she's very unhappy,' he suggested mildly.

'I thought you were a cynic. You're a sentimentalist.'

'Have you only just discovered it?'

The door was slowly opened, pushed wide, silently, and Louise stood in the doorway. She did not come forward. She did not speak. She looked at Fred, and a faint, shy, deprecating smile hovered on her lips. You could see that she was nervous. Her whole body seemed to express a timid uncertainty. It had, as much as her face, an air of appeal. Fred stared at her. He did not move. He did not ask her to come in. His face was sullen and in his eyes was a cold and relentless hatred. The little smile froze on her lips and she seemed to give a gasp, not with her mouth, but with her body, as though a sharp pain pierced her heart. She stood there, for two or three minutes, it seemed, and neither of them moved an eyelash. Their eyes met in an insistent stare. Then, very slowly, and as silently as when she opened it, she drew the door to and softly closed it on herself. The two men were left alone once more. To the doctor the scene had appeared strangely, horribly pathetic.

chapter twenty-nine

The *Fenton* sailed at dawn. The ship that was to take Dr Saunders to Bali was due in the course of the afternoon. She was to stay only just long enough to take on cargo, and so, towards eleven, hiring a horse-cab, the doctor drove out to

194

Swan's plantation. He thought it would be uncivil to go without saying good-bye.

When he arrived he found the old man sitting in a chair in the garden. It was the same chair as that in which Erik Christessen had sat on the night when he saw Fred come out of Louise's room. The doctor passed the time of day with him. The old man did not remember him, but he was spry enough and asked the doctor a number of questions without paying any attention to the replies. Presently Louise came down the steps from the house. She shook hands with him. She bore no sign that she had passed through an emotional crisis, but greeted him with that composed and winning smile that she had had the first time he saw her on the way back from the bathing pool. She wore a brown sarong of batik and a little native coat. Her very fair hair was plaited and bound round her head.

'Won't you come inside and sit down?' she said. 'Dad is working. He'll be along presently.'

The doctor accompanied her into the large living-room. The jalousies were drawn and the subdued light was pleasant. There was not much comfort in the room, but it was cool, and a great bunch of yellow cannas in a bowl, flaming like the new-risen sun, gave it a peculiar and exotic distinction.

'We haven't told grandpa about Erik. He liked him; they were both Scandinavians, you know. We were afraid it would upset him. But perhaps he knows; one can never tell. Sometimes, weeks after, he'll let fall a remark and we find out that he's known all along something that we thought we'd better say nothing about.'

She talked in a leisurely manner, with a soft, rather full voice, as though of indifferent things.

'Old age is very strange. It has a kind of aloofness. It's lost so much, that you can hardly look upon the old as quite human any more. But sometimes you have a feeling that they've acquired a sort of new sense that tells them things that we can never know.'

'Your grandfather was gay enough the other night. I hope I shall be as alert at his age.'

'He was excited. He likes having new people to talk to. But

195

that's just like a phonograph that you wind up. That's the machine. But there's something else there, like a little animal, a rat burrowing away or a squirrel turning in its cage, that's busy within him with things we know nothing of. I feel its existence and I wonder what it's about.'

The doctor had nothing to say to this, and silence for a minute or two fell upon them.

'Will you have a stengah?' she said.

'No, thank you.'

They were sitting opposite one another in easy chairs. The large room surrounded them with strangeness. It seemed to await something.

'The *Fenton* sailed this morning,' said the doctor.

'I know.'

He looked at her reflectively and she returned his gaze with tranquillity.

'I'm afraid Christessen's death was a great shock to you.'

'I was very fond of him.'

'He talked to me a great deal about you the night before he died. He was very much in love with you. He told me he was going to marry you.'

'Yes.' She gave him a fleeting glance. 'Why did he kill himself?'

'He saw that boy coming out of your room.'

She looked down. She reddened a little.

'That's impossible.'

'Fred told me. He was there when he jumped over the rail of the veranda.'

'Who told Fred I was engaged to Erik?'

'I did.'

'I thought it was that yesterday afternoon when he wouldn't see me. And then when I came in and he looked at me like that I knew it was hopeless.'

There was no despair in her manner, but a collected acceptance of the inevitable. You might almost have said that there was in her tone a shrug of the shoulders.

'You weren't in love with him, then?'

She leaned her face on her hand and for a moment seemed to look into her heart.

'It's all rather complicated,' she said.

'Anyhow, it's no business of mine.'

'Oh, I don't mind telling you. I don't care what you think of me.'

'Why should you?'

'He was very good-looking. D'you remember the other afternoon when I met you in the plantation? I couldn't take my eyes off him. And then at supper, and afterwards when we danced together. I suppose you'd call it love at first sight.'

'I'm not sure that I would.'

'Oh?' She looked at him with an air of surprise, which changed to a quick, scrutinizing glance, as though for the first time she paid him attention. 'I knew he'd taken a fancy to me. I felt something I'd never felt in my life before. I wanted him simply frightfully. I generally sleep like a log. I was terribly restless all night. Father wanted to bring you his translation and I offered to drive him down. I knew he was only staying a day or two. Perhaps if he'd been staying a month it wouldn't have happened. I should have thought there was plenty of time, and if I'd seen him every day for a week I daresay I shouldn't have bothered about him. And afterwards, I didn't regret it. I felt contented and free. I lay awake for a little while after he left me that night. I was awfully happy, but, you know, I didn't really care if I never saw him again. It was very comfortable to be alone. I don't suppose you'll know what I mean, but I felt that my soul was a little light-headed.'

'Have you no fear of consequences?' asked the doctor.

'How d'you mean?' She understood and smiled. 'Oh, that. Oh, doctor, I've lived on this island almost all my life. When I was a child I used to play with the children on the estate. My great friend, the daughter of our overseer, is the same age as me and she's been married for four years and has had three babies. You don't imagine sex has many secrets for Malay children. I've heard everything connected with it talked about since I was seven.'

'Why did you come to the hotel yesterday?'

'I was distracted. I was awfully fond of Erik. I couldn't believe it when they told me he'd shot himself. I was afraid I was to blame. I wanted to know if it was possible that he knew about Fred.'

'You were to blame.'

'I'm dreadfully sorry he's dead. I owe a great deal to him. When I was a child I used to worship him. He was like one of grandpa's old Vikings to me. I've always liked him awfully. But I'm not to blame.'

'What makes you think that?'

'He didn't know it, but it wasn't me he loved, it was mother. She knew it and at the end I think she loved him, too. It's funny if you come to think of it. He was almost young enough to be her son. What he loved in me was my mother, and he never knew that either.'

'Didn't you love him?'

'Oh, very much. With my soul, not with my heart, or with my heart, perhaps, and not with my nerves. He was very good. He was wonderfully reliable. He was incapable of unkindness. He was very genuine. There was something almost saintly in him.'

She took out her handkerchief and wiped her eyes, for while talking of him she had begun to cry.

'If you weren't in love with him, why did you become engaged to him?'

'I promised mother I would before she died. I think she felt that in me she would gratify her love for him. And I was very fond of him. I knew him so well. I was very much at home with him. I think if he'd wanted to marry me just when mother died and I was so unhappy I might have loved him. But he thought I was too young. He didn't want to take advantage of the feelings I had then.'

'And then?'

'Daddy didn't very much want me to marry him. He was always waiting for the fairy prince who would come and carry me off to an enchanted castle. I suppose you think daddy's feckless and unpractical. Of course I didn't believe in a fairy prince, but there's generally something behind daddy's ideas. He has a sort of instinct for things. He lives in the clouds, if you know what I mean, but very often those clouds glow with the light of heaven. Oh, I suppose if nothing had happened we should have married in the end and been very happy. No one could have helped being happy with Erik. It would have been very nice to see all those places he talked about. I should have liked to go to Sweden, to the place where grandpa was born, and Venice.'

'It's unfortunate that we ever came here. And, after all, it was only a chance; we might just as well have made for Amboyna.'

'Could you have gone to Amboyna? I think it was fated from all eternity that you should come here.'

'Do you think our destinies are so important that the fates should make such a to-do about them?' smiled the doctor.

She did not answer and for a little while they sat in silence.

'I'm terribly unhappy, you know,' she said at last.

'You must try not to grieve too much.'

'Oh, I don't grieve.'

She spoke with a sort of decision, so that the doctor looked at her with surprise.

'You blame me. Anyone would. I don't blame myself. Erik killed himself because I'd fallen short of the ideal he'd made of me.'

'Ah.'

Dr Saunders perceived that her instinct had come to the same conclusion as his reasoning.

'If he'd loved me he might have killed me or he might have forgiven me. Don't you think it's rather stupid the importance men, white men at least, attach to the act of flesh? D'you know, when I was at school in Auckland I had an attack of religion – girls often have at that age – and in Lent I made a vow that I wouldn't eat anything with sugar in it. After about a fortnight I hankered after something sweet so that it was positive torture. One day I passed a candy shop and I looked at the chocolates in the window and my heart turned round inside me. I went in and bought half a pound and ate them in the street outside, every one, till the bag was empty. I shall never forget what a relief it was. Then I went back to school and denied myself quite comfortably for the rest of Lent. I told that story to Erik and he laughed. He thought it very natural. He was so tolerant. Don't you think if he'd loved me he would have been tolerant about the other, too?'

'Men are very peculiar in that respect.'

'Not Erik. He was so wise and so charitable. I tell you he didn't love me. He loved his ideal. My mother's beauty and my mother's qualities in me and those Shakespeare heroines of his and the princesses in Hans Andersen's fairy tales. What right have people to make an image after their own heart and force it on you and be angry if it doesn't fit you? He wanted to imprison me in his ideal. He didn't care who I was. He wouldn't take me as I am. He wanted to possess my soul, and because he felt that there was somewhere in me something that escaped him, he tried to replace that little spark within me which is me by a phantom of his own fancy. I'm unhappy, but I tell you I don't grieve. And Fred in his way was the same. When he lay by my side that night he said he'd like to stay here always on this island, and marry me and cultivate the plantation, and I don't know what else. He made a picture of his life and I was to fit in it. He wanted, too, to imprison me in his dream. It was a different dream, but it was his dream. But I am I. I don't want to dream anyone else's dream. I want to dream my own. All that's happened is terrible and my heart is heavy, but at the back of my mind I know that it's given me freedom.'

She did not speak with emotion, but slowly and in measured terms, with the collected manner that the doctor had always found so singular. He listened attentively. He shuddered a little within himself, for the spectacle of the naked human soul always affected him with horror. He saw there that same bare, ruthless instinct that impelled those shapeless creatures of the beginning of the world's history to force their way through the blind hostility of chance. He wondered what would become of this girl.

'Have you any plan for the future?' he asked.

She shook her head.

'I can wait. I'm young, When grandpa dies this will be mine. Perhaps I shall sell it. Daddy wants to go to India. The world is wide.'

'I must go,' said Dr Saunders. 'Can I see your father to say good-bye to him?'

'I'll take you to his study.'

She led him along a passage to a smallish room at the side of the house. Frith was sitting at a table littered with manuscripts and books. He was pounding a typewriter, and the sweat pouring from his fat red face made his spectacles slip down his nose.

'This is the final typing of the ninth canto,' he said. 'You're going away, aren't you? I'm afraid I shan't have time to show it you.'

He had forgotten that Dr Saunders had fallen asleep while he was reading his translation aloud to him, or if he remembered was undiscouraged.

'I am nearing the end. It has been an arduous task, and I hardly think I could ever have brought it to a successful conclusion but for my little girl's encouragement. It is very right and proper that she should be the chief gainer.'

'You mustn't work too hard, daddy.'

'*Tempus fugit*,' he murmured. '*Ars longa, vita brevis.*'

She put her hand gently on his shoulder and with a smile looked at the sheet of paper in the machine. Once more the doctor was struck by the loving-kindness with which Louise treated her father. With her shrewd sense she could not have failed to form a just estimate of his futile labour.

'We haven't come to disturb you, darling. Dr Saunders wants to say good-bye.'

'Ah, yes, of course,' said Frith. He got up from the table. 'Well, it's been a treat to see you. In this backwater of life we don't often have visitors. It was kind of you to come to Christessen's funeral yesterday. We Britishers ought to stick together on these occasions. It impresses the Dutch. Not that Christessen was British. But we'd seen a great deal of him since he came to the island, and after all he belonged to the same country as Queen Alexandra. A glass of sherry before you go?'

'No, thank you. I must be getting back.'

'I was very much upset when I heard. The Contrôleur told me he had no doubt it was the heat. He wanted to marry

Louise. I'm very glad now I wouldn't give my consent. Lack of self-control, of course. The English are the only people who can transplant themselves to strange lands and keep their balance. He'll be a great loss to us. Of course he was a foreigner, but all the same it's a shock. I've felt it very much.'

It was evident, however, that he looked upon it as much less serious for a Dane to die than for an Englishman. Frith insisted on coming out into the compound. The doctor, turning round to wave his hand as he drove off, saw him with his arm round his daughter's waist. A ray of sun finding its way through the heavy leafage of the kanari trees touched her fair hair with gold.

chapter thirty

A month later Dr Saunders was sitting on the little dusty terrace of the van Dyke Hotel at Singapore. It was late in the afternoon. From where he sat he could see the street below. Cars dashed past and cabs drawn by two sturdy ponies; rickshaws sped by with a patter of naked feet. Now and then Tamils, tall and emaciated, sauntered along, and in their silence, in the quiet of their stealthy movement, was the night of a far-distant past. Trees shaded the street and the sun splashed down in irregular patches. Chinese women in trousers, with gold pins in their hair, stepped out of the shade into the light like marionettes passing across the stage. Now and then a young planter, deeply sunburned, in a double-brimmed hat and khaki shorts, walked past with the long stride he had learnt tramping over the rubber estates. Two dark-skinned soldiers, very smart in their clean uniforms, strutted by conscious of their importance. The heat of the day was past, the light was golden, and in the air was a crisp nonchalance as though life, there and then, invited you to take it lightly. A water-cart passed, slithering the dusty road with a stream of water.

Dr Saunders had spent a fortnight in Java. Now he was catching the first ship that came in for Hong-Kong, and from there he intended to take a coasting vessel to Fu-chou. He was glad he had made the journey. It had taken him out of the rut he had been in so long. It had liberated him from the bonds of unprofitable habits, and, relaxed as never before from all earthly ties, he rejoiced in a heavenly sense of spiritual independence. It was an exquisite pleasure to him to know that there was no one in the world who was essential to his peace of mind. He had reached, though by a very different path, the immunity from the concerns of this world which is the aim of the ascetic. While, like the Buddha contemplating his navel, he was delectably immersed in his self-satisfaction, someone touched him on the shoulder. He looked up and saw Captain Nichols.

'I was passin' by and saw you sittin' there. I came up to say 'ow d'ye do to you.'

'Sit down and have a drink.'

'I don't mind if I do.'

The skipper wore his shore-going clothes. They were not old, but they looked astonishingly seedy. He had two day's growth of beard on his lean face, and the nails on his hands were rimmed with grime. He looked down at heel.

'I'm havin' me teeth attended to,' he said. 'You was right. The dentist says I must 'ave 'em all out. Says 'e's not surprised I suffer from dyspepsia. It's a miracle I've gone on as long as I 'ave, according to 'im.'

The doctor gave him a glance and noticed that his upper front teeth had been extracted. It made his ingratiating smile more sinister than ever.

'Where's Fred Blake?' asked Dr Saunders.

The smile faded from the skipper's lips, but lingered sardonic in his eyes.

'Come to a sticky end, poor young chap,' he replied.

'What do you mean?'

'Fell overboard one night or jumped over. Nobody knows. He was gone in the morning.'

'In a storm?'

The doctor could hardly believe his ears.

'No. Sea was as flat as a mill-pond. He was very low after we come away from Kanda. We went to Batavia same as we said we was goin' to do. I suspicioned 'e was expectin' a letter there. But if it come or if it didn't I don't know, and it's no good askin' me.'

'But how could he go overboard without anyone noticing? What about the man at the helm?'

'We'd 'ove to for the night. Been drinkin' very 'eavy. Nothin' to do with me, of course, but I tell 'im he'd better go easy. Told me to mind me own bloody business. All right, I says, go your own way. It ain't goin' to disturb my night's rest what you do.'

'When did it happen?'

'A week ago last Tuesday.'

The doctor leaned back. It was a shock to him. It was so short a while since that boy and he had sat together and talked. It had seemed to him then that there was in him something naïve and aspiring that was not devoid of charm. It was not very pleasant to think of him now drifting, mangled and terrible, at the mercy of the tides. He was only a kid. Notwithstanding his philosophy, the doctor could not but feel a pang when the young died.

'Very awkward it was for me, too,' continued the skipper. 'He'd won nearly all my money at cribbage. We played a lot after we left you, and I tell you the luck 'e 'ad was unbelievable. I knew I was a better player than 'im; I'd never 'ave took him on if I 'adn't been as sure of that as I am that you're sittin' there, and I doubled the stakes. And d'you know, I couldn't win. I began to think there was somethin' phoney about it, but there's not much you can teach me in that direction, and I couldn't see 'ow it was done if it was done. No, it was just luck. Well, to cut a long story short, by the time we got to Batavia 'e'd took off me every penny I'd got for the cruise.

'Well, after the accident I broke open his strong box. We'd bought a couple when we was at Merauke. I 'ad to, you know, to see if there was an address or anythin' so as I could communicate with the sorrowin' relatives. I'm very particular about that sort of thing. And d'you know, there wasn't a shillin' there. It was as empty as the palm of my 'and. The dirty little tyke carried all 'is money in 'is belt and 'e gone overboard with it.'

'It must have been a sell for you.'

'I never liked him, not from the beginnin'. Crooked 'e was. And mind you, it was me own money, most of it. You can't tell me 'e could win like that playin' on the square. I don't know whatever I should 'ave done if I 'adn't been able to sell the ketch to a Chink at Penang. It looked like I was bein' made the goat.'

The doctor stared. It was a queer story. He wondered if there was any truth in it. Captain Nichols filled him with repulsion.

'I suppose you didn't by any chance push him overboard when he was drunk?' he asked acidly.

'What d'you mean by that?'

'You didn't know the money was in his belt. It was quite a packet for a bum like you. I wouldn't put it past you to have done the dirty on the wretched boy.'

Captain Nichols went green in the face. His jaw dropped and a glassy stare came into his eyes. The doctor chuckled. That random shot of his had gone home. The scoundrel. But then he saw that the skipper was not looking at him, but at something behind; he turned round and saw a woman slowly ascending the steps from the street to the terrace. She was a shortish woman and stout, with a flat, pasty face and somewhat protruding eyes. They were strangely round and shone like boot-buttons. She wore a dress of black cloth that was a little too tight for her, and on her head a black straw hat, like a man's. She was most unsuitably dressed for the tropics. She looked hot and out of temper.

'My God!' gasped the skipper, under his breath. 'My old woman.'

She walked up to the table in a leisurely manner. She looked at the unhappy man with distaste in her eyes and he watched her in helpless fascination.

'What 'ave you done with your front teeth, captain?' she said.

He smiled ingratiatingly.

'Whoever thought of seein' you, my dear,' he said. 'This is a joyful surprise.'

'We'll go and 'ave a cup of tea, captain.'

'Just as you say, my dear.'

He got up. She turned round and walked the way she came. Captain Nichols followed her. His face wore a very serious expression. The doctor reflected that now he would never know the truth about poor Fred Blake. He smiled grimly as he saw the skipper walk in silence down the street by his wife's side.

A faint breeze rustled suddenly the leaves of the trees and a ray of sun found its way through them and danced for a moment by his side. He thought of Louise and her ash-blonde hair. She was like an enchantress in an old tale whom men loved to their destruction. She was an enigmatic figure going about her household duties with that steady composure and with serenity waiting for what would in due course befall her. He wondered what it would be. He sighed a little, for whatever it was, if the richest dreams the imagination offered came true, in the end it remained nothing but illusion.

W. Somerset Maugham
Cakes and Ale £2.50

Cakes and Ale was the book by which Maugham most wanted to be
remembered. As he traces the fortunes of a famous writer and his
extraordinary wife, Maugham's superb ironic skill combines with a
great lyrical warmth to make a uniquely unforgettable novel.

The Razor's Edge £2.95

The story of three of Maugham's most brilliant characters – Isabel,
whose choice between passion and wealth has lifelong
repercussions . . . Her uncle, Elliott Templeton, a classic American
snob . . . and Larry Darrell, Isabel's ex-fiancé who leaves his
stockbroking life in Chicago to seek spiritual peace in a Guru's
ashram in Southern India.

Theatre £2.50

The world of the theatre was one known intimately to Maugham,
and its blend of glitter and guile provided the finest material for his
fiction. This novel – one of the author's own favourites – traces the
story of Julia, an actress touched with genius, ravishingly lovely, and
at the peak of her career. As her son struggles into manhood and her
husband lapses into middle age, Julia meets Tom – whose gauche,
shy charm masks a callous and predatory smile .

All these books are available at your local bookshop or newsagent, or can be ordered direct from the publisher. Indicate the number of copies required and fill in the form below.

Send to: **CS Department, Pan Books Ltd., P.O. Box 40, Basingstoke, Hants. RG21 2YT.**

or phone: 0256 469551 (Ansaphone), quoting title, author and Credit Card number.

Please enclose a remittance* to the value of the cover price plus: 60p for the first book plus 30p per copy for each additional book ordered to a maximum charge of £2.40 to cover postage and packing.

*Payment may be made in sterling by UK personal cheque, postal order, sterling draft or international money order, made payable to Pan Books Ltd.

Alternatively by Barclaycard/Access:

Card No.

Signature:

Applicable only in the UK and Republic of Ireland.

While every effort is made to keep prices low, it is sometimes necessary to increase prices at short notice. Pan Books reserve the right to show on covers and charge new retail prices which may differ from those advertised in the text or elsewhere.

NAME AND ADDRESS IN BLOCK LETTERS PLEASE:

....

Name ————————————————————————

Address ————————————————————————

————————————————————————————

————————————————————————————

————————————————————————————

3/87